"I am not a hero, Cate." He tried to pull away.

She held on, resting their joined hands against her chest. "Never said you were. You're a flesh and blood man."

And this close, she could smell the soap on his skin and see the darker streaks in his green eyes.

"Very much so." His breath seemed to hiccup. "So . . ."

When his voice trailed off she got a taste of what it felt like to have someone drop the end of important sentences like she often did. But she didn't think he tried it or that he was playing games.

"Now you're the one who should finish the sentence." Her voice came out in a breathy whisper.

"We're in a tense situation. Stress sometimes disguises itself as something else."

The words crashed into her brain, wiping out every other thought. She pulled back a bit, but kept holding his hand. "What are you talking about?"

His gaze traveled over her face now, landing on her mouth. "How much I want to kiss you."

By HelenKay Dimon

the Protector

Games People Play

HELENKAY DIMON

AVONBOOKS

An Imprint of HarperCollinsPublishers

THE PROTECTOR. Copyright © 2018 by HelenKay Dimon. All rights reserved. Printed in the United States of America. No part of this book may be used or reproduced in any manner whatsoever without written permission except in the case of brief quotations embodied in critical articles and reviews. For information, address HarperCollins Publishers, 195 Broadway, New York, NY 10007.

First Avon Books mass market printing: August 2018

Print Edition ISBN: 978-0-06-269223-8
Digital Edition ISBN: 978-0-06-269222-1

Cover design by Amy Halperin
Cover photograph by Yasmeen Anderson Photography

Avon, Avon & logo, and Avon Books & logo are registered trademarks of HarperCollins Publishers in the United States of America and other countries.

HarperCollins is a registered trademark of HarperCollins Publishers in the United States of America and other countries.

FIRST EDITION

18 19 20 21 22 QGM 10 9 8 7 6 5 4 3 2 1

To my family in Pennsylvania: This is not about you.
It's fiction. I promise.

the
Protector

CHAPTER 1

Cate Pendleton dumped her grocery bags on the kitchen counter and glanced around the living room area of her small one-bedroom condo. Flattened pillows. Magazines spread across the coffee table. A blanket in a ball on the floor from where it slipped off her last night while she watched television. The remote stuffed between cushions.

Everything was exactly where she left it when she took off on her store run an hour ago. But something struck her as off. She felt it rather than saw it. A violation of her sacred space. A lingering menace. The sensation of unknown hands skimming over her things. A shiver skated through her at the thought.

With her keys sticking between her fingers like a weapon, she walked around the condo, peeking in the closet and looking inside the bedroom. The journey ended back where she started. She approached the couch nice and slow. She listened for footsteps, but the only sound came from the hiss of her clunky, usually malfunctioning icemaker.

She leaned toward the cushions, just a bit, and sniffed. There it was. Aftershave. Faint, but present. Since a man hadn't been in the condo for weeks, the smell was out of place. And this was not the first time this had happened. She came home two days ago to the same scent. A mix of musk and orange. The last time it happened in the evening. This time in the morning.

On that first day, she found her patio door unlocked. Living in a city, she didn't take her personal safety for granted. Being two floors up, tucked behind rows of government buildings and a few blocks back from the National Air and Space Museum in downtown Washington, DC, she kept her guard up. The neighborhood served as home to many congressional staffers. Traffic, both human and the car variety, moved in a steady beat. But she knew better than to assume everything was fine. She locked her doors. All of them and all the time, but someone got in.

A punch of awareness moved through her as she brushed her fingertips over the arm of the chair. The idea of someone snooping through her stuff, standing in her space, made her gag. Last time nothing was stolen, so she skipped calling the police with that fear. Wrote the whole thing off as faulty memory. She knew something strange had happened, but she blocked it and pretended otherwise. But this was different. From the first whiff of that cologne, the trembling started deep down in her stomach, spun up to her head and would not stop.

She forced her mind to focus. Someone kept getting in without leaving much of a trail. They didn't stick around, and for that she was grateful. Nothing stolen. Not obviously, anyway.

Her sister. That's what this had to be about. Cate thought back to the last six weeks and all the ground she'd covered. She poked around, asked uncomfortable questions and clearly upset someone. She got too close, which was exactly her plan. Maybe she uncovered some piece of information she hadn't realized yet. But she would.

If someone broke in thinking they'd figure out her strategy or grab every lead she'd collected, they miscalculated. No way would she make it that easy for anyone to destroy her work or derail her.

She'd called the police in the past. Years ago. Not about this, but about a much bigger unsolved horror and it led nowhere. A call today likely would end the same way. They would ignore her, write her off as *the crazy one with the dead sister.* Add to that, her complaint wouldn't pinpoint any clear evidence. This was about a *sense* of a presence, of being spooked, and she would become the new lunchtime story for the officers.

But she knew. He had been there. He or she. The person knew how to get in and was playing with her. The next time she might come home too soon.

Despite her worries and the downsides, she picked up the phone and dialed the one person who might be able to help her, the mysterious DC fixer. The guy no one ever saw who went by one name—Wren.

"WHAT ARE YOU doing here?" Damon Knox stepped up to the foul line in his slouchy navy blue sweats and took a shot. The ball bounced off the rim and landed close enough for him to run it down again.

"Waiting in the middle of a YMCA gym, watching one of my closest friends drown in self-pity," Wren said from his seat on the bottom row of the bleachers.

Damon refused to fight with Wren because Wren was not a man who lost very often, if ever. Known by different names to different people, he'd always be Levi Wren to Damon.

They came from different places and met in their twenties when they both believed they were out of options—him on the run and Wren looking for revenge. They'd been taken in by Quint, a former undercover operative in some quasi-governmental organization he never talked about, a man who trained them and three others. Coached them on how to shoot, how to set fires and not get caught, how to hide, and then he taught them that all of those skills, while helpful, ended in jail or a death sentence. He encouraged them to funnel their anger into legal pursuits. To learn other skills. Wren did and was now the elusive, mostly anonymous fixer that every rich person and government turned to for help.

But Damon wasn't in the mood for a walk down Memory Lane. He didn't want to talk about any subject, really. Just wanted to shoot some hoops in peace. "If you're here and not at your desk it must be a slow day for trouble in DC."

"There's no such thing." Wren leaned forward with his elbows resting on his knees. "I had to wander outside because you've been ignoring me."

"Apparently not hard enough." The basketball bouncing off the rim echoed the sentiment. Hell, he could not even hit a foul shot these days. When everything went wrong, it went *really* wrong.

Wren blew out an exaggerated breath. One that said he was already bored the conversation wasn't going his way. "As if I'd take 'no' for an answer."

"I believe my exact response to your summons was 'kiss my ass' but the result is the same." Damon took a good look at his friend. So much had changed in the guy's life over the past year, but he still managed to be the most well-dressed, put-together person in the room. "Nice suit, by the way."

"Grown-ups wear them." Wren groaned as he got up, but since he had just turned thirty-five, the noise likely meant he was annoyed.

"Interesting life advice. I'll keep that in mind."

"We need to talk about—"

"Nope." Damon slammed the ball against the court as hard as he could. The loud thud before it soared into the air filled him with an odd satisfaction.

Wren caught it and threw it back to Damon. "What kind of answer is that?"

"The same one I gave on the phone."

"You do realize I'm standing right here." Wren held his arms out to his sides, showing off that expensive black suit.

"Tough to miss you with that fancy green tie." But Damon noticed something else—the file in Wren's hand.

"Then you also know that I'll keep hunting you down until we have a civilized conversation."

Damon balanced the ball under his arm and studied one of the handful of people he trusted in the world. "Let's do the abbreviated version. You want me to work for you again and the answer is no."

"This is your mess."

"Hardly." A door opened behind them, grabbing both of their attention, then closed again without anyone stepping inside. "Speaking of hunting, how did you find me? Please say you haven't put a tracker on me."

Wren snorted. "Come on. I stopped using trackers on my friends two years ago. Now I serve you irradiated liquor when you come to my house and keep tabs on you that way."

Damon looked for signs of amusement but didn't really see any. "From anyone else I'd think that was a joke. From DC's mysterious big-time, powerful fixer? Who the hell knows."

"You're trying flattery to throw me off topic?"

"Is it working?"

"Never." Wren took the opportunity to reach in and steal the ball.

Damon didn't fight him, because why bother? "Tell me why Emery stays with you."

Emery Finn, the woman who had Wren turned

around and thinking about walking down the aisle. She'd chased her own demons, and dealt with a huge load of family dysfunction, but she calmed Wren. Made him happy, and that's all that mattered to Damon.

Wren smiled. "I have no idea but I'm not questioning my luck."

The no-shit expression on Wren's face made Damon laugh. "One of these days you'll be smart enough to ask her to marry you."

"It's amazing to me that all of you guys, my supposed friends, think I haven't tried to nail marriage down. Last time I mentioned the possibility, she held up her hand and said, 'we'll see' and then gave me a lecture about how I needed to be less controlling."

Damon could almost hear her voice. "I love her."

"That makes two of us." Wren set the ball on the floor and held it there with his foot. "And nice try at redirecting the conversation."

"It was worth a shot." Damon knew it wouldn't work. Not with Wren. He was not a man who ever got knocked off stride.

Wren glanced at the basket. "Better than your foul shooting."

"You try, old man."

"We're basically the same age." Wren swore under his breath when Damon continued to stand there, not saying a word, then he dropped the file and picked up the basketball again. "Fine."

Stepping up to the line, Wren aimed and sank the

shot. Despite the suit jacket and no warm-up, he sank it. It never touched the rim. Figured. There was little this guy couldn't do.

Damon watched the ball bounce until it rolled to a stop against the wall. "Impressive."

"I have many skills."

"I know. We spent years training together, remember?"

"Damon, we can go round and round here but the result will be the same. You can't outrun this." Wren picked the file off the court and held it out to Damon. "Take it."

Nothing piqued Damon's interest like a mystery that needed solving, but he held firm. "You underestimate me, my friend."

Wren hummed. "This is about Sullivan."

The mention of The Sullivan School sent Damon's heart rate speeding off at a gallop. His past tied him to the people and the land . . . and the horror he barely escaped. But if he jumped even a little, Wren would be all over him, so Damon forced his voice to remain flat and he did not reach for the folder. "Not interested."

"They're coming after her."

"I don't know who you're talking about and I'm not asking for details. I don't want to know anything." And that was an understatement. If the thought caught hold in his mind, if he read and wanted to read more, he was a goner. He'd step in, and that could not happen.

Wren had tried to lay out some of the facts in his call. One mention of the school and Damon's mind had blanked. This strange echoing started in his ears, blocking out all sound. Now he knew one more fact. A woman needed help. Wren knew just the right thing to say to entice him.

Wren shook his head. "They will not let this drop."

"Of course not. That's what they do. Intimidate people into bolting . . . or worse."

"You're going to let an innocent woman get trapped by those monsters?" Wren asked, pushing that guilt button a second time.

That time the punch hit harder. "Don't do that."

Damon had to clamp down on the need to ask questions, to want to run in and help. The idea of anyone being hunted, man or woman, started a ball of anxiety spinning in his stomach. Something about a woman thrown into the role of survivor due to the school kicked up his protective instincts. And Wren knew him well enough to know that.

"I can give you details," Wren said.

"I'm not listening." But he was. Damon's mind already started setting out a plan to get back in and help this woman—whoever she was—out again. At least that's what he assumed the problem was. Another person who thought the school sounded good, got sucked in and trapped. The pattern had repeated itself so many times over the years, despite all the news coverage from thirteen years ago.

"You are and you know I'm right." Wren continued to hold out the file with a steady hand.

"I'm not taking it. Shred it for all I care."

"Cate Pendleton," Wren said, rattling off facts.

Damon wouldn't forget her name now, which he guessed was the point. He'd have to beat back the urge to do a simple internet search for more information. "You're not going to stop with this, are you?"

"What do you think?"

The guy was relentless. Damon grabbed the file but didn't open it. "What did she do to piss someone off?"

"She went to Salvation, Pennsylvania. Your hometown."

Damn. "Most inappropriately named place ever."

"She's looking for her sister's killer."

"Fuck me." Damon shoved the file back at Wren. When he didn't grab it, Damon pressed it to Wren's chest, messing up that perfectly straight tie.

Wren took the file back. "I'm in a committed relationship, but thanks for the offer."

"Listen, I can't go back there." Even now, standing in the middle of a hot gym, hearing the mumbled voices from the hall, Damon had to fight off the memories. How the classes turned into something else. The gunfire. The bloodbath. "No way."

"You're the only one who can."

"You forget the old rumors about how there's a bounty on my head." He'd been twenty. By the time the legal wrangling ended five years later, Damon didn't have anything left but the Quint Five, the five friends he trained with under their mentor. Slowly, time passed and the public's memories of what happened blurred. He'd tried to go back, to talk with the few people he still cared about, but couldn't force his body to walk through the school's front gate. Eventually, he found some peace and experienced good times but, at thirty-four, the sensation that it could all be taken away in a flash lingered.

"That's why they'll open the gates for you. No one else will be able to breach the exterior face they show off and dig underneath."

He made it sound so simple. For Wren, it was. He was a man who dealt in strategy and who made things happen. For Damon, it potentially meant the end of everything. Wren likely wanted him to have some sort of closure but Damon knew some wounds never healed.

"You're sending me on a dangerous mission. You know what happened there before. Maybe not all of it, but I've clued you in on some of the shittier parts." Because one night in a drunken rant, Damon had spilled the truth about most of what happened back at Sullivan. Not what the press knew or even what the police knew. The actual rundown. He'd talked about growing up in Salvation. About his family and the so-called college.

"You escaped." Wren let out a long, ragged breath. "Her sister didn't."

Tempting . . . "The answer is still no."

"I'm going to leave this top secret, for-your-eyes-only file right here on the basketball court." Wren dropped it at his feet with a *thwap*. "The type of file with information no one else should see."

"I'm not picking it up. You can't reel me in on this one."

Wren put his hands in his pockets and took a step back. Then a second. "You'll make sure no one else gets ahold of it, right?"

Well, shit. "Does this game usually work for you?"

Wren's expression said it was a fifty-fifty shot. "When you go in, I'll keep you safe."

"You can't make that promise." That anxiety threatened to overtake Damon now.

"Name one time I've lied to you." But Wren didn't wait for an answer. "You know I wouldn't ask if I thought there was another way, if I didn't think it was important for Cate Pendleton and for you."

There it was—forced closure. Damon wasn't interested. "I'm immune to guilt."

"I'm telling you, I will protect you. Burn the place down from the inside if you're in danger and I'll still get to you in time if I have to rush in with a grenade launcher." The conviction in Wren's voice said it was a promise.

But Damon heard something else. Wren didn't throw around meaningless words. He meant what he said. "Holy hell. You already have someone on the inside."

"True but not close enough." Wren nodded at the file sitting on the court. "Read the file on Cate and her sister."

"The answer is still no."

This time Wren started walking. He headed toward

the door to the right of the basket. "You know you can't resist the challenge."

"Watch me." Damon could hear his voice rise. The panic hovered right there.

"Come to dinner before you leave for Pennsylvania. Emery would like to see you." Wren turned around and opened the door. The noise from the hallway spilled onto the court.

"You're using your girlfriend to lure me in?"

Wren lifted a hand in the air. "I'm desperate."

"You can't see me but I'm giving you the finger." Damon yelled to make sure Wren heard him.

Wren didn't even turn around but he gave a little wave as he turned the corner. "I'll take that as a yes."

CHAPTER 2

Cate heard the knocking sound and looked around the windowless conference room to track it. Nothing obvious stuck out as she swiveled her chair from one side to the other, but the knocking stopped. That pretty much fit with her experience in the building so far. Plush and bustling with people inside. Outside, a nondescript beige building near Capitol Hill. She only knew the business's official name—Owari Enterprises—due to the small plaque in the lobby. Not exactly where she'd expected the mysterious, everyone-wants-his-help DC fixer to work.

Uncrossing and recrossing her legs, she went back to studying the files in front of her. The same ones she'd collated, created and read at least a hundred times each. Police reports. Interviews. Piles of paper that purported to tell Shauna's story but really only told the pieces that people assumed explained how and why she died. Cate knew better.

The door opened behind her. She didn't look up, choosing to focus on the paperwork instead. Then her visitor's legs came into view. Long, like stupid long.

Her head jerked up and she caught a peek at the rest of him. Tall and sleek in his slim-fitting black pants and black short-sleeve shirt with thin white stripes.

She tried to look away, not see how fit he was. Ignore the way his biceps strained the hem of sleeves. Pretend she didn't notice how those pants balanced low on his hips, highlighting his long torso and flat stomach. The light brown hair and his shocking green eyes. So green. Like grass-on-a-summer-afternoon green.

So far every man she met in this office gave off a hottie vibe. Men in suits. Men in casual clothes, all walking around, seemingly working hard with chiseled faces to match their impressive muscles. Almost like it was some sort of employment requirement.

"Cate Pendleton?" The guy's deep voice floated through the room.

The knocking started again right after. This time it beat in time with the smack of her knee against the underside of the desk. The second she realized she was the one causing the noise, she stopped fidgeting.

She gestured at the chair across from her at the wide conference table. "Take a seat."

But he didn't move except for his eyebrow, which kicked up and somehow managed to make him look amused. "I'm guessing that means you actually are Cate Pendleton."

"Yes." She assumed that was clear, but maybe there was more than one conference room with a lone woman on the edge in this place. "I have—"

"Hello."

Good grief, that smile. He could sell anything to anyone with that dimple. Except her. She didn't fall for that sort of thing. "What?"

"I thought we'd do the old-fashioned thing and introduce ourselves." He stuck out his hand. "I'm Damon Knox."

"Okay." Her gaze followed his arms and those long fingers. For a second all she could do was stare as mindless chatter rattled around in her brain. It took a few blinks for her to snap back to reality, shake and drop her hand to the table again. "Are you ready now?"

"Sorry I got delayed. How are we doing in here?" Garrett McGrath said as he stepped into the room behind the other guy.

She'd met this one before. He was Wren's right-hand man and the one she dealt with because getting in to see Wren one-to-one proved impossible.

She nodded toward Doug . . . wait, was that it? Her mind blanked out when he started talking. Not a state she was accustomed to. She blamed the secrecy covert crap she had to do to get on Wren's radar. "Your guy is big on formal introductions."

"That doesn't sound like him." Garrett winked at her then closed the door and took the chair at the head of the table. He glanced at Doug, Dan . . . whatever his name was. "Sit."

He listened to Garrett and took a seat. Then he pointed at the shiny band on Garrett's finger. "Congratulations. Gotta say, I never thought you'd get married."

Garrett laughed. "We were looking at takeout menus

one night and I suggested we go to Vegas and get the deed done. Once she said yes, I couldn't get her there fast enough."

"Couldn't risk her changing her mind to that romantic proposal?"

Garrett's laughter only got louder. "Exactly."

Damon! Seeing the men go back and forth, paying her the same attention they paid to the plant in the room, sparked something and the name popped right into her head. One problem down. Now, on to the next one. "You two know each other? I mean, as more than fellow employees."

"Fellow employees?" Damon asked, stringing each word out likely as a signal he didn't love the phrasing.

Garrett shrugged. "Sure."

"Wait." Damon turned to Garrett. "Are you Wren's guy on the inside of Sullivan?"

"I'm sitting right here, so no."

Enough boy talk. The whole conversation raced by without her understanding the context. She'd picked up the Sullivan reference, but little more.

"Excuse me." They both stared at her now. "I'm not sure if this is some sort of men's-club thing, but is there any chance one, or both of you, would consider filling me in on what's happening? Me being the client and all."

If Garrett was offended, he hid it well. At her slight outburst, he pivoted the conversation and focused on her. "Sorry about that. But yes, Wren has used Damon on other missions."

"How formal you sound," Damon mumbled, not even trying to keep his voice low.

"And he'll be with you on this until he heads into Sullivan to collect intel," Garrett said, almost talking over Damon. "I'll be your contact on the outside."

She wasn't convinced about this Damon guy or any plan to put him in Sullivan. Being hot didn't qualify him for anything other than hotness, but he had said something pretty interesting. "But he mentioned you already have an inside man."

Damon nodded. "She's not wrong. I did."

"If there's a person inside, I should just skip . . ." She let her voice trail off when Damon frowned at her. "Well, I should work directly with that person and Damon can go do . . . whatever it is he does."

Garrett glanced at Damon. "I see you've made quite an impression on her."

They'd gotten way off track. She tried to steer them back to the case and Sullivan and this idea of an "inside" person. "I'm not trying to be offensive but—"

"We should start over." Damon leaned back in his chair and talked louder as the metal or wheels or something underneath him creaked. "I'm the one who's going to look into your case with The Sullivan School and then I intend to charge Wren and Garrett, here, a boatload of cash for my valuable services."

Just what she needed, some guy with billable hours on his mind. She didn't have that much money left. Her deal with Wren included a steep discount from his usual rate but she didn't have any sort of agreement with Damon. "I hope not since that bill would get passed on to me."

"Take it up with Wren." Damon lifted one of his hands then let it fall again. "Billing is not my department."

That was not the answer she wanted to hear. She needed to redirect and get them to come to an understanding. They needed to get moving. She didn't have the time or will to postpone this last push one more minute with fights over money.

She stood up and looked at Garrett. "May I see you in the hall for a minute?"

"No." The sharp word came from Damon. He gave his answer that sounded like an order, then stopped talking.

Garrett actually rolled his eyes. "Oh, Damon."

With a heavy sigh, Damon leaned forward, balanced his elbows on the table and stared her down. "Look, I get that I'm not what you were expecting, even though I did put on my fancy clothes to meet you."

"You are . . ." Watching him now, getting hit with full intensity by those sexy eyes, words failed her.

Garrett shook his head. "The right word will never come to you, so just stop there. Trust me."

"Probably true," Damon said then kept right on talking. "I didn't ask for this assignment. I'm doing it as a favor to Wren and to you."

She almost swallowed her tongue. "To me?"

"You need someone intimately familiar with Sullivan. Someone who can get in and look around. Someone who can get the intel out of the people in there and use Wren's inside source."

She had to give him credit because he had her attention now. "And that's you?"

He didn't blink. "That's *only* me."

This conversation got more interesting by the second. "Why you? What is so special about being Damon?"

He shook his head. "You need to trust me on this."

She snorted. "I don't think so."

"That would be a mistake on your part."

She couldn't figure out if he'd slipped into blowhard mode or if the comment was genuine. From the look of him, all sure and not-trying-to-impress, he struck her as the kind of guy who could back up his boasts. But she'd been down wrong roads and followed so many false leads in the effort to find answers about Shauna's death. The idea of getting lost in hope one more time only to find the promising direction led nowhere zapped the energy out of her. She'd tried for so long and this really felt like the last viable trail.

But the sureness in his voice lured her in. Something about that confidence, almost cocky, made it tough for her to immediately discount him as a pretty face and move on. "Your ego is impressive. I'm wondering if the rest of you is."

The corner of Damon's mouth kicked up in a sly smile. "Try me."

"Well." Garrett clapped as he shifted in his chair. "On that note, why don't we take a breath and figure out where we are."

But Damon didn't back down. He never broke eye contact with her. "Not until Cate tells me how she got Wren's attention."

Luck, pure luck. "Meaning?"

"He's elusive and particular about the cases he takes. Most people assume his existence is a rumor and not real. The rest of us know he works for governments and powerful people. Charges a crap ton of money for his services, which explains how he can afford to be choosy and mysterious." Damon ticked off his arguments on his fingers. "None of that explains you. How did you get him to take on your case?"

"I can be persuasive. You need to trust me on this." She smiled as she threw his words back at him. When Damon didn't move, didn't say a word, she realized she sucked at this game. "And my neighbor is a friend of his."

"Who?"

Cate searched her mind for a reason to hold back this bit of information, but she couldn't come up with one. And when Garrett nodded at her, she took that as approval to keep talking. "Senator Sheila Dayton."

Damon blinked for the first time. "Ah, yes."

"Maryland. Tough with two kids and a husband who's a professor at Howard University." Garrett smiled. "And an old friend of Wren's."

"I know who she is," Damon said without looking away from Cate. "You asked her for help?"

"Begged." Cate refused to act like finding the information she needed didn't matter, as if she could easily forget Shauna and move on. "That's what you need to understand. I will do anything to get to the truth."

Silence filled the room. For almost a minute, the only sound came from the muted voices on the other side of the closed conference room door. Then Damon's voice broke through the tense quiet. "Including lunch?"

She looked from Damon to Garrett, hoping to get a little help since her Damon-to-English deciphering tool seemed to be malfunctioning. "What are you talking about now?"

"The changing-the-subject thing?" Garrett shook his head. "He does that a lot."

Damon stood up. "Let's get some food and you can fill me in on what you need and hope to gain here."

"But . . . but . . ." She looked at the stacks of files highlighting years of hard work sitting in front of her, all perfectly compiled so that she could walk him through the issues in a clear way. "Everything we need is right here. Police reports. The interview transcripts and the . . . the . . ."

"I'll review it all but first I want to hear what you need directly from you. Lines on a page only tell me so much. Your passion, your commitment, will tell me what I need to know."

She wasn't sure how to respond to that. "Okay."

Garrett snorted. "Really? That speech worked for you?"

"Sort of." She figured it was easier to concede because she didn't really care about food. And once she got him talking she might get a peek into what made him so confident and supposedly knowledgeable about Sullivan.

Pick your battles. Her mother's voice echoed in her brain. That's exactly what she intended to do here, and she had a feeling with Damon she'd be picking quite a few as she struggled to hold her ground against his whirlwind of stubbornness.

"We'll be back." Damon was already around the table and headed for the door.

"So, I don't get lunch?" Garrett asked, the amusement clear in his tone.

"If Cate and I are going to work together, we need to be sure we can survive lunch." Damon motioned for her to precede him through the door.

"If he's not coming, who's paying?" she asked but she had a feeling she knew the answer.

"I like you, Cate." He guided her into the hallway. "And the answer, of course, is you."

Just as she thought.

CHAPTER 3

A half hour later, Cate looked ready to jump out of her chair. They sat in a self-professed American bistro a few blocks from Wren's office. Damon picked it for proximity and name, but if the food tasted half as good as this place smelled, he'd be happy.

It wasn't even noon on a weekday and most of the tables were full. Waiters and waitresses bustled around the white-and-black checkered floor. From their table in the back, Damon could see it all, including the very antsy, very pretty woman in front of him.

Her shiny, straight black hair fell over her shoulders. As she crossed and uncrossed her legs, her body shifted around. One minute she fiddled with her napkin, the next she wrapped her fingers around the armrests of the chair and held on as if she rode the wildest roller coaster.

Damon wasn't sure what was happening in her head. Probably a back-and-forth about him and whether he would be any help to her at all.

He cursed Wren for putting him in the ill-fitting

and always uncomfortable role of savior. He'd spent his life disappointing people. Apparently, now it was Cate's turn.

She finally broke the silence on a loud exhale. "We've studied the menu and ordered, had a few sips of water and looked around. Would now be a good time to get to work?"

As she spoke, she pinned him across the table with a fiery look in those deep brown eyes. He'd been waiting for her to take control again, and she did not disappoint. Except for her meal choice. "You ordered a grilled cheese and salad."

She frowned. "So?"

Her quick glance toward the door leading to the street suggested she was toying with the idea of making a run for it. Damon couldn't blame her. He'd had the same *run like hell* sensation racing through him since Wren handed him her file.

"It's a burger place. The word *burger* is actually in the name of the restaurant." Which was the main reason Damon picked this restaurant instead of something more out of the way and quiet.

"I bet they have the unique skills required to make things with cheese."

Sassy, verbally punching out . . . he liked it. Even though she looked ten seconds from punching him, his initial thought was that he liked *her*. She fought him, didn't back down and bullied her way into meeting Wren—or whatever name he used when they met.

She used her contacts to hunt down the one person who might help her. All smart. Those were the moves of a survivor.

Studying her wasn't exactly a hardship either. The file Wren handed him listed her mother's name as Emi Asato. A single mother who put herself through college while she raised Cate and her sister. Born in Ohio to parents who came to the US from Osaka, Japan, the woman buried one daughter while the other fought to find out the truth. Those facts made him respect the whole family. That kind of tenacity and strength always made him look twice.

The rest of Cate, the long legs and sexy pronounced collarbone where her thin gold chain balanced, the way her white V-neck T-shirt highlighted high, round breasts and trim waist . . . well, those worked for him, too. From the way she walked to the way she talked, she intrigued him. He found himself wanting to know more about how she lived and what, other than her dead sister, mattered to her.

He appreciated every inch of her, including that big brain that she didn't hesitate to use to best him whenever possible. That was some pretty sexy shit right there.

"Are you not a meat eater? Because that's something I should know up front." The kind of thing Wren should put in her file. Damon didn't think that was too much to ask.

As predicted, she frowned at him. Shot him one of those you're-wasting-time looks that she'd been using on him nonstop since they met. "Are you serious right now?"

"Because I eat a lot of burgers and if that's going to offend you, I can eat something else. I won't like it, but I will." Her fidgeting must be rubbing off on him because he picked up his fork then set it down again.

She leaned across the table. "How many burgers?"

Now this was a topic he could handle. Especially since she asked the question in a soft voice, as if they were sharing a secret. "Every day."

She sat back hard in her seat again. "You do not eat a hamburger every day."

He ignored the horror in her voice. "True. Some days I mix it up and order a cheeseburger. If I'm feeling particularly frisky I'll have a steak sandwich."

"That seems like an invitation to heart disease." And she was back to shifting around. She crossed and uncrossed her arms before she grabbed for her napkin again.

He could not stop watching her. Energy buzzed off her. He found the mix of tough talk and nervous fidgeting unexpectedly hot. "You'd think, but no."

"I'm going to pretend you're kidding."

"I'm not."

She cleared her throat. "Shauna."

They could circle back to food because she had his attention now. He refused to joke about this topic. "Your sister."

"She's three years older."

He noticed she didn't use the past tense. Shauna

died ten years ago and Cate still saw her as an "is." For Damon, that meant treading carefully. "And you are . . . ?"

"Twenty-nine."

He knew that answer before she said it, but thought keeping her to facts might help her emotionally wade through the next part. He'd helped Wren with other cases and this piece—dealing with the grief—never got easier. Damon had a load of grief and guilt of his own piled on top of hers, so he got it.

He nodded to her. "Go ahead."

"The questions you ask don't seem that pertinent."

"I'm going to be honest with you." He started to lean forward when the waiter came by and dropped off their food. The smell of grilled hamburger filled his senses as he reached for his folded napkin and threw it across his lap.

She didn't move. "That would be a good way to start."

"Wren already gave me a file he had on you. The man is an expert at collecting information and then making Garrett put it together in a nice big, easy-to-understand breakdown of what happened and when."

For a few seconds she sat there, quiet, as her gaze moved over his face, studying him. "Then why are we here doing the get-to-know-you thing?"

"First, I'm hungry. That happens a lot. The need-to-eat thing. So, you'll need to get used to it." He popped a french fry in his mouth.

"You aren't . . . I mean, you look . . ."

Interesting. "I'm pretty excited to hear how you finish that sentence."

She waved a hand in front of her. "You're fit."

"Oh, really?"

"Don't get excited. That was an objectively factual statement."

"Objectively factual?" He didn't even know how to decipher that. If she found him sexy she should absolutely say so because *damn* was that a mutual feeling.

"You know what I mean."

Rather than risk saying the wrong thing and wearing her salad, he switched back to the food. That seemed like a safe topic. "I have low blood sugar and get cranky when I don't eat."

"So, you eat burgers all the time."

"I like pleasure."

She bit her top lip as if she were fighting off a smile. "You sound like you're five."

"And protein." All this talk about food and seeing the burger *right there*, all he wanted to do was pick it up and take a bite, but he waited. "My point is that this—here, right now, us eating together—is about getting to know each other."

That buried smile disappeared. "Why do we need to?"

"Why?" Good lord, she was serious. He could tell from the confused expression. Nothing about her tone or demeanor telegraphed amusement or suggested she was joking.

"It's a job. You go in and do it." She shrugged. "I'd rather spend our time this afternoon with you telling me your big plan so that we can figure out what we do next."

They appeared to have very different views on who was going to be in charge of this operation. He was very clear, but she seemed to be confused. "Let me understand this. You think *we* need to agree on strategy?"

"Of course."

"That's not how this works." Not in his world. Not ever. When he took on a job he ran it alone, not by committee.

She shoved her plate to the side and leaned on her elbows, inching closer to him across the top of the two-seat table. "Do you understand what's at stake here?"

"Likely a silent promise you made to your sister that you would make sure her killer didn't go free." It was a guess, but an educated one. He'd dealt with grieving family members before. He'd seen both sides of the battle lines. So, when her eyes widened he knew he'd scored. "And your peace of mind."

She glanced down at her salad then at the two men at the table next to them who were locked in an argument about football season tickets. When she finally looked back at him again, some of the stress around her eyes had disappeared. "You get it."

"I know guilt when I see it." Worse, he knew how it ate away at a person, not needing darkness to creep and spread. Yes, it stole sleep but it haunted the daylight hours, too. Any free minute when his mind wasn't bombarded with other thoughts, the doubts moved in and took hold, and he knew his experience was not unusual.

"I'm not—"

"Let's try it this way." He decided to jump in, make it clear he knew the basics and save her from having to relive them. "You and your sister were raised by a single mom. You grew up without money, so Shauna looked for alternative ways to fund her education. She stumbled onto Sullivan and its promise of providing an education while learning skills and working her way through."

He knew the story by heart because it played over and over in so many faces, so many people, all sorts of backgrounds at Sullivan. The so-called school thrived on being the place to land for people who craved security and wanted to make a better life. Many went on to do just that, didn't get sucked into the rest. But for those who did . . . something sinister filled that need for security.

Cate's eyes narrowed a fraction. "You sound like a brochure for the place."

Once, a long time ago, he'd memorized the thing. That was one of his jobs—to talk up Sullivan. "But nothing was as it seemed at the school."

"Understatement."

"Two years before the ATF stormed the place and closed it, making it the very private, no-trespassers-

allowed commune it is now, your sister died there."
Damon knew he should tiptoe through this part, be
more patient than he could usually muster.

"She was murdered."

"That's your theory." And her mother's and a few
others. But louder, more powerful voices overwhelmed
the accusations, shutting down any talk until the official school and all that good press ended in a storm
of bullets two years later.

"Do you know better?"

As someone who prided himself on collecting intel, this was one time he knew too much. "I start
from a place where I don't have a preconceived answer about what happened to your sister. I listen to
the evidence and follow it."

Cate took a quick look around before leaning in a
little more. "They said she fell off the water tower.
Lost her balance."

Damon blocked the noise of the busy restaurant.
The clanking of dishes and low hum of conversation
faded away as he looked at her. "You don't buy it."

"She was deathly afraid of heights. There's no way
she would have been on that ladder, thirty feet off the
ground."

Sounded pretty convincing to him, but he didn't
want her to get her hopes up. She'd been battling this
case for years. The idea that he could rush in and fix
it all even with Wren's considerable power and backing struck Damon as ridiculous. Life didn't work that

way and she didn't really need a white knight. He got that now. What she needed was answers.

"Is that your total case against the official story?" he asked.

"If we do this, I need to know you're on my side." She thumped her finger against the table, rattling the water in the glasses. "I can't have any questions about your loyalty."

Wrong answer. "If you want blind devotion without regard to facts, I'm not your man."

"Okay." She nodded before rolling up her napkin and throwing it on the table. Then she was on her feet.

Fury pounded off her. Every muscle tensed. He'd failed her. The vacant look in her eyes said that much without uttering the actual words.

This woman exhausted him. "But if you want someone who will literally risk everything to find an answer, then you want me, Cate."

She ignored the curious glances from a few people sitting around them. Damon guessed they looked as if they were engaged in a lovers' quarrel or fight of some sort. Even the waiter who had been headed for their table completed an abrupt U-turn and walked away.

Smart bastard.

Emotions moved across her face. Anger, frustration and finally resignation. Another minute passed before she blew out a long breath and sat back down. She didn't bother to say anything but she picked up her fork, which he took as a sign that they had overcome a roadblock, even though he wasn't clear how.

"Well, Cate Pendleton. Do you want me or not?" The comment came out more provocative than he intended.

Before he could clean it up, she nodded. "For now."

She might be annoying, but he did like her style. Noncommittal and making him work for every inch forward. The combination had him reeling and wanting to know more. "That response doesn't sound promising."

"Trust needs to be earned." She dropped her fork and reached across the table to snatch a few of his french fries.

Okay, that move made him like her a bit less. "So, you're one of those."

"What?"

"French fry stealer. You could have ordered your own but chose to take mine instead."

She shrugged as she grabbed two more fries that had fallen off the edge of his plate and onto the place mat. "Maybe you're being a bit dramatic?"

"You'll learn fast."

"What?"

When she reached over again, he moved his plate closer to him and the edge of the table. "That if you want something, all you have to do is ask."

She blinked a few times. "I don't . . ."

"Do you often just drop the back end of your sentences?"

She winced. "Unfortunately, yes."

That might have been the most endearing admission he'd ever heard. "Well, my point still stands. Ask."

"Are we still talking about food?"

He gave in and spun the plate around while pushing it toward her. The move gave her an easy line to the fries. "Excellent question."

CHAPTER 4

Cate had never seen anyone get so much joy out of a hamburger. She kept stealing Damon's fries just to prevent him from going overboard and starting to moan. But that was fifteen minutes ago. Now they were back in the conference room, sitting in the same chairs they'd left before they ate, with Garrett looming over them. Staring and smiling.

Her mood flipped as a familiar wariness settled inside her. Garrett looked like a man with a secret and she'd never found that to end well for her.

Garrett's gaze moved from Damon to Cate. "Congratulations. I see you survived lunch."

She wouldn't go that far. "Sort of."

"It's been a rocky almost two hours of knowing each other, but at least I'm no longer hungry." Damon shrugged. "Not right now, anyway."

"Sounds like this relationship is off to a great start." Garrett took one folder off the stack in front of him and shot it across the table toward Damon. The other landed in front of her. "Speaking of which . . ."

Damon opened it but didn't look down to see what was inside. "What's this?"

"Your cover."

Damon shut the file just as quickly. "Excuse me?"

Two words were all it took for most of her wariness to slip away. When she got a good look at Damon's expression—open mouth and wide eyes—she almost laughed. A you've-got-to-be-kidding vibe thrummed off him.

She guessed her smile matched Garrett's. "He thought he was in charge."

Garrett shook his head. "Yeah, well, he's wrong."

She couldn't help it. She had to take a peek, see what Garrett had in mind. If the contents had the power to knock Damon speechless, she was in. In the short time she'd known him, he hadn't exactly been quiet.

Damon slid the folder back toward Garrett. "You are not assigning us a—"

"No way." She blinked a few times as the lines on the page in front of her came into focus. "This is a joke, right?"

Damon frowned. "What does it say?"

"We're dating." Her voice rose, and she didn't even try to calm it back down. "Each other."

Damon stopped in the middle of reaching for his folder again and stared at her. "And the thought of that is what has you screaming?"

"You're missing the point." Like, he wasn't even in the same universe as she was right now.

Garrett's eyebrow lifted. "It was an interesting reaction. Explains a lot about the sad state of Damon's dating life. Apparently, women run away screaming in horror. Who knew?"

She decided to ignore any reference to Damon's dating life. But now she knew he was single, not that she cared because she refused to care. "You basically threatened to have me arrested for eating your french fries."

Garrett made a humming sound. "You didn't touch his hamburger, did you?"

"She's exaggerating. A little." Damon held up a finger as if he was making some grand point. "And it was, like, ten fries. Not just a few."

"That many? Oh, sure. That makes your reaction completely reasonable." The sarcasm dripped off every word Garrett said.

Enough food talk. She needed them to focus on kicking this idea so they could come up with a better one. "We can't pull this off."

"You sure?" Garrett winced. "Because Thanksgivings growing up sounded a lot like this. The screeching and arguing. Feels like family to me."

Damon stood up with an exaggerated sigh. "I'm suddenly worried about your marriage."

"If you'd sit back down we could go over this," Garrett said as he eyed the now empty chair.

"No." Damon shook his head as if to emphasize his point.

"This time I agree with him." And that made her nervous.

Garrett leaned back in his chair. Didn't seem to care that he tipped it far enough that the chair looked ready to fall over. "You can't just walk up to the locked gate and knock."

"But we can . . ." Nothing else came to her. Not a single word.

Garrett stared at her. "Yes?"

She looked at Damon for assistance. "I was hoping you would finish the sentence for me."

Wasn't he supposed to be the big-time covert ops guy? Actually, now that she thought about it, she didn't know what his skills were. He talked about strategy, so he could use that pretty head of his and come up with one.

Damon dropped back into his chair. "With that bossiness, maybe we are married."

She snapped her fingers at him. "Focus. He's suggesting we go in there and . . ." She hadn't gotten past the first paragraph on the page, so she didn't actually know what came next. "What?"

"Damon knows people at Sullivan," Garrett said.

All the questions bombarding her brain disappeared in a flash. Now she had a bunch of new ones. She went with the obvious first one. "How?"

"Let the man finish telling us about his stupid idea," Damon said through what looked like a locked jaw.

"You're saying you're going to answer my question once he finishes?" She didn't buy that for a second.

"No, I just think the sooner he finishes we can come up with a better idea." Damon turned to Garrett. "Go ahead."

"Under this cover, you two met each other when Cate kept bugging you for information on Sullivan." Garrett's smile never slipped as he looked from Damon to Cate. "See, since you've been asking questions and causing trouble, they are going to know you and not want you on the grounds."

"He makes a good point," Damon mumbled under his breath.

She decided to ignore that comment, too. She was starting to think that might be her best defense mechanism until all of this was over. "But you think because I walk into Sullivan with Damon here, the fine people of Sullivan will welcome me."

"No, I think you can sell the story that you fell for each other and Damon is taking you there to meet some people and prove to you that your theory about your sister is wrong."

"It's not wrong." She was murdered. The words ran through Cate's brain nonstop these days.

Garrett frowned at her. "Do you understand what a cover story is?"

She had too many questions to make any sense of the plan. The biggest one kept echoing in her head. She glanced at Damon. "Why will they let you in?"

His expression stayed blank. "I have a way with people."

Garrett snorted. "Hardly."

They were pushing her off topic. She could see it. Garrett used humor. Damon avoided. They knew things she didn't, and she hated that.

"What aren't you telling me?" She didn't care which one of them answered so long as one of them did.

"Here's an idea." Garrett tipped his chair forward again to rest his elbows on the edge of the conference room table. "You two will have plenty of time together, in tight quarters because people who are dating would share a room, and you can ask and answer all the questions about each other then."

For a few seconds, no one said anything. She fought to come up with another plan—any other plan—and nothing came to her. When she looked at Damon she didn't exactly see him jumping up to offer suggestions either. The only sense of satisfaction in the entire room came from Garrett. He practically reeked of it, which made her hate his plan even more. "He thinks he won."

Damon looked at Garrett then nodded. "He's annoying like that."

She tried one last time. "What was your plan for getting into Sullivan?"

"I go to the gate and yell until someone opens it," Damon said.

Garrett nodded. "Brilliant. We'll call that Plan D."

There was no way that was the sum total of his plan to help her . . . right? "Once you were done yelling what did you think would happen?"

"Knowing the people I know at Sullivan? Someone would shoot me."

She waited for him to laugh or joke, but no. "That's ridiculous."

"True, but I like the plan better now." Garrett made a note in his file. "I'm moving it up to Plan B."

Damon made a strangled sound. "I agreed to take this case about ten minutes ago, so forgive me for not having the perfect entrance strategy and cover story all mapped out."

She stared at him for a few more seconds before glancing at Garrett. "I don't have a choice about this fake relationship, do I?"

Garrett's smile only widened. "You could pretend it's a fake engagement instead."

Her stomach rolled over. "Yeah, that's not better."

DAMON WAITED UNTIL Cate excused herself to go to the bathroom to turn on Garrett. In any other building, he would have gone after her. Assumed she was running and understand, but still stop her. Not here. Wren kept this place locked down. No one could get in or out without a badge, and she didn't have one.

Damon tapped his fingers on the folder in front of him. "Fake relationship?"

Garrett shrugged. "It was Wren's idea."

Of course it was. This nonsense had Wren's fingerprints all over it. "You know the chances of us getting away with this are slim."

"People have been trying to lure you back to Sullivan for years."

"Some. Others have been really clear I should stay

away." Damon could remember the yelling when he left the property years ago. The smell of gunfire and the darkening sky. He'd gotten into the back of the police car, waiting for the ground to open and swallow up all of them. Nothing less would have washed the ground clean again.

"And now you'll have a chance to visit with all of them," Garrett said.

"No one is going to believe I'm there to say good things about the place to my fake girlfriend." Not after all the years of being away. Not after all the accusations he'd made and the arrests.

"No, but if you put on a good show they will believe you're willing to go through some shit to make Cate happy."

"What kind of cover is that?" Maybe better than he wanted to admit because that totally sounded like something he'd do. He'd gotten so good at keeping his distance, at using people, that the guilt that used to swamp him now amounted to little more than a twinge most days.

"As a newly married man, I'll take the Fifth. But, really, you'd be amazed what I'd do for Lauren."

Damon struggled to stay pissed off while Garrett wore that silly grin. "But you're in a real relationship with Lauren. I've spent less than two hours with Cate and I'm pretty sure she'd be happy to run me over with her car."

"I've known you for a decade and feel the same way."

Damon blew out a long breath. Tried to silence the

protests screaming in his brain at the idea of heading back into Sullivan and pretending he *wanted* to be there. "I'm serious."

"There's no covert way to do this. People at Sullivan know you. They are aware of her. If you want to get in there, look around and ask questions, you're going to have to go in through the front door. That means having a cover that makes you two being together make sense."

"Or I could sneak in without her." That had been his plan. Half-assed, sure, but solid in that if he got caught it was just him. She would be safe. Sullivan had already claimed one Pendleton sister. It didn't deserve another.

"And then what? Eventually someone would see you. You're kind of tough to miss, plus you want to be able to look around and ask questions. Make them feel comfortable so they mess up. Get into rooms and buildings you wouldn't otherwise be able to access. None of that can happen with you sleeping in a tree and running behind rocks to keep from being seen."

Garrett had thought through all the angles, which was not good for Damon's argument at all. "I hate it when you sound reasonable."

"It happens now and then. Because, you know, I actually do this for a living."

So did Wren, and Damon noticed he didn't seem to be around today. *Interesting.* "Yet I'm the one heading for Pennsylvania."

"Life isn't fair."

Damon opened and closed the file again. He didn't bother scanning the lines this time either. There would be time for intel and more planning tonight. "This better work."

"I like your enthusiasm."

"What you're hearing is frustration."

"Oh, I know." Garrett stood up. "Enjoy Salvation."

"Not possible."

CHAPTER 5

Two days later, Cate and Damon pulled into the parking lot of a one-story motel with rooms all lined in a row. It sat fifteen miles outside of Salvation, Pennsylvania, almost hidden in a cluster of trees, like the rest of the county.

A few diners and gas stations dotted the road that connected the series of tiny towns in the middle of the state. She knew because they'd passed quite a few before setting up in Montour. The town stretched out in a tiny corner along a lake, at the base of a mountain. Exactly two hundred and two people lived in Montour, or that's what the welcoming sign on the highway said. No one knew the exact number for Salvation next door because no one knew how many people still lived up on the mountain ridge at Sullivan.

Cate understood the beauty of coming here. Well, in a way. The seclusion and all that rich greenery. The smell of cut grass and the open farmland. Fresh air and the lack of traffic, so unlike where she grew up in Baltimore. In the fall, the mountains were ablaze in color. Dotted in deep reds and bright yellows. She'd seen the photos both before and after Shauna decided to invest her time in Sullivan.

All of those facts sped through Cate's mind as she looked at the maps spread out on the round table in front of her. Damon picked adjoining rooms that consisted of little more than a bed and dresser in each. A small pole on the wall outside the bathroom and two hooks formed the closet. Damon had opened the door between the rooms and dragged the small round tables from under the windows to the middle as a makeshift battle station. That kept the door open between their beds and killed off any sense of privacy, but she doubted they would be here for very long.

When he stepped out of his bathroom, drying his hands on what looked like a washcloth, she pointed at the documents on the table closest to him. "These are the blueprints for Sullivan."

He made a strange humming sound before shrugging. "Sort of."

The comment didn't surprise her. He challenged her on every last thing. She still hadn't recovered from his insistence this morning that cereal was not real breakfast food. The guy had an opinion on everything.

Rather than argue, she skipped ahead to a statement. "I'm not asking you. I'm telling you."

He threw the cloth on the top of the dresser, clearly not caring that it landed on his baseball hat. "Well, I'm telling you these are off."

"I got them from the county." She was pretty sure

Garrett had seen them and not questioned them. "They're accurate."

"These are the ones that comply with all the local regulations." Damon finally tore his gaze away from the documents and glanced up at her. "That doesn't make them factually correct."

Tiny drops of water beaded on the ends of the hair laying on his forehead. She figured he'd washed up after their drive and had to beat back a wave of envy. She had the sweaty, pretty-sure-she-smelled grungy feeling that she got whenever she went on a road trip. Even pulling her hair back in the ponytail hadn't helped. She blamed the mix of wariness and excitement for the way adrenaline kept whipping through her.

One minute she ached to get near Salvation faster, hoping closure waited there. The next she thought about all the lies and cover-ups and how little she knew about Damon and then her stomach flipped over in panic. The idea of getting here, right to the edge of the place where she could finally get answers, and then failing made her want to heave.

She forced her mind to stay off the "what-ifs" and all the years of kicking herself for not fighting harder to keep in touch with Shauna. They had bigger issues to handle over the next few weeks.

"The architect's signature is right there," Cate said, pointing to the small boxed-off area on the bottom of the blueprints.

He snorted. "Because that can't be faked."

She noticed all of him then. The faded blue jeans

and light gray T-shirt that fit him like a second skin. He'd worn a zip-up hoodie in the car but that had disappeared. Somewhere along the line he'd done an informal striptease and she'd missed it.

She closed her eyes for a second, trying to block out all the stray thoughts and her unwanted attraction to a guy who viewed hamburgers as a food group. When she opened them again, he hadn't moved. Despite the unintended closeness, she kept her voice steady. "Explain what's wrong."

"This wasn't a food storage facility." He pointed to the outline of a building constructed in the side of a hill. The natural lower temperature of the ground and moss and umbrella of trees surrounding it likely kept the area cooler, hence preserving the food. "This was where they kept the weapons."

"Under the deal with . . ." *Weapons?* Those were supposed to be gone but he sounded so sure. She didn't know what to think about that fact. "Was?"

"In the past."

"Believe it or not, I wasn't asking for a definition of the word. How do you know where they were and that they're still there?"

"Educated guess." He returned to pointing. "Weapons. Bunkhouse for new students, and I use that term loosely. They were more like cabins, actually very homey. Sullivan is not about living a monk-like existence." His fingers moved around the page, highlighting the strategic use of each area. "These are guard posts and this is the firing range."

Her head started spinning. The more he spoke, all clear and sure, the dizzier she became. "Damon."

"Maybe some things have changed, but I'm right about Sullivan really being more than a school or commune. It always was."

Her mind flashed to his use of the past tense then to the comment about an inside man. Damon wasn't supposed to be the person buried deep within the Sullivan operation, but he spoke with far too much knowledge. Nothing about his tone suggested he was guessing or merely passing on gossip. "When?"

To his credit, he didn't pretend not to understand the question. "Back then."

Personal intel but "then" could mean any time period. But he possessed the kind of information that had proved so difficult to obtain. Not the type she'd shared or gotten from any discussion she'd had with any of Wren's people. Which meant it came from somewhere else. "What are you talking about?"

"Its real purpose under all the teaching and behind the awards Sullivan won back when the school was in the press and touted as a new means of educating—less expensive and more practical—wasn't knowledge."

The guy spent a whole lunch arguing about french fries and most of the drive here on unimportant topics, like the best rock band of the last decade, but he skipped over this part. "Okay, stop."

"I thought you wanted inside information."

"That's supposed to be coming from someone on

the inside, not you. Which makes me wonder what you do know and how you learned it."

He shrugged at her. "I'm a smart guy."

She seriously considered punching him every time he lifted his shoulders. Who knew a simple gesture could be so freaking annoying? "You're being cryptic."

"Not if you listen."

She hit that unseen line where her temper blew. All the building frustration spewed over until her sole focus became getting him to stop rambling and answer her questions.

She stepped over to her bed and dug around in the duffle bag she brought with her. She took out the one thing she thought would guarantee they jump off this odd conversational train to nowhere and get back to where she needed them to be.

She turned around to face him and took aim. "Let's try this again."

Instead of being scared or worried, his expression morphed into something else. He basically shot her a you-are-not-impressing-me frown as his hands moved to his hips. "You have a gun?"

"For protection."

"From?"

"Right now? You."

This time he rolled his eyes at her. "Come on. You know I'm not dangerous. Well, not to you."

"Uh-huh. Just keep in mind that I know how to use it and can if you don't start answering my questions in a way that makes sense." She'd taken lessons and went to the range.

"I've been trained to take it from you before you can blink." He made a noise that sounded like a snort. "So there."

"I can't believe you've gotten this far in life without someone shooting you. I've wanted to shoot you ten times in the last hour." And that was not much of an exaggeration. Not something that would hurt too bad. More like a ping across his ear to let him know her patience had expired.

"I never said I had." When she tried to ask what that meant, he talked over her. "Is it loaded?"

"Maybe."

"Which I assume means no and that's not smart." He shook his head. "You could wave that in front of the wrong person."

She wasn't sure if he was stalling or not. "Like?"

"Someone who is carrying and thinks you're really a threat." He blew out a long breath, as if he were the one struggling with frustration. "Now, tell me what your protection worry is about. Did someone threaten you?"

He sounded serious, maybe even concerned, which sucked away most of her anger at him. "Someone broke into my place."

He took another step closer and put his hand on the side of her gun to point it away from him. "When did that happen?"

"Stop moving around." She realized then he could

have taken the weapon and chose not to. It was possible he sensed she needed to hold it, needed to feel in control. Of course, it was also possible she was giving him far too much credit for "getting" her.

He shook his head. "You aren't going to shoot me with what I'm assuming is an unloaded gun."

"Don't be so sure." But she was sure and she clearly was not fooling him.

"First, you're not a dumbass. Second, killing me means you have to beg Wren for another person to help you. Even though he is sympathetic to someone in your situation, he doesn't have so many friends that he can afford to have a bunch of us killed off."

That made sense . . . which ticked her off all over again. "I should shoot you on principle."

"Honestly, that thought is going to be in your head a lot while we spend time together. So long as you don't follow through on it, we're fine." He held out his hand.

She didn't fight it. She put it in his hand but vowed not to lose sight of it because she needed to make sure she got it back if they ever managed to get back to her simple question about his knowledge of the blueprints. "Who are you? Not the cover story. I mean, really."

"Damon Knox. I'm pretty sure Wren told you that at some point. Or Garrett, maybe."

He'd hit on a touchy subject but she doubted he knew that. "I never actually got to meet Wren. As far as I know, he's made up."

Damon smiled. "You met him."

It was official. He could make any sentence annoying. "I actually didn't."

"He likely went by another name, but you met him."

That couldn't be true . . . or could it? She thought back to Garrett, then to the guy she met before Garrett. Brian Jacobs. He seemed to be big at Owari. Now she wondered if one of those two really was *the* guy, Wren. "That's ridiculous."

"Trust me, I've told him that many times." Damon rolled his eyes. "He has some excuse about the business being dangerous and this ensuring the protection of his staff and the people he cares about. I think he's just a paranoid bastard. But since he's a millionaire and always buys my dinner when we go out, I ignore the numerous-names thing character flaw."

"Is Garrett really Wren?"

"Nope. Two different men."

So, it was Brian. Part Asian, she could see it in his face just like she saw the hints of her ancestry in her own every morning. "This is a confusing mess."

"People have reasons to change names." Damon pulled out one of the wooden chairs at the table and sat down. He set the gun down in front of him, but not before checking to see if she was right about it being loaded.

But she focused on what he said. "People . . . like you?"

"Admittedly, Damon Knox is not my real name, but—"

"Stop." She cut him off because, come on. "Most normal people don't have more than one name."

"We clearly know different people."

The weird thing is, that the answer didn't surprise her. From him, she half expected a convoluted response. Of course he had more than one name and ran with a group of people who operated in the same way. That fit with the little she knew about him so far. "I don't understand why Wren would send you to me. None of this makes sense."

"I've known Wren for more than a decade." Damon leaned back until the front two legs of the chair left the carpeted floor. "Yes, the millionaire superman who can make all problems disappear is actually a friend of mine. It's a long story and before you ask, I'm not telling it. But the relationship means shooting me is never going to be the right answer for you."

"Is everything going to be this hard with you?" She reached for the gun to put it back in her bag.

"More than likely, yes." He trapped the gun and her hand under his. "Let me keep the weapon."

"I need it for protection."

"That's what I'm here for."

"Are you sure? I don't feel all that secure right now." But she let go of the gun, fully intending to steal it back from him later.

Pick your battles.

"We're using two different words." He moved the gun closer to his side of the table but didn't pick it up. "Tell me about the break-in thing."

"You're going to think I'm the nervous type or making it up."

His expression suggested she might be right. "Try telling me first then I'll come up with a response."

"Twice I've been out of my condo and come back to the faint smell of men's cologne or aftershave. I can't quite nail it down, but it's a scent that should not have been there."

He didn't laugh or roll his eyes. Didn't give her the *poor little lady* wince she'd gotten from the police about her sister long ago. "Sounds like an amateur move."

She wasn't sure if he was talking about her or the intruder. "Meaning?"

"People hired to do this kind of work blend in. You shouldn't be able to pick up any clue that they've been there."

"Everything else looked the same." Only that one thing hinted at an intruder.

"Still, the scent might help us in the future."

"How?"

"Do you live alone?"

"You know I do." He'd already admitted to reading a file on her, so she refused to play that game. "Nothing was missing that I could tell, but it felt like someone had looked around."

"For what?"

"My guess? Some intel on what I've found on Shauna's case."

He nodded. "What exactly have you found?"

That none of the pieces fit together. That the police and FBI made leaps and seemed to accept Sullivan's story without much research or investigation. It was all in her notes in the file she kept on the case. The same one she'd intended to show him that first day they met but then he'd insisted they go out to eat instead. "We'll get to that."

"That's an annoying answer."

"How does it feel to be on the receiving end of a nonresponse?"

His mouth screwed up in a frown. "Not great."

She heard the amusement in his voice. Just a touch and it left as quickly as it came, but she was pretty sure she'd made her point. Just to make sure, she rubbed it in a little. "See?"

"So, no one touched you but they touched your stuff. Walked around, looked through everything, likely sat on your bed and—"

The wave of nausea hit her out of nowhere. "Don't . . ."

The blood left her head. She felt it whoosh right out of her. Her balance faltered and she fell against the edge of the bed, managing to catch herself from taking an embarrassing tumble by grabbing on to the edge of the mattress and lowering her body the rest of the way down.

He was up and out of his chair a second later. On his knees next to her, rubbing her arm. "Cate?"

She bent over with her arms dangling between her widespread legs and her eyes closed. "I'm going to be sick."

"Whoa. Let's not do that." His hand slipped over her back and up to the base of her neck. He massaged her with a gentle touch.

"I can't . . ."

"Breathe in and hold it until I tell you to let it go." He stood right next to her, counting and guiding her. "There it is. Now exhale." He held her hand and breathed with her. "Again."

They went through the calming exercise three more times. He never rushed her or questioned her. His entire focus seemed to be on getting her body to relax while it tried so hard to rebel on her.

After a few more deep breaths, the urge to throw up on him subsided. She slowly lifted her head but kept her eyes closed just in case the room continued to flip-flop. "I'm okay."

"Of course you are." His hand rubbed up and down her back in a soothing rhythm.

She leaned into him, letting him shoulder a bit of her weight. "This is embarrassing."

"No one is watching but me."

She opened one eye and peeked over at him. "I can't tell if you're being condescending."

"Honestly, I'm not that transparent. You'll know when it happens."

She let her head drop back as she stared up at the bland off-white ceiling. "That was—"

"A panic attack."

She lowered her head and stared at him then. "I do not panic."

"You're human, Cate. You think your sister was killed in a secretive school that enjoyed protection from the local government and police for years." He shifted until he sat on the bed next to her. "A lot of people have been covering their asses about Sullivan, so you're allowed to panic."

"One second you're likeable then the next you're . . ."

He laughed. "A dick?"

Not quite that bad, but she was sure he could head there without trouble. "That pretty much sums it up."

His hand dropped to the mattress between them. "You'll get used to it."

Maybe, but right now her head thumped from the aftermath of the panic. She knew from experience the blinding headache would soon hit. She needed low light and loads of caffeine. But she also wanted him to understand. "I've spent years trying to figure out what happened that night at Sullivan."

"Were you two close?"

The comment struck her with the force of a hard slap. "What does that mean?"

He held up his hands as if in mock surrender. "It's a simple question, not a test or a value judgment. I'm trying to figure out if you were able to communicate with her during the two years she was there. If so, if you have any insight on what was happening with her."

"That's not how Sullivan worked."

His gaze searched her face. It smoothed over her cheeks and down to her mouth. Then he got up and sat on the table across from her. "Tell me what you think you know."

The move was so abrupt she could actually feel a breeze of air blow between them when he moved away. That fast, she missed the warmth thrumming off him. But his words grabbed her attention away from all that comfort. "The way you say things makes it clear *you* know about the inner workings at Sullivan."

"Let's stick to your sister."

She took that as a *yes* but didn't battle him. At this rate, it would take two weeks for them to have a full conversation on any topic. "For now."

"It's cute that you think we're negotiating."

"Once she was at the school, or whatever it really was, she would call. That lasted for the first year but eventually, right before she died, that stopped. I wrote a few letters near the end but I never heard back, which made me think she didn't get them." That soft-coated her feelings back then. Cate had felt abandoned. That her sister had moved on and no longer had to worry about Mom's work hours or how they would pay all the bills and still eat.

In Cate's head, Shauna was off having fun and making friends. She'd moved on and left Cate behind.

"You're right. With the timing of when she broke off contact and what was happening at the school, it's likely she didn't see the letters. Things had turned by then, become less subtle."

Cate wanted that to be true but she was afraid to let her mind go there. After all the years of strangling guilt about not stepping in and asking questions sooner, she was not ready to be let off the hook. "And how would you know about all those changes?"

"That's how cults work."

The word settled in Cate's head. For a second she didn't say anything. Couldn't because relief raced through her, stealing her breath. "You're one of the few people willing to use that word."

"Seems obvious." He shrugged. "It started out fine but things slowly changed. Before the shoot-out that ended it all, the so-called students were kept on campus, very insular. Trips outside the school were limited."

"But by whom?"

"The Sullivan family started the school two generations ago. The original idea was to teach practical skills in this bucolic environment. Keep the costs low by having the students provide labor and produce goods." He stared off to her right, into the distance, as if he were disconnecting from the words as he spoke them. "The idea turned out to be successful. Too successful."

She'd never heard anyone explain the school's history quite this way before and was eager for him to go on. "Meaning?"

"In the most recent generation, the two sons stepped up. One took over the education and theory and helped the school's reputation and reach grow. The other brother handled the production end." Damon rocked the chair back and forth on those back two chair legs. "The place flourished. It was held up as an example of a new type of educational thinking."

"And then people started to die." Not just her sister. Others.

"Right." Damon focused on her again. "The first time the FBI and the ATF stormed the place, it was viewed as law enforcement overreach. Then the paranoia set in. Years passed and something changed. The place became less of a school and more of a locked-down facility."

She wasn't convinced it was ever really a school, but she knew what it was when her sister died. "Like a cult."

So much of the story had been in the press. Professionals dissected every move, trying to figure out how everyone missed the signs. Fourteen years ago, that initial attack on the school was referred to as a rogue operation based on wrong information. Sullivan was cleared and FBI procedure changed and the school continued to thrive. Then, years later, her sister died and that barely made a blip in the national news. Then another death. Then came the showdown that ended the school. Now it was a private commune.

But those were the basics. A man who could spy wrong blueprint details likely possessed a deeper understanding of what happened there. "How am I supposed to trust you when you won't tell me how you know what you know?"

He let the front two legs of the chair fall to the carpet again. "You're paying me."

He was big on the payment arrangements. Those were the least of her concerns, except for the part where she couldn't afford any of this and was halfway through her sixty-day special leave from the office from the insurance company. Most of her fellow employees used the time to travel or take classes. One adopted a baby. She used it to hunt down old leads. "Wren is paying you, though I suspect that cost will get passed onto me."

"He's a millionaire for a reason."

"Then answer this. Is everything you know about Sullivan from the file Wren gave you?"

"No." For a few seconds, Damon didn't say anything else, which had to kill him because the man loved to talk. Then he filled in a few more blanks. "Sullivan was in the news. There's a paper trail. Theories. A documentary, even though it doesn't offer much that wasn't already public."

"I'm not sure you answered my question."

"Complaints against Sullivan either got lost or were quickly closed without much in the way of an investigation. Then a congresswoman started asking questions. The result was the altercation with FBI and—"

"You're calling the first government intervention fourteen years ago an altercation? Two people died."

He nodded. Even looked a bit relieved, as if he was

happy she got that without him having to explain it. "That fact tends to get lost in the legal battle that came after. Sullivan's PR machine went into overdrive with all the talk about private land and government interference. The argument touched off a national conversation about interference since the FBI came to ask questions but fired the first shot."

"There's some debate over that." At least there was in her head.

"Maybe." He sighed. "Eventually, a teacher broke off with Sullivan and started talking. This time when ATF and the FBI stormed the place—the second time—the result was a bloodbath. That was eight years ago."

Arrests were made and what happened there slipped and became little more than a footnote in history books except to the antigovernment crowd that still considered every move at Sullivan to be part of some bigger government conspiracy. "All of that was in the news."

He traced over the cracks on the top of the table with his finger. "It was."

"What do you know that wasn't put out for the public to see? You're hiding something."

He groaned. "So many things, yes."

Things he didn't intend to tell her, at least not yet. She picked up on that. Really, she couldn't blame him. She wasn't a fan of you-show-me-yours either but they had to start somewhere and the bits and pieces of information she had didn't provide any direction. "What's the plan now?"

"We get closer."

"We haven't even talked about . . . there are files. You know." She knew that was a mess of a thought, even for her.

"I'm going to pretend that was a full sentence." He pushed back from the table and stood up. "We'll have plenty of time to review paperwork tonight. Right now we need in-person intel."

"You think we're going to knock on the front door and they'll let us in." Man, she would be so happy if that worked, since she'd been sneaking around the outside fence, looking for an easy way in.

"I think we're going to have an early dinner."

She swallowed a groan. "Again with food? Maybe I should buy you a box of energy bars."

"There's a diner near the front gate of Sullivan. We're going there."

A strange feeling flickered inside her. She barely recognized it, but the spiraling sensation reminded her of hope. "Because you're hungry."

"Yes, but that's not why. We're going because everyone knows the best place to be seen is at a diner."

That sounded like he had a plan. She tried not to get too excited over the idea. "Is that a Pennsylvania thing?"

"A small-town thing." He walked over to the bed and tucked her gun back into her duffle bag. "If you're right that a person has been in your condo, snooping around—and I don't doubt you for a second—then we want to send a message."

She watched every confident move he made. "What message?"

"It's simple."

Nothing about him, this case or her life fit that description. "Fill me in."

"You're saying, *here I am.*"

Anxiety started whirling around in her stomach. "Couldn't we say something a little less provocative? Maybe something subtle."

He just smiled at her. "That's not my style."

CHAPTER 6

"This is a terrible idea."

Damon started keeping count. This was the second time Cate made the same comment since they got to the diner fifteen minutes ago. This time she added a heavy sigh. He fought the urge to mimic her. "I've had worse."

"I believe that," she mumbled as she deconstructed her turkey club sandwich. First, she removed half of the meat. Next, she put the middle piece of toast to the side. When a piece of lettuce dared to sneak out of the side of the sandwich, she pulled out most of that, too.

"At least this one comes with a side order of onion rings." He picked up his patty melt. The only question is if he'd have the chance to eat it.

She finished putting her meal back together and looked up at him. "Are you ever serious?"

"All the time."

"Then what's with the jokes?"

He stopped before taking a bite. They engaged in banter, he joked, but this topic was deadly serious. "You're not the only one who panics near danger."

She snorted. "You panic?"

"I am human." Most days he didn't feel like it. Years ago, the emotions had been burned right out of him. He'd stepped up, pulled a trigger and everything changed. He'd tried after to issue warnings about what was happening at the school but no one listened, and he spiraled, unable to help anyone. But he had to believe some bit of caring and humanity still lingered inside him. "Though some believe that I don't feel anything. Would you prefer that?"

She waited a few seconds to answer. "I'm thinking."

He picked up on the lightness of her voice. "Sounds like I'm not the only one who likes to joke."

"I'm trying to keep up with you."

He watched her eat. She even managed to look enticing doing that. The way she moved, sometimes all nerves and awkwardness, other times confident and strident. She managed to be this complex mix without ever once losing her smarts or her determination to get answers for Shauna. Compelling and sexy with just a touch of kick-ass I-don't-need-you bravado to have him thinking about her when he should be concentrating on other things. Like eating.

He turned his plate around to silently offer her an onion ring. "I thought you were a genius."

She grabbed one then another and stacked them on the side of her plate. "Did the file Wren gave you say that?"

"Not exactly, but your job sounded fancy." The type where she wore a suit and celebrated office birthday parties and attended meetings. Maybe even had an assistant who answered her phone. At least that's how it worked on television. He had no clue how it worked in real life.

"I'm an actuary."

He only had a vague idea of what that meant. "Numbers and math, right?"

"I analyze costs and risks for companies, everything from how much insurance should a museum carry to the potential risk of a business investing in a new product."

That sounded impressive in a not-really-saying-anything kind of way. But since he punched things for a living and got to shoot a gun now and then, he wasn't exactly in her league. "Sounds impressive."

"It's not hard to figure out why I chose it." She picked up one of the onion rings and studied it before peeling off a piece of the batter. "Psychologically speaking, I mean."

Funny, but he thought it was kind of hard. "I might need a clue or two."

She dropped the onion ring without eating it. "I grew up with uncertainty. Not enough food or money. So, when it came time for me to plan my life—"

"Which was when?"

"When I was about fourteen."

"Ah." He figured she might say something like that. At fourteen he'd been shooting beer cans off logs for fun. Clearly, they'd had different teen experiences. "Go ahead."

She hesitated, as if she were trying to decide how much to share. "I read this article about careers and actuaries were considered to be in safe jobs with good pay. Actuary actually was listed as *the* top-rated job, so I decided to do that."

She stopped talking and for a few seconds he didn't say anything. He was impressed and a bit in awe of her determination. "It's interesting you realized the reasoning behind your choice. That's very . . . self-aware of you."

She lifted her water glass and silently toasted him. "That's what six years of therapy will do for a person." After a sip, she lowered the glass again. "It doesn't matter because I'm not working right now."

"Did you hit the lottery?"

She picked the last stray piece of lettuce out of her sandwich. "I'm on leave."

Since he'd never really held down an office job, he wasn't clear on what that meant. One of the benefits of being an independent contractor of sorts is he picked his schedule. Usually Wren or one of the other Quint Five tried to fill it. He assumed it was their way of keeping him out of trouble. But, technically, if he ever wanted to take a vacation he could schedule one in. Not that he was a lounge-on-the-beach guy, but the idea of riding his motorcycle across country without anyone texting him or bugging him or sending him out on some potentially fatal mission like this one, didn't sound bad.

"You're taking sick leave?" he asked.

"My company offers this special sixty-day time off period every five years. It's a morale booster, an employment incentive sort of thing. My boss believes in people bettering themselves."

"And you can accomplish that in sixty days?" Just the idea of that made him laugh. "I haven't managed to do that in thirty-four years."

"I think it's more theoretical than realistic. But if someone wanted to travel or try a serious cooking class or go off and live in the woods, they could do it with pay."

"That might convince me to try cooking."

She smiled. "Do you ever cook?"

He ordered and grabbed takeout. The one time he'd tried a serious grocery run, he threw away almost every item he bought at the end of the week on trash day. He wasn't exactly the type to burn through money for fun, so he stopped that shit and focused on his strengths. "I grill."

"Burgers, right?"

"And steaks. I have skills with the entire meat family."

She laughed and shook her head at the same time. "That's very manly of you."

"Thank you for noticing." The bell dinged above the door and he glanced up, expecting to see another group of seventy-something older men like the three other times he looked. But no. "Well, that didn't take long."

The smile faded from her face but she didn't whip

around to look. No, she had more sense than that, but her eyes did grow huge. "What?"

"We have company." Company he recognized. Company who wore long-sleeve shirts in summer, so who knew what weapons they hid.

Two men stepped inside the diner. Both with broad shoulders and football lineman builds. They looked like they worked the land, possibly flipped tires for fun. The type to skip any job that would put them in front of a desk, preferring to use their hands.

They didn't glance around or look for a table. One stayed by the door, leaning against the glass with his arms folded over his chest. The other headed right for them in a faded navy cotton shirt and dark blue jeans.

The utility boots and hair snarled from a mix of working outdoors and fingers running through it. The look flipped Damon back fourteen years. A few less lines around the eyes and a slimmer build and he could be looking in a throwback mirror.

He'd performed this ritual back then. More than once, he'd gone to a motel room or this very diner and had an "honest" talk with someone looking for a loved one. It looked like the Sullivan informal communications system was up and running just fine despite the school being closed.

The man didn't falter in his steps. He walked over and stopped at the end of their booth. His gaze stayed on Damon with a brief flicker to Cate, but he didn't say a word.

"Hello." Damon started the conversation because

there was no way to avoid this. Not that he wanted to. He brought Cate to this exact diner, hoping to get a reaction. The speed of it was all that surprised him.

"It's been a long time." Their guest nodded toward Cate's side of the booth. "May I sit?"

Probably on instinct, she slid into the corner, giving him room. "A long time?"

"I expected someone to swing through and say hello, but not you." Damon didn't see a reason to pretend not to know their guest, so he didn't. But he couldn't stop and fill in Cate now. "It has been a long time."

"Not long enough."

"It hurts when you say things like that." Damon made a joke but deep down he wondered if there was a spark of truth behind the words. He never regretted leaving this place, but it shaped him. Remained a part of him. From the second he crossed the county line, he could feel the hum of the land in his heartbeat.

"I'm here to offer a friendly reminder that there's nothing left in Salvation for you."

"You guys are the ones who insist Sullivan isn't a prison." Damon glanced at Cate and saw her hanging on every word. Her gaze flipped back and forth across the table. She seemed to be taking it all in, and if the slight frowns that floated across her face were any indication, she assessed each comment as she heard it.

Vincent Barton. He was a walking, talking memory from Damon's past. The fact that he showed up meant someone at Sullivan already knew Damon was in town.

Vincent's gaze never left Damon's face. "No one knows but me and a few others. Keep moving before it's too late. Before something happens that can't be undone."

Knowing Vincent, he meant that more as a friendly suggestion than a threat . . . right now. But the harsh sound of his voice and the way he moved forward on the booth seat as he talked hinted that he would follow through, unload, the second he was ordered to.

Damon just wasn't sure who was giving the orders these days or what those orders were. And he would find out. He'd made a personal vow when he read the file from Wren and agreed to help with Cate. No matter what anyone at Sullivan fired at him, he would go down swinging and kicking, protecting her with his last breath. "I don't think so."

"We both know you shouldn't be here after all these years and all that happened." Vincent shook his head. "Come on, don't do this. You're asking for trouble."

"What does that mean?" Cate asked.

"He knows." Vincent stared at Damon's plate for a few seconds before looking up again. "What name are you using these days?"

"Same one. Damon." But he would bet Vincent knew that. "What's with the threats?"

Cate frowned. "So, you two—"

"Are you saying you just happened to be in the neighborhood and aren't really here to poke around Sullivan?"

Damon snorted. "I'm not really the poking type."

"Definitely no poking. We're just having an early dinner and engaging in awkward conversation." Cate popped the smaller onion ring in her mouth as if to prove her point.

She had Vincent's attention now. He watched her with a gaze that bounced up and down, assessing with a blank expression. "And you? You're not the wife, so what's your story?"

"The wife of what?" She didn't say *you've got to be kidding* but it was written all over her, from the stiff way she held her shoulders to the tension snapping in her voice.

"You have to like her spunk." Damon sure did.

She was tough as hell. Vincent's size intimidated most people. Damon had wrestled with the guy growing up and almost always lost thanks to Vincent's thirty-or-so-pound advantage. But Cate didn't hide in the corner or behind her plate of food. She was actively engaged, not missing one minute.

Vincent exhaled. His frown suggested he had no idea what to make of her. "Her being here, attitude or not, is not going to help either of you."

That only made Cate's eyes narrow even more. "You have a very threatening tone."

Damon decided to jump in before she smacked Vincent with a spare onion ring. "That's the point. He's here as a warning. Aren't you, Vincent?"

Cate's eyes narrowed. "Finally I hear a name. I'm Cate, by the way."

"Sorry." Damon sent her a small smile. The sarcasm

in her voice and the way she held it together were the best things about this cryptic and mildly threatening conversation.

Vincent leaned in, bringing his body in closer to Damon's across the table. "I'm trying to protect you."

"From?" she asked, clearly refusing to be ignored.

Damon started talking faster to prevent Vincent from circling back and filling in that blank. "How did you know I was here?"

Vincent shrugged. "You should assume people here keep track of your location. For obvious reasons."

Not a surprise but no less creepy. "You must have better things to do up here. Chopping firewood. Cleaning weapons in case the apocalypse comes."

"This isn't funny." Vincent glanced back at his buddy standing by the door. "Your coming back makes people antsy."

"I'm not back permanently. This is a short visit." Not on anything more than a temporary basis. But it was official, he hated this assignment. Wren would pay for this.

Cate was staring at Damon now. "Back?"

Vincent pointed at Damon's plate. "Eat and move on and we'll forget this meeting ever happened."

"We?"

Before Vincent could answer, Cate asked a question of her own. "Who are you exactly?"

"An old friend."

She treated Vincent to an eyeroll that might have been more impressive if he had been looking in her direction. "Are you sure you know the definition of that word?"

Damon knew what she was doing, keeping the guy talking while she memorized his face. Even now he could see her mentally searching her files to see if his name or anything about him sparked a memory.

"Let's make this easy." Vincent motioned for the waitress by making a check signal in the air. "I'll even pay the bill."

As if Damon would agree to owe anyone in this town anything. "No thanks. We're good."

"You stay, the past gets dredged up. Old wounds open. Angry people remember why they're angry," Vincent hissed. "I can't let that happen."

Vincent kept his deep voice at a low whisper. His hands rested, open, on the table. Nothing about his demeanor or tone was overtly threatening, but the words he kept dropping telegraphed only one message— get out.

Well, there was nothing subtle about that.

"Maybe I'm angry." The comment wasn't exactly an overreach. Damon swam in a river of guilt and disappointment every day. He'd tried to wash it away by warning about Sullivan all those years ago. Thought it was a penance of sorts. When that didn't work, he moved to burning it out with alcohol. Now he'd developed a shield of complete indifference. He pretended not to care about anything. Most days he could pull it off.

"Are you looking for a showdown, Damon?"

Cate jumped in with that. "No."

"Maybe," Damon said at the same time.

"Well, I delivered the message. I saw you and tried to step in before anything escalated. What you do from here is your choice." Vincent slid to the end of the booth as he talked.

That comment made Damon think there were cameras stationed all over town in addition to informants of the human variety. "I'm eating a burger."

The corner of Vincent's mouth twitched. "Meat?"

Thanks to the moment of understanding, some of the tension twisting Damon's gut eased. "Things change."

Sullivan ran on a strict no-meat policy. It stemmed more from a need to eat what they could grow than a deep belief in something. The school long ago decided keeping animals added a new level of commitment and strength, so they kept mostly to gardening.

Fourteen years ago, days started early with the choice of an apple or a previously boiled potato followed by a hike. Every morning followed the same pattern. After hours of labor, by the time he got to lunch, even lentils had sounded good.

"We all cheat sometimes," Vincent said.

That mentality was a change. The Vincent that Damon knew, the one where they called themselves cousins but weren't actually related by blood, followed every single house rule. The idea of Vincent sneaking out for a hot dog almost made Damon laugh.

"Good to know." Damon sobered as he thought back to Wren's comments about having an inside contact. Vincent wasn't the most likely candidate to go against the commune but there wasn't a long list of people it could be either. "Anything else we need to talk about?"

For a second Vincent looked confused. His forehead wrinkled a bit, making him look older than thirty-five, which Damon remembered him to be. But when Vincent didn't continue on or drop a hint, Damon silently ruled him out as the inside person, the one Wren somehow got into the middle of Sullivan's insular operation.

"I'm done." Vincent didn't waste time on more chitchat. He stood up. "Just think about what I said. Nothing good can come from a nostalgic walk through the past."

But him being there might prove uncomfortable enough for the right people and get them to talk. That's what Damon was counting on . . . you know, if he lived through this.

Vincent nodded to Cate. "Ma'am." Then his long legs carried him back to the door and his snooping friend and they left.

With him gone, the noise of the diner filtered back into Damon's head. Dishes clanked all around them from the other booths. The fake leather from the seat across from him squeaked as Cate shifted into her original seat.

She shoved her plate to the side and leaned in on her elbows. Those big eyes stared him down. "Want to tell me what that was about?"

He thought that was pretty obvious. "A warning."

"For me?"

"Both of us, but mostly me." The people in charge at Sullivan had been tracking him. The informal snitch circle likely kicked into gear the second he came back into the county. People were talking. Vincent knew that this wasn't about driving across a few state lines to get this particular patty melt. It was good but not that good. Not risk-your-life good.

"Are you ready to tell me what your ties are to Sullivan?" she asked in a voice barely above a whisper.

She deserved to know the truth. Maybe not every last detail, but this was a big piece and he couldn't hide it. "I used to live there."

"In Salvation or at Sullivan?"

"Both." He'd spent every minute of his life there until he turned nineteen.

Cate shook her head as if questions pummeled her and she fought to figure out which one to ask first. "Did you know my sister?"

It's the first question he would have asked, so he didn't blame her. "I was gone before she got there."

That was the honest truth. They never met. He hadn't heard much about her because he'd been gone well down his path of self-destruction by then. Only Quint and his friends pulled him back, and even that had been close. Some days the darkness consumed him. The memories would gnaw and bite until they swamped him.

Blocking, ignoring, pretending it was all in the past.

He'd employed every defense mechanism. Letting go proved impossible. That's why he understood Cate's insistence about needing answers. Others might call it an obsession, but he knew caring was a thousand times better than not being able to feel anything at all.

"But you went to school there?" Cate asked the question nice and slow, drawing out each word as if she couldn't believe she hadn't asked earlier.

"Worse." He watched the color drain out of her face. "I can get on the inside because I know exactly what the inside looks like."

"What are you saying?"

"I got out." When she continued to stare at him, he clarified. "I grew up here. Sullivan was my home until the day it ceased to mean anything to me."

"When was that?"

He shoved the plate away from him now that his appetite had vanished. "Fourteen years ago, right after the first shoot-out with the FBI."

"So, your knowledge about the place is . . ."

"Firsthand."

CHAPTER 7

A half hour later, standing alone in the middle of her musty motel room with the green shag carpet, a thousand questions bounced around inside Cate's head. Damon, or whatever his real name was, had lived there, at The Sullivan School. He knew what he knew about it from the inside out. His talk about guns and blueprints wasn't about guessing. He'd been walking her through his memories.

His connection to the place seemed like a pretty important nugget of information to keep quiet about. At the very least, Garrett or Wren, or Wren pretending to be Brian—someone—should have filled her in. Finding out over a turkey sandwich with some random guy sitting in next to her was not the optimal time to learn important new facts.

Really, these covert guys needed to pick one name and stick with it. Then they could work on telling the truth now and then. Images flashed in her mind and she didn't know what to call anyone, except Vincent. She'd nicknamed him Mr. Spooky Pants in her head.

It made him slightly less scary to give him a stupid nickname than to think about his huge hands and how he likely could crush her neck with one and wouldn't care. Hell, he'd barely spared her a glance at the diner.

Thanks to him she left her sandwich behind. She'd managed to get one onion ring down before Damon slapped cash on the table and dragged her out of there. The only good thing was that he didn't take one bite of his hamburger so, technically, he hadn't had his required amount of red meat for the day. Maybe that would teach him a lesson.

The racing around, the half stories, *the thing about him growing up here,* all had her on the verge of exploding. She hated the secrecy. He'd withheld so much . . . admittedly, for only a few days and they barely knew each other, but still. She was not in the mood to be rational right now. Or alone, which had her peeking out the peephole into the parking lot and dark night beyond.

She'd tried to argue with him in the car but he'd shut down. He didn't respond at all, which had to be the number one most annoying male trait in the world. He just sat there, taking it. The lack of a response had her anger winding down, and she really wasn't ready to forgive him yet. She certainly refused to let him win an argument by default because he had exhausted her or bored her to death.

He'd gone out to do a walk around the buildings. Muttered something about checking the perimeter before he closed the door behind him. The longer she stood there, the more the questions piled up. She wanted answers now.

She texted him and waited all of ten seconds for him to respond. When he didn't, she unlocked the door and opened it, searching the darkness for his familiar gait. Nothing moved or made noise in the parking lot in front of the motel. Nothing looked to be out of order either.

The rooms lined up in a straight row, all connected to each other. The manager's office sat more than twenty feet away to the right. Lights burned in the window but the curtains kept her from seeing anything and she figured she should be grateful for that.

There were only three cars parked on the gravel and one of those was the rental Damon insisted they get before they drove here. Something about him not wanting to put the miles on her car or pile a bunch of stuff on his bike, which she took to mean motorcycle, but who knew.

Then there was the kicker, how he didn't want to make it easy for anyone to trace their license plates. If he wanted to scare her with that, it worked. Since someone had made it a habit of breaking into her place and sitting on the couch, she was very much in favor of not being easily tracked.

A memory, some idea she couldn't grab hold of, tickled in the back of her mind. Her gaze switched back to the manager's rooms. Something about . . . no, she couldn't get her brain to kick into gear and fill her in. She rubbed her arms, trying to ignore the goose bumps. She needed that gun. Holding it would make her feel better.

She turned, right as the memory sparked in her brain—the lights. The outside ones at this end of the motel were dark. The rooms around them . . . nothing but darkness. Just as the thought registered, she heard the footsteps. Looking up, she saw Damon turn the corner and head toward her. He glanced behind him, out into the parking lot. Everywhere but in her direction.

"Where have you—"

His eyes widened as they focused on something behind her. "Get down!"

Another male body came barreling toward her from the opposite direction. Big and brawny. Wide shoulders. Fury echoing in the grunting sound he made as he quickened his pace. And a black mask where his face should be. It was as if he stared through her. His attention appeared to be locked on Damon.

Anxiety welled inside her. She was stuck in the middle.

"Cate, move!" Damon ran now. He started from farther away but was gaining ground. Just not enough.

Her hand shot out as she pushed the door open behind her, thinking to squeeze inside and grab her gun. That might be the only thing to equalize a battle between Damon and this other guy. Adrenaline fueled her steps but not fast enough. She'd just crossed the threshold when the attacker slammed his hand into her chest, pushing her out of his path. At the last second, she lifted her head, just avoiding a hard smack to the face that likely would have knocked out her front teeth.

He passed close enough for his hot breath to skim across her cheek. She tried to take a step back and her knees buckled. Off balance, she started to slide down to the small porch in front of the door. She reached out, trying to break her fall, keep on her feet, but her butt hit the wood and she sat down, turning to see what happened to the attacker.

She blinked, trying to take in the chaos of two men battling less than two feet away. The mass of bodies and all that grunting. While she flailed, they struck out at each other and swore. Two twists and Damon had the attacker in a headlock.

The other man grabbed at Damon's arm, raking his nails over Damon's skin, but Damon didn't make a sound. They struggled and punched each other. The attacker managed to hook his leg behind Damon's and trip him up. They both went down in a rush.

The porch shook as their bodies crashed into it. A crack rang out from the force of the fall, but no one came running. Every motel room door stayed shut. The whole time, she struggled to sit up, to think. She needed the gun and a phone, which she dropped or lost because it was no longer in her hand.

She struggled to think of the right thing to do next as the men rolled off the porch and crashed into the dirt and gravel below. In a second, they were back up again. Damon landed a crushing blow that had the other man's head shooting back. Taking advantage of the blind spot, Damon nailed him with a roundhouse kick right to his stomach.

The guy's legs seemed unsteady and his balance off as he stumbled backwards. He held out a hand as if to call for some sort of weird time-out.

"Take off the mask." Damon's stern voice whipped around the parking lot.

The guy shook his head. He bent over as if he were trying to catch his breath. When Damon took a step toward him, the guy bolted, all injuries seemingly gone. He ran toward the tree line and blended in with the darkness.

Damon didn't even try to catch him. "Damn it."

The door to the manager's office opened and the guy shouted into the now relative quiet. "Everything okay out here?"

Damon waved as he gulped in air. "She slipped. We're fine."

The attack, the fight—it all happened in superspeed. While she watched, it felt like it dragged and she kept trying to get up so she could help, but she realized now that the whole thing hadn't lasted a minute. When the rush and chaos ended she could hear the heavy pounding of breathing and knew it came from her.

"Hey." Damon stepped onto the porch and crouched down in front of her. "Look at me. Are you okay?"

There was only one of him, which she took as a good sign. Except for his ruffled hair, he looked fine.

She didn't think that was fair at all since she's been reduced to a lump on the ground. The headache hammering her skull was not welcome either.

"Why did you tell the manager that?"

"Do you really think he didn't watch the whole scene from his window?" Damon exhaled. "For all we know, he's the one who tipped off Vincent and whoever that guy was."

"That guy wasn't Vincent." She'd sat next to the man in the diner. He smelled like he'd been standing close to a fire, despite the warm weather. The attacker's scent was much different. "He didn't smell right to be Vincent."

"I'm not going to try to argue with that logic." Damon brushed his fingertips over her arm and across the side of her face. The touch, so gentle and soft, had her leaning closer to him even though she realistically knew he was checking for injuries.

"Damon." The need to return the soothing gesture hit her. Somehow, she conjured up the energy to lift her hand and traced her fingers over his cheek. Down to his mouth. To that inviting lower lip. "That man appeared out of nowhere."

"I heard noises, so I went around the back of the motel. That's when . . ." Damon shook his head. "I'm sorry I didn't get him before you came outside. Did he hurt you?"

"More like he pushed me out of the way." Which didn't make sense to her. Why go to the trouble of making sure she was out of the fray? She turned slightly, trying to make out his figure in the darkness, and pain flashed across the top of her eyes. She reached up to touch the spot and hissed when her fingers skimmed her temple.

"Is it your head?"

"I think that was me. I slipped and . . ." She actually wasn't sure what happened and didn't try to make it up. All that registered was the distinct sense the attacker beelined for Damon, not meaning to do more than shove her out of the way.

"Jesus." Damon shifted as he got to his feet and put an arm around her. "Let's get you up and checked."

But the haze had begun to clear. The pain in her head still thumped but fear no longer raced through every vein. She could almost feel the adrenaline seep out of her, leaving her boneless and dragging. Little more than deadweight.

She leaned on him until they got inside then she stood by as he locked each lock, knowing anyone who really wanted to get in could. A few steps and they were in the bathroom. He put the lid down and guided her to the toilet seat as he studied the back of her head. He kept the probing and poking gentle, so she tried not to squeal when he hit that one spot that was sore.

"I'm not a doctor or concussion specialist, but I think you're clear. He did rattle your head pretty good though."

Not exactly how she would describe the moment, but sure. "Again, I did it."

"I prefer to blame him." Damon swore under his breath. "Now we just have to figure out who that was."

She needed him to concentrate on her and this moment and not mentally run off seeking revenge. "So, your family is one of the original families at Sullivan."

His eyes widened. "We're going to have that conversation now?"

It might be the only time she could catch him off guard enough to answer. "I figure you feel bad about what just happened and—"

"Like shit, yes." He leaned back against the sink, putting a little bit of distance between them in the small room, but not much. "You shouldn't have been—"

"How were you supposed to know someone dressed in ski gear was going to attack you by going through me? Now I know this small town is no safer than DC, which is a little weird." She'd prefer to have this conversation just about anywhere else, but she suspected if she moved he would take advantage of the break and try to not answer what she asked. "But you should feel compelled to answer my questions. Consider it your punishment for the silent treatment in the car ride from the diner then running away on your big walk before I could corner you in the motel room."

His grip tightened on the edge of the sink behind him. "I thought that was slick."

"No." It was as if they were having some big marital spat without ever going through the marriage part.

Now she knew why her mother stayed single. "The thing about you being a lifetime Sullivan resident and kindergarten buddies with Vincent. Go."

"That's not . . ." Damon shook his head. "Damn, don't say it that way."

Poor baby. "Tell me the truth or I hunt down the gun."

He nodded toward the main room. "It's in the safe."

In just a few words he'd strayed off topic. She recognized the strategy now because he used it a lot, but this time she let it happen because she wanted to prove a point about him being all covert putting them both in danger. "I'm supposed to guess the combination?"

"It's your birthday."

She felt the air rush right out of her. Of course he knew her birthday. He probably knew things she'd forgotten thanks to Wren and that file of his. Okay, then. "Do you get how frustrating it is for you to know stuff about me but I don't get to know anything about you?"

He had the good sense to wince. "Yeah, that would probably tick me off."

"So?"

He shrugged. "I'm private."

"And unbelievably annoying."

That stern frown flipped and he shot her a bright smile. "I think I'm growing on you."

Her stomach tumbled, which was not a good thing at all. She was used to the sensation when something upset her or that one time she went on a boat and *never again*. Having it tumble over some dude's smile was not okay with her.

To block whatever superpower he was using on her, she looked anywhere but at his face. The rip in his T-shirt at the collar. Those forearms. Then she saw the trail of red and slowly got to her feet. "You're bleeding."

"Is that a pickup line? Because it's kind of weird."

"It's reality." She turned his arm to show him the lines of blood running down his elbow.

"It's a scratch."

It was more than that. She thought back to the fight and remembered the attacker using his nails, but now she knew that's not really what she saw. These cuts were from a blade. The attacker used a knife on Damon.

"Maybe we should call the police. Make a report." She realized it was a ridiculous idea as soon as she said it. Years had passed but she'd bet some of the same police who ignored her sister's murder were still here. Yeah, no thanks.

Ignoring her own comment, she turned him around and cleaned off the blood in the sink. The warm water ran over the underside of his arm and her fingers.

"This actually does look like the kind of place the police need to visit pretty often." He reached for a towel and pressed it against the wound. "You probably didn't get a great look at the manager but he gives off a *Psycho* vibe."

"Naturally, you brought me here."

His head shot up and he stared at her in the mirror. "I'll protect you."

"I'm not a damsel in distress."

"Never thought you were." The serious expression morphed back into a smile as he stepped out of the bathroom. "My guess is you could kick my ass."

"You should keep that in mind." She was about to call him back when he reappeared in the doorway with a first aid kit. "And of course you have one of those. I assume that's a statement about how often someone tries to kill you."

He nodded. "Pretty much."

"Answer this . . ." She opened the kit and rummaged around for something to clean the wound and a bandage. She didn't see him move but she felt the touch of his finger under her chin.

He lifted her head until their gazes met. "You actually have to say words now."

"Is this what you do for a living? Pick up a fake girlfriend and race into small towns across America to solve old crimes?"

His thumb slipped over her chin. Back and forth in a rhythmic beat. "You make me sound like a bad television show."

"I'm serious. I'm trying to figure you out." And fight off the tremble that started in her muscles and threatened to take over her entire body. "You're this messed-up puzzle with all these odd pieces."

"Now that's definitely a pickup line."

"One minute you're joking around. The next you're fighting off attackers." She hadn't heard him coming until the other guy went flying. Damon was tall and all muscle and, she guessed, fully trained for this sort of work. "You have a connection to this place but you got out. From the few things you've said, it's clear that anyone who gets out of here runs, which means it's dangerous for you to be here. Yet here you are."

"Wren hired me."

She covered his hand with hers. She meant to push it away and force him to talk to her but the minute their fingers touched, they entwined. "I'm not buying it. This gig with me is not a way for you to score a few easy bucks."

"I am not a hero, Cate." He tried to pull away.

She held on, resting their joined hands against her chest. "Never said you were. You're a flesh and blood man."

And this close, she could smell the soap on his skin and see the darker streaks in his green eyes.

"Very much so." His breath seemed to hiccup. "So . . ."

When his voice trailed off she got a taste of what it felt like to have someone drop the end of important sentences like she often did. But she didn't think he tried it or that he was playing games. He stared, un-blinking, at her and her own breath stuttered in her chest.

"Now you're the one who should finish the sentence." Her voice came out in a breathy whisper.

"We're in a tense situation. Stress sometimes disguises itself as something else."

The words crashed into her brain, wiping out every other thought. She pulled back a bit, but kept holding his hand. "What are you talking about?"

His gaze traveled over her face now, landing on her mouth. "How much I want to kiss you."

Ah, okay. That sounded better.

"I thought we were talking about your past."

He shook his head. "Nope."

"About the risks you're taking." The conversation about his past and this assignment had dwindled away, as predicted. If this was his way of changing the topic it sure worked. Her entire focus centered on him and how good it felt as he rubbed his thumb over the back of her hand.

He really was an evil genius.

"So long as you stay in Salvation, I stay." His foot slipped between hers.

Forget the headache and the attack. All she wanted was this—him—right now. "But you still say you're not a hero."

"Just a man who wants to kiss you."

She almost shouted *yes* but somehow kept her voice calm and steady. "Do it."

"Cate, I don't—"

He was making this way harder than it needed to be. "Now, Damon."

She moved first, dropping his hand and bringing hers up to cradle his throat. As her eyes closed, their lips met. Not soft and sweet. No, when Damon Knox kissed, he went for it. His arms wrapped around her and the blood left her head.

He kissed like he walked, full of confidence. His mouth covered hers, moving and learning, first licking along her bottom lip then swooping in. She felt picked up and spun around but her feet never left the ground. The kiss reeled her, made her forget her questions and concerns, and had her wanting more.

When he lifted his head a few seconds later and stared down at her, all she wanted was the feel of his warm mouth against hers again. Her tongue swept over his as the kiss started anew. Her stomach rolled and bounced as if she were on a sexy, wild roller coaster. Her fingers slid into his hair as a hot little grumble sounded from the back of his throat.

She was just about to wrap a leg around his when he cut off the kiss and lifted his head. His heavy breaths echoed around her and he didn't let go, but he wasn't watching her. His focus switched to the locked door.

She strained to hear what he heard. Tried to figure out what he saw, but gave up. "What's wrong?"

"Someone's outside."

"You saw . . ." No, not saw. He probably sensed it and that was good enough for her. She tried to remember where the safe was in the room. "I need my gun."

There was one loud knock.

The sound stopped her. "Do attackers usually ask to be let in?"

If Damon heard her, he didn't show it. He was too

busy standing at the side of the door. Maybe he thought someone would kick it in. She had no idea but this time she would have a weapon ready. She just needed for him not to get himself killed before she could load it.

"Get away from there," she said in a strained whisper. Her fingers pressed in the lock code and she reached for the weapon.

But he already had his hand on the knob and pulled. The open door blocked her view to the outside but she saw Damon freeze.

His mouth dropped open. "Oh, shit."

That was good enough for her. She stepped around the door and aimed her gun at the guy standing there. Barely even saw him except for the male face part.

Damon moved lightning fast. His hand came up and he pushed the barrel down toward the floor. "Cate, no."

"I don't . . ." She realized the tension had left his face. In reaction to his sudden calm, her shoulders relaxed, and so did her stranglehold on the gun. "Why not?"

He smiled at her. "Because you're about to shoot our inside man."

CHAPTER 8

Damon saw the guy on the other side of the door and couldn't help but smile. He should have known this was coming. Of course Wren sent Trevor Gault, one of the Quint Five, a friend for more than a decade. And one lethal son of a bitch.

Through a combination of smarts and charm, Trevor could sneak in anywhere and somehow fit. Based on sarcasm alone, the guy should have been shot and killed long ago. But he bounced back. He was *that* guy. The one who could run into a raging fire and come out petting a kitten.

Trevor held up a bag from a fast-food restaurant and shook it. "I brought dinner."

The lightness in his tone. The dirty blond hair that always looked a few weeks past haircut time. That sunny surfer-boy smile he'd been flashing around for more than thirty-three years despite the fact he grew up in Pittsburgh and now lived in the mountains. The open-front plaid shirt he wore over a T-shirt, even in summer, as if neither the heat nor the cold touched him.

Some things never changed, and Trevor was one of them.

The longer Cate stared at Trevor, the more confused she looked. "Who exactly are you?"

Trevor's relaxed demeanor didn't falter under the scrutiny. "A friend."

"You guys grew up together at Sullivan?" she asked, clearly not ready to mentally declare Trevor a friend rather than a potential attacker.

"Hell, no. That place produces some seriously messed-up folks." He smiled at Damon. "Just saying."

She joined Trevor in glancing at Damon. "He seems smarter than you."

Trevor winked at her. "I like you."

Rather than risk another shoot-out or accidentally make Trevor into a life-sized target by standing in the open, Damon motioned for him to come inside. With the door shut and locked, Damon started introductions. "Cate Pendleton, this is Trevor Gault." Damon winced. "Or are you using a different name?"

"Yeah, you guys clearly are friends." She rolled her eyes as she walked back into the main living area. "Same general disheveled-but-hiding-a-killer-underneath look. The annoying multiple names thing."

"Whoa. I am much prettier." Trevor followed her. Stood across from her and dropped the bag on the table between them.

"Trevor and I trained together after I left Sullivan," Damon said, hoping to cut off too many questions.

She dropped into the chair next to her. "Trained for what?"

Damon answered her with a sigh.

The noise started Trevor laughing. "Oh, come on. You had to know she would ask that. You opened the damn door to that question."

"Combat." There. Damon figured that was a good enough answer in light of the fact he already got attacked by an unknown knife-wielding assailant today.

"Right." She treated him to a second eyeroll. This one went way up, like the kind of eyeroll that could give a person a headache. After the dramatic presentation, she stared at the bag right in front of her. "You brought food?"

Trevor must have found her tone inviting because he sat down across from her. "I know you left the diner without eating."

"How?" She tugged down a corner of the bag, as if trying to take a peek inside.

"I have people everywhere." Trevor lounged in his chair with one ankle crossed over the other knee, but he stayed alert. His gaze followed Cate's every move.

Not that she noticed. Nope. She was too busy slipping a french fry out of the bag.

She snorted. "See, you guys say stuff like that and I think *you* think it's comforting."

The longer Trevor watched her, the more he smiled. "No?"

"Not even a little."

"That's too bad because I love saying it."

The bag crinkled as she started snooping in earnest. After taking a few wrapped items out she looked at Trevor. "You brought him a burger, I'm guessing."

"Two."

Damon was pretty sure he could eat the bag at this point. "Good man."

"Heaven forbid he eat chicken," she mumbled under her breath.

Damon thought about ignoring her, but it was so much more fun to tease her. "I was stabbed tonight. That's enough punishment."

Trevor uncrossed his legs and his foot fell to the floor. "Stabbed?"

"You missed our visitor." Damon came the rest of the way across the room and met them at the makeshift work area he'd set up between the rooms. "He shoved Cate and took a whack at me. Unfortunately, he held a knife at the time."

"Motherfucker." Trevor sat up straight, all signs of amusement gone as he looked at Cate. "Are you okay?"

"Nothing that a few french fries won't solve." She saluted him with one.

"I'm fine, too. You know. In case you care." Damon noticed how Cate helped herself to a few from each bag of fries. "You're sharing those, right?"

"Maybe." Then she popped two fries in her mouth.

"There's plenty of food in the bag." Trevor took over distribution duties. He had all the food spread out on the table, complete with napkins and condiments in two seconds. "Now, someone tell me what happened."

Cate unwrapped her burger and went to work deconstructing it. The onion was the first to go. "Big guy, over six foot. Bulky build. He manhandled me and cut Damon's arm."

Trevor's gaze shot to Damon. "Did you recognize him?"

"He was wearing a mask but Cate said it wasn't Vincent. Because he didn't smell right." Damon touched her shoulder to get her attention as he settled in the chair next to her. "Correct?"

She didn't look up from repositioning the tomatoes from the top bun to the bottom one. "You got it."

Trevor held up a hand as if he were asking for permission to talk, which was something he would never do. "Smell?"

Cate eyed up Trevor over the top of her burger. "Who exactly are you? And, to be clear, I'm not asking for a list of your pseudonyms. I mean, really. What's the reason you're here?"

Trevor's eyes widened. His gaze flipped from her burger to her face, as if he didn't know what he should talk about first. "First, Trevor really is the fake name."

She frowned at him. "Of course it is."

Trevor looked at Damon, who could only shrug. His entire life had been like this since he met her. She asked questions and led him around in circles. She made it clear the whole protection thing did not impress her.

"I've been embedded at Sullivan since the first time you tried to reach Wren."

That one seemed to stump her. "What?"

Damon had to admit he hadn't expected the answer either. "That timing seems early."

If he understood Trevor, that meant Wren had been playing a really long game here. He'd set up a mission at Sullivan long before Cate's final demand to see him. Damon wasn't sure what any of that meant.

Trevor shook his head as he continued to stare at Cate. "You went looking for Wren. He checked your background, realized your story was legit and wanted me to gather any intel I could."

She pointed at Damon. "But he is the one with a connection to the place."

"Which is why Trevor is here instead." Damon knew that much.

"I work the grounds, keep my head down and listen to every conversation anyone has anywhere on the property. Then I report back," Trevor said.

"Because that's your training."

Trevor didn't seem upset by her comment or subtle digging. "I also like to blow up things now and then."

When Trevor looked as if he intended to go into details, Damon cut him off. "She doesn't need to know about that."

She'd been spooked in her own house and thrown around outside the motel. Somehow, she held it together. She didn't scream or cry or beg to go home. If he were her, he probably would have done all three. They were perfectly legitimate, rational civilian things to do. The fact she didn't show more fear actually worried him. She struck him as a survivor. She'd need those skills to face off with the folks in charge of Sullivan these days.

"Fast-forward to you contacting Senator Dayton." Trevor balanced his weight on the back two legs of the chair and reached over to the small fridge. In a perfectly orchestrated case of putting this arm here and that leg there, he managed to open the door and grab a bottle of water. "At that point, Wren had already collected intel and decided your sister likely was murdered, which is why he let the senator arrange the meeting."

Cate made an odd noise that sounded a bit like *humpf.* "That's a lot of manipulation."

Trevor screwed off the water lid. "Welcome to our world."

"Let's go back to the part where your friends believe me." She shot Damon a you-are-the-problem-here frown. "Which is a nice change."

Trevor followed her gaze back to Damon. "Why is she glaring at you?"

"He has to be convinced of the facts surrounding Shauna's death." She sounded as unimpressed as a person could possibly sound.

Trevor took a long swig of water. "Oh, he gave you the I-need-evidence speech? Classic Damon."

"Excuse me?" Damon threw that in there but he had to admit Trevor was not wrong. He did collect information. The one time he didn't—he just blindly believed—he wasn't the only one who paid the price.

"You, too?" she asked. "I thought only I got that treatment."

Trevor shook his head. "It's his *thing*. Me, I charge in based on gut. Damon needs more."

That was enough of this topic. Damon reached for one of the burgers. "That's not true."

"He has trust issues," Trevor said, getting one more shot in.

But Damon really hated people talking about his supposed trust issues, so he tried to put an end to the conversation . . . again. "He also has ears and is sitting right here."

"And as much as I want to continue talking about Damon while he listens and tries not to implode, I have to get back to Sullivan." Trevor put the lid back on the water bottle. "I've stuck close to the place since I got there and don't want to act differently now that you're in town."

"How did you get out of the commune?" Such a soft word for such a terrible place, but Damon used it anyway. He adamantly refused to call it a school because it hadn't been that for years, if ever.

"It's not a prison. Honestly, it would be easier if it were because then we could call in law enforcement— ones we trust, not any that still might be on Sullivan's payroll after all this time and after everything that happened—and take that place apart piece by piece." Trevor sounded intrigued by the idea. His voice actually rose a bit with excitement as he talked.

"Is it dangerous there?" Cate asked between bites.

Trevor looked like he was thinking through the question, turning it over in his mind. "Not that I can see. But, honestly, it's nearly impossible to get good intel."

"Why?" Damon asked.

"They don't exactly let the new guys count the ammunition or look at hidden bank books." Trevor shook his head. "All Wren could do was get me in. To do that, he provided the right cover and produced a fake recommendation from a former Sullivan resident who no longer lives in this country. That got me on the property, but even his reach doesn't work inside. I'm listening, and all the talk so far is about legitimate issues and concerns."

Her eyes narrowed. "Then how do you know there's still a problem at Sullivan."

"Instinct," Trevor said without hesitation. "There's a bit too much gunplay by some of the members for my liking."

That quick, the amusement moved back into her face. She shook her head. "You two even sound alike."

"You say something like that after I brought you dinner?" Trevor joked then sobered a bit as he looked over at Damon. "Point is, ten minutes after you hit town a buzz of activity started at Sullivan. Lots of people in closed-door meetings. Whispers."

Not a surprise, really. Damon had actually hoped that would happen. All except the physical attack part. "That explains how Vincent tracked me down."

"That and the guy who owns the diner is tied to Sullivan," Trevor said.

Damon nodded. "Always was."

"Well, you wanted to get their attention." Cate finished the first bag of fries and reached into the second one. "I say that while not being sure who *they* actually are."

Trevor held up a hand. "Though I have to say that I'm not sure whatever happened here tonight was about Damon."

Damon snorted as his hand moved to his side. "Sure felt like it."

"What does that gain them to immediately go after you? They don't know why you're here." Trevor asked as he continued to play with the lid to the water bottle, screwing it and unscrewing it. "They attack you and miss and now you can cause trouble."

Seemed obvious to Damon. "I'm assuming they didn't expect to miss."

"Then they would have sent more than one guy."

Trevor made good points, Damon hated to admit, because that meant the threats to them originated from different directions. He could fight on one front, no problem. On two? That made things harder.

Cate glanced over at Damon. "Exactly how many people in Salvation hate you?"

"It's likely a high number." Trevor aimed all of his attention at her. "But, no. Tonight was something else, and I fear it could be about you."

"Me?" She looked wide-eyed and startled at first but then she nodded her head. "Someone who doesn't want me to poke around and ask questions about Shauna's death."

She was smart. She got it. Damon just wished she'd act a bit more concerned about being a target. "Someone with something to lose. Which means you're leaving here."

He couldn't be clearer than that. She had to know—

She was already shaking her head. "That's not happening."

"We'll discuss this later." And by that he meant he'd pack the car and argue with her on the way out of town, but they were going.

She didn't even pretend to be interested in the food now. "You mean we'll fight and I'll win."

Trevor whistled. "Man, I wish I could be here for that, but I have to head out."

"What if someone sees you?" she asked.

"I'm kind of an expert on sneaking around. My truck is parked a good distance away and hidden. I waited until the manager got on the phone and ducked in the shadows. Even took out the light next to your door to hide my coming here." Trevor listed off his subterfuge like it was the most natural thing in the world.

"You sound like a man who goes into a situation with a plan." She glared at Damon as she spoke.

"You mean, unlike your fake boyfriend here? And yes, I know about your cover and it's hysterical." Trevor pointed toward Damon with the end of the water bottle. "Before I sneak out of here and back to Sullivan, can I speak to you for a second?"

"Boy talk?" she asked.

Trevor shook his head as he led the way outside. "An unrelated message from Wren."

With everything that had happened, Damon didn't like being out in the open or leaving her alone. Anyone who wanted to get to her would have to fit through the small bathroom window and he'd like to think he'd hear that noise. But it was more likely she'd shoot the person before he could rush back in.

They walked across the porch into the suffocating darkness, while they both scanned the area. The dark night made seeing too far out difficult. Close in wasn't that easy either. Damon made a mental note to replace the missing lightbulbs along the porch.

They ended up at the edge of the parking lot, wedged between the end of the rental car and the porch leading up to the now shadowed motel room door. It wasn't the best space but it provided a limited amount of cover. Damon decided it was good enough for a quick talk. "What does Wren want? And it better be to apologize for getting me into this assignment."

"I made that up to get you out here." Before Damon could comment, Trevor continued, "But I am worried about this. With all the secrets around here, Salvation is not a place you should be."

Damon knew Trevor meant Sullivan, Salvation and the state of Pennsylvania. The whole area provided an opportunity to fall down a hole Damon wasn't sure he could climb back out of again. "You think I don't know that?"

"We both know you would have turned this job down if there wasn't a tiny piece of you that wanted to come back here for some sort of fucked-up show-down."

No way was Damon admitting to that. That kind of death wish would land him back in observation. No thanks. "People seem to think I need *closure*."

Trevor scoffed. "I have never heard you use that word."

Because he hadn't. He wouldn't. It didn't mean anything to him. Not in the real world where wounds didn't close and some didn't deserve to. "Does it really sound like something I would say?"

"Tonight's close call means your mere presence in the county is enough to push someone into making a bad move." Trevor continued to play with the water bottle. Peeled and picked at the label. Tightened the cap until it made a cracking sound. "I get it. I've felt the same way around you, but I wouldn't act on it. This person already has."

"You just sold the idea that this attack was linked to Cate." Damon didn't understand the new tactic. Looking to Cate meant tying the attack to her sister's death. Now Trevor seemed to be hanging it on a much older sin—Damon's.

"Does it matter? The result is the same—danger. And if someone kills you, who is going to save your girlfriend?"

The word screeched across Damon's brain. "She's not—"

"Fake or not, I don't care." Trevor, usually so calm, shifted his weight around as if anxiety had his insides churning.

Damon couldn't really hear much. His mind kept zooming back to the girlfriend thing then misfiring. In one sentence, Trevor had managed to get so much wrong. Damon rushed to correct some of the mistakes. "She's not weak or looking for someone to swoop in and solve all of her problems. She needs help and asked for it, but she is not backing out of this investigation and handing it over. I've already learned that about her."

Trevor exhaled as his shoulders fell and the intensity in his voice eased back to normal. "Can she catch a bullet with her bare hand?"

Even Damon had to admit the argument made sense. He tried to think of a good comeback as he looked around them, checking for predators of the two-legged and four-legged varieties. "You made your point."

"I'll stick around but you should think about getting her at least a hundred miles away from this place until we know who visited you two earlier."

It was a good plan. Solid. But still potentially very unhealthy for Trevor. "You made it sound like you'd have to take some pretty big risks and potentially blow your cover to get more intel."

For the first time in a few minutes, Trevor smiled. "I thrive on stress."

Damon picked the one topic that could get Trevor

to rethink this plan. "What will Aaron say about you sticking to this assignment?"

Trevor wiggled his eyebrows. "That he has a hot, lethal boyfriend."

"No one wants to take on your guy-who-pretends-to-be-an-engineer boyfriend." The guy had this nerd look about him with the dark glasses and all, but Damon had once gone to their condo not knowing they were back from vacation. You know, just to borrow a bed for the night, and Aaron had him slammed against the wall with an elbow to his throat before Damon could shut the door behind him. No fucking way did that guy sit at a desk all day.

Trevor's smile only grew wider. "He really is an engineer. He's also a retired sniper who did some very dirty undercover work overseas, so yeah. I wouldn't mess with him."

"He knows you're here?"

Trevor nodded. "I told him I was keeping you out of trouble."

"Excellent. I can hardly wait for him to track me down after you accidentally blow your cover and get yourself shot."

Trevor sighed. The loud you're-an-idiot kind. "Your lack of confidence in my skills makes me sad."

"You are definitely sad."

"Once you figure out where you're going, leave a note for me with the manager." Trevor downed the rest of the water bottle then handed his empty to Damon.

He took it, but only because the comment stunned him. "The motel manager?"

"He was hired to watch over you. To make sure you didn't get yourself killed before you got into Sullivan and all that."

Well, shit. "He didn't even open his curtains when I was getting thrown around the parking lot."

"He probably thought you had it under control."

Right. "He looks like a serial killer, by the way."

"I'm pretty sure he was a marine." Trevor snorted. "But who knows."

"I don't need a bodyguard."

"That would be more convincing if you hadn't gotten stabbed tonight." Trevor reached into his front jeans pocket and pulled out a handful of something that made a crinkling noise in his palm. "And, here. I didn't put them in the food bag because I have some decorum."

"What are . . ." Damon held out his hand and stared down at the packets stacked there. "Condoms?"

"I'm happy you've seen them before and recognize them."

There had to be twenty of them. The choice made Damon wonder exactly what Trevor thought was happening during this mission. "This is a fake relationship. She's not actually my girlfriend."

"Do you only have sex with official girlfriends?"

"My point is, I don't need these." But Damon couldn't seem to hand them back. A small voice in his head told him to pocket them and be grateful.

"I was in the room with the two of you for five minutes and I know you need those, or you hope you will." Trevor snorted. "Even a gay man could see the sexual tension pinging between you. You look at her when she's not looking at you. You tease each other. From what I can tell, straight people flirting is a lot like fifth grade."

Damon refused to deal with any part of that comment and skipped to the point. "I'm on the job."

"In a motel."

All true, but still. "It's not like that."

Maybe a part of him wondered what *that* might be like, but no. He couldn't protect her if he got caught under her. He needed a clear head. And she needed something other than him. Feelings, emotions, building ties—all that had been burned out of him long ago. He had a handful of friends and keeping up with them proved exhausting enough. He wasn't looking for more human contact. Not the type that lasted for more than a few hours, and with her it would make it last longer.

Trevor shook his head. "I will never understand straight guys."

"Go."

"You really should think about being out and away by tomorrow morning."

The plan made sense to him. He could get her out of danger and regroup. "Is that an order?"

Trevor wasn't smiling or joking now. "If that's what it will take, yeah."

CHAPTER 9

Cate stayed in the chair, polishing off the last of the french fries. She'd thought about saving Damon a few then remembered how he held back the information about his ties to Sullivan and she kept on eating. But she picked her seat carefully. She figured the food would lure Damon back inside and she'd be waiting next to it. Then he'd have to deal with this. With her.

As predicted, Damon came in after about ten minutes and locked the door behind him. Without hesitation, he headed straight for the hamburger. It was cold by now but he bit into it, not appearing to care. He didn't even bother to sit down.

When he didn't say anything, she started. She had a feeling she'd have to be the one to lead them through all the tough conversations. "You have interesting friends."

"You have no idea."

She actually liked Trevor. Found him charming in an odd sort of way. He was a fraction taller than Damon, maybe six-three. They glanced at each other throughout their informal meeting, sharing frowns that supported the claims that they had been friends for a long time.

But she didn't know the specifics. Not about anything, actually. Damon tended to limit his explanations and answers to brief responses that didn't say much. That needed to end now. "I'm betting you won't provide any other details."

"The basics aren't very exciting or a secret. I met Trevor a few years after I left here." Instead of joining her at the table, Damon kicked off his shoes and sat down on the edge of his bed. "We were . . . I'm not sure how to say it. Lost boys together? Something like that."

Huh . . . "I feel like I'm missing a reference here."

"Growing up at Sullivan I had certain skills. I'd been homeschooled and took classes with some of the professors who used to come in and out. Mostly, I learned survival skills. Even those weren't enough to keep me out of trouble, but when I spun out of the mess I'd created I got a second chance."

That was not the upbringing she'd expected. The press for Sullivan had boasted about bringing in expert lecturers and engaging in *a new way of thinking*, which included mandatory work projects for the students to offset the cost of attendance. In all of that PR spin, she created this picture in her mind of rolling green hills and students sitting on a quad. Progressive in its teaching strategies, maybe, but with a sort of educational snobbishness.

Nothing about talk of survival skills fit in with the version she'd dreamed up. But it did match the rumors of a closed-off facility stormed by government officials. That happened at least twice that she knew of, the first being chalked up to government interference, but not the second.

She'd assumed Damon grew up in the ivy-covered college version but now she wondered if it was more like an armed camp. Either way, she wanted to know more. "Did you get that second chance here?"

"A long way from here." He finished off his burger in a few bites then rested his hands on his lap. "A man named Quint owned a security company. He started this program where he took in wayward twenty-something males and tried to teach them the skills to keep them out of jail or a casket."

"Them?"

"There were five of us. Wren was one. So was Trevor."

"That's the training you were talking about."

"Yep." Damon stared at his hands in a moment of awkward silence before looking up again. "In between learning the basics about financial dealings and other things, I figured out that revenge and anger weren't really great job skills, so I found some others."

"How did Trevor end up with Quint?" She thought maybe it would be easier for him to talk about someone else, to hold back on the rest of *his* story for now, even though she ached to hear it.

"We all got there the hard way." Damon smiled

as if he were reliving a memory only he could see. "Trevor had a self-destructive streak."

Not exactly the answer she was hoping for but she didn't push. She understood how a family could look one way on the outside and be very different on the inside. How someone could come across as sure and put together as a way to hide how internally they were a crumbling mess.

Her sister suffered from that duality. A fact Cate didn't understand until it was too late to stop being angry and feeling abandoned to give Shauna what she needed. Damon had that edge. If she had to guess she'd say it ran through Trevor as well, though he hid it better, under a pile of sarcasm and quick responses. "Does he still act that way?"

"No, he's all domestic and basically married to a great guy who gets him. Aaron lets Trevor run wild on a small scale—handling jobs and taking on more risk than he needs to—then Aaron pulls Trevor back in before he gets into too much trouble. It works for them."

Now that was interesting. So much for her preconceived notions about macho guys and what they would tolerate about their friends. Nothing in Damon's reactions suggested he cared if one of his closest friends were gay. One more thing to like about him.

"I guess Trevor was lucky." He'd found a peace of sorts. She knew from personal experience how difficult that could be.

"We all were. We weren't on a path headed for survival, but it happened."

The harsh rumble of his voice called out to her. "You're serious."

"Very."

The reason Wren picked Damon to help her became a bit clearer. At first, she thought working together amounted to a mismatch that would set her back instead of move her forward. Now she knew differently.

Damon tried to pull off this air of disinterest. Acted like he was a loner who blew into town and helped out on cases for a paycheck then blew out again. Someone not tied to, or responsible for, anyone.

She didn't buy any of that careful cover now. She had at first, before the drive to Pennsylvania and before seeing him in action against the attacker. He struck her as hot and tough and the exact kind of guy she should run away from—fast. But digging deeper she saw the truth. He had friends and made personal connections. He left Sullivan for reasons he hadn't yet shared but she could see the pain move through him when he talked about life here. Forget the shallow act, life affected him.

No longer comfortable with sitting five feet away from him, she curled the burger wrapper into a ball and went over to him. Dropped down on the bed next to him. "I'm guessing you also know how important it is to have answers. Some of us can't move on without them."

He shot her a sly smile. "I see what you did there."

"Then you also know I'm not running away from this, right?"

He sighed hard enough to blow a puff of air across her cheek. "Trevor is worried about your safety."

"And what are you worried about?"

He lifted his hips and pulled a handful of condoms out of his pocket. "He gave me these."

Sex. The word flashed through her head. Kissing was one thing but she'd intended to stop the attraction there, focus them back on her sister's case and keep their lips apart. But now the thought bounced around up there. A release. The warmth of a body next to hers. For an hour, maybe a night, letting her mind empty of thoughts of death and disappointment and just feel.

She tried to remember the last time she'd been touched. Greg, a lawyer in the building next to her office. They met at the lobby coffee cart a few times, she thought by accident until he admitted he waited for her.

He was cute and shy and a good guy . . . and she wished every day she'd had the energy for a relationship, the space in her heart for something other than this drive and obsession for answers. But she didn't, so they ended.

That was almost a year ago. Twelve months suddenly seemed like a *really* long time.

She picked up one of the condoms out of his hand then let it drop. "There sure are a lot of them. Nothing subtle in that message."

"Trevor is many things, subtle is not one of them."

"Are you hoping to use all of them?"

"Tonight? Woman, I'm not a machine." Damon leaned forward and dumped the pile on the edge of the table.

"I meant with me." She'd blurted that out. She was not a blurter. She didn't just drop sex talk into a conversation with a guy she barely knew. Not while they wallowed in danger and confusion and a whole mess of other unsexy things.

"Ah." He threaded his fingers together. "I guess that depends on you."

She couldn't figure out his mood. His expression bordered on a smile but it was not quite there. "You don't get a say?"

"I'm kind of a sure thing where you're concerned."

She decided right then she would never understand men. He looked on the verge of rolling his eyes every time she spoke. He argued with her, at times she was pretty sure he did it just to see her reaction. Only a guy would think that signaled interest. "I thought you found me annoying."

He nodded. "Definitely."

That time she saw him smile. Her first thought was that he should do it more often because it lit up his face and eased away the tension that seemed to linger around his eyes.

"Then there was your theory about separating work from sex." Apparently now that she mentioned sex, she was just going to keep on mentioning it. "Your idea not mine, by the way."

He put a hand on his chest. "Did I really say something so stupid?"

"You balked."

"Looking at you I'm not sure why. You're hot and annoying. Smart and a bit quirky. Sexy as fuck."

"Is it because I smell like a hamburger and you're confusing your love for those with an attraction to me?"

"I'm pretty clear on what I want to do to you." He lifted her leg until it rested over his. "While I could say something dirty about eating you, you should be clear that you are far more intriguing than a burger."

Her heart jumped at the contact. His hands, those long fingers. They mesmerized her. She had to blow out a little breath to calm the racing sensation inside her. "That's high praise coming from you."

His hand settled on her knee. "You have no idea."

The warmth of his touch burned through her jeans. The conversation kept flipping around. She let the threads fall away and concentrated on him. The scent of his shampoo, like evergreen, and the musky heat of his skin. Their arms balanced against each other, their thighs touched. Little space remained between their bodies. Despite the shortness of time they'd known each other and the danger whirling around them, this felt right. Safe . . . and a little not safe, exciting and risky. Not words she usually associated with her sex life, but she suddenly ached for a change.

Instead of pulling back like any smart-thinking, head-in-the-game person would do, she slid her leg over his thighs until she straddled him with a knee on either side of his hips on the mattress. The move brought their faces close and had their hands skimming over each other.

"You know, you talk tough, but you seem a little shaky." She traced her finger around his mouth and felt him shiver.

She couldn't think of anything sexier than a big, tough dude being felled by the skim of a fingertip over his bare skin.

"I'm on a job. I usually don't have sex on a job." He winced while he said the words.

She chose hers with purpose. "Is that a hard rule? Like, no sex at work ever. Is there wiggle room?"

A breath stuttered in his chest. She could see it, hear it.

"Are you going to wiggle for me, Cate?"

The back and forth, the sexy innuendos . . . all of it was new to her. She'd had fun before, enjoyed time with a few good guys, but this had a different feel. Raw and a little wild, like she'd been spun up in a frenzy she couldn't quite control. "Is that your thing?"

He shook his head but his hands went to the sides of her waist. "I'm trying not to be a dick here. Being back near Sullivan has my defenses down. Being with you would be so easy."

"I never agreed we were having sex." She said the word every ten seconds now.

He looked down at the sliver of space between their upper bodies. "You're on my lap."

"You're comfortable."

A muscle in his cheek jumped as he sat there, watching her, his gaze sweeping over her and always landing back on her mouth. "I can't risk someone else coming here and then getting caught naked and—"

"Are you talking yourself back to that place where you think sex between us is a bad idea?" She hated that. The flirting freed her and suddenly she did not want to lose that.

"There might be a battle between common sense and *damn, I want her* happening in my head right now." His hands clenched and unclenched against her waist until his fingers slipped under the hem of her shirt to rest on bare skin.

"Stop thinking." She pulled back as far as his hold would allow, which was not far. "Unless you're not interested."

"You're sitting on my lap. I'm pretty sure you know I'm interested."

Oh, she could feel him. His hardness pressed against her inner thigh. That had to be the cause of the harsh breathing beating in her lungs. "I mean, I don't want to mess with your vow of work celibacy or . . . whatever."

He dropped his head until his cheek rested against hers. "You're killing me here."

"Should I get up?"

If anything, he tugged her in closer. "No."

She waited for him to make the move. She'd been clear. Being with him there on the bed was the only thing that did make sense to her tonight. She opened her mouth to point that out when the room spun around her. With an arm locked on her waist he turned her, easing her back down onto the mattress.

His shoulders blocked the overhead light as he loomed over her. When he dipped his head, she lifted her shoulders and met him halfway. The kiss burned through her, wiping out every thought except the sensation of his fingers tunneling up her shirt and his leg trapped between her thighs.

His weight anchored her to the bed as his hand cupped her cheek, holding her still for his blinding kisses. She bent her leg with her foot flat against the mattress and cradled his body against hers.

The lights dimmed as his mouth moved down her neck. He trailed kisses over her collarbone to the hollow at the base of her throat. Everywhere she touched she felt miles of rock-hard muscle. Wanting nothing between them, she tugged his shirt up his back. He lifted his chest off her just long enough to strip it off and throw it on the floor. Then he was back, his hands roaming over her, igniting every nerve ending he brushed over.

His hands settled on her breasts. That expert mouth pushed her shirt to the side and nuzzled the bare skin he found underneath. Her earlier frustration gave way to a new kind of tension. It ratcheted up inside her, thumping harder when one of his hands slipped down her body to land on the zipper of her jeans. With a few flicks of his fingers he had the button open and his hand slid inside.

He took his time savoring her nipple with his mouth

as his finger swirled over the outside of her underwear. The move from meeting to this had been crazy fast but her brain had shut down. Pleasure rocked through her when his finger slipped under the elastic band. The tip swirled over her before he slid it inside her.

Her hips arched as his finger moved. The rhythmic in and out beat in time with the pounding in her chest. She grabbed on to his forearms trying to push back the sensations swirling through her, to make it last longer. Nothing stopped the tightening. It wound inside her until her heels dug into the mattress and her teeth snapped together.

One last lick of his tongue over her nipple and her body bucked. The pulsing took over as her orgasm crashed over her. She could smell him, feel him, and when she lifted her head and buried her face in the space between his shoulder and neck, she could taste him.

The trembling finally stopped as she settled back in the bed. She looked down the length of her body and saw her shirt shoved to the side and her bra undone with his hand still inside her jeans. He once called her a genius but she was pretty sure that was him. He had her half undressed and panting and she did not have a single regret.

He pushed up on his elbow and balanced his body over hers. "Well then."

"That worked." Her body still trembled as the last wave of pleasure settled deep inside her.

"We need to take showers and get some sleep." His voice sounded rough and scratchy.

She took that as a compliment as she looked him over. That bulge in his pants was hard to miss. "We're really not using the condoms to take care of that?"

"Not tonight."

Part of her still believed he was joking. Like, pretending he had all this self-control but would fold in the end. "You prefer to save condoms until Thursdays or something? Is this a rule?"

"We need some rest if we're getting on the road tomorrow."

Good grief, he was serious.

"You can rest with that?" She brushed the back of her hand over his length and his body jumped in response.

"I was kind of hoping you'd take care of it in the shower." He shrugged. "Or I can."

Or he could and she could watch. She couldn't believe how sexy that idea sounded. He'd probably prefer her mouth on him, but she vowed to circle back to the watching-him option later, another night since he seemed determined to hold on to his control tonight . . . for some reason.

"Once we're away from Salvation then we can—"

Again with this? "No, Damon."

He pushed up higher on his elbow. "We're heading out of here, Cate. As much as I hate to admit it, Trevor is right. It's too risky being here."

It was a little hard to take the harsh tone seriously with his hand still trapped between her legs. "You're going to find I don't do well with being ordered around."

"And you'll see that I won't think twice about wrapping you in a sheet and carrying you to the car if it means keeping you safe."

That was kind of sweet. In a really weird way that she wasn't quite ready to admit. She also refused to back down on this. "The answer is still no."

"This is not up for debate."

She put her hand on his cheek and brought him in for a lingering kiss. "Agreed."

He pulled his hand out of her jeans and rested it on her bare stomach. "Cate."

If they stayed in this position too long she might give in, so she sat up. "I'm showering." Since he looked so confused and disgruntled, she kissed the wrinkles on his forehead. "We can either keep fighting or you can join me."

He groaned. "That's not fair."

She threw her legs over the side of the bed. For a second she wondered if her legs would hold her. He'd sapped her strength and reduced her muscles to mush. "Is that a yes?"

He was around the bed before her feet hit the floor.

An hour later, she lay in bed with her back pressed against his front. He wore his briefs and she put on a pair of bikini bottoms after the shower, but that was their only nod to the willpower it took not to use the condoms tonight. She'd gotten on her knees in the bathroom then he returned the favor once they were back in bed.

It was now after midnight and she couldn't move.

Didn't really want to. The air conditioner blew a light breeze over the bed as it provided white noise for the room.

She had just started drifting off when she felt his arm tense around her. The palm on her stomach curled into a ball. She turned to look at him. "What's wrong?"

He lifted his upper body off her and the mattress and stared into the darkness of the room. "I thought I heard something at the door."

"I really hate this motel." She fell back into the mattress as she tried to ready her body for another fight. So much for resting and just enjoying the feel of him pressed up against her until morning.

"Which is why we're leaving." He took the verbal shot as he got out of bed and hugged the wall on his way around the room. "And do not move."

"You are relentless."

"I'm going to pretend you meant that as a compliment." One second he stood there. Then the next, he ducked down over at the couch, out of sight.

She was about to jump out of bed when he popped up again. He had what looked like an envelope in his hand. "What is that?"

He turned it around a few times before opening it. "A note."

"The guy who tried to slice you into pieces is sending us thank-you notes now?" She really did not understand Salvation at all.

"Someone is." He walked back to her and sat down on the edge of the bed as he scanned the note.

Something about his slumped shoulders tipped her off to a problem. Anxiety welled in her gut. He'd relaxed the tension right out of her earlier, but now it was back. At first in waves, but she knew a tsunami was coming.

"Want to fill me in?" she asked, though she really didn't want to know. A little ignorance might be a relief right about now.

"Not really." He turned the envelope over and studied the back of it. "It's an invitation to visit Sullivan."

She scrambled to her knees on the bed and held the thin sheet up to her chest. "What?"

"Later this morning." He shook his head and his voice sounded hollow, almost far away. "We're invited to go to Sullivan."

Hope flickered inside her. "I guess that settles it."

He frowned. "Meaning?"

"This is exactly what we wanted. It's why we're here." She'd gotten close before only to have a witness shut down. Not this time. She'd be more careful, maybe a bit more graceful. Definitely abandon the rush to get answers and, instead, let people divulge whatever they needed to say but on their own terms. In her excitement for answers she couldn't forget any of that . . . or that she was supposed to be in love with Damon. "We can't leave because we have a date with potential killers this morning."

His hand fell to his side and the note landed on the bed. "That's not funny."

He grumbled under his breath as he dropped back

into the pillows. She thought about responding but decided he wasn't really looking for a conversation.

A few seconds later, his arm slipped around her waist again. She was about to tell him goodnight when he whispered against her neck, "I'm never going to be ready to go back there."

That made two of them. "I'll be with you."

"That's part of what scares me."

CHAPTER 10

Damon stood in front of the gates to the Sullivan property and fought for breath. Being this close caused the memories to crash in on him. Running around with the other kids. Sitting through lectures about behavior. Being dragged away in handcuffs.

Cate got it right last night. Getting a welcome invitation inside was huge. But now that it had happened, Damon realized the truth—he hadn't been prepared for how this would feel.

"Hey."

Cate's soft voice slipped past the images racing through his mind. The here and now came floating back to him as she brushed her hand up and down his arm. She hadn't left his side since they got out of the car.

The whole drive over he kept up a running monologue, listing all the reasons coming here sounded good but was not smart. Too risky. Too many variables he couldn't control. Too out in the open. Also too closed off behind gates. Too many people with guns. Too . . . everything. She'd listened to all of it, not even complaining when his voice rose or he swore in a combination that even he hadn't put together before. He hadn't aimed any part of the tirade at her and her silence said she got that.

His fingers slid through hers and he held on even though he knew he should step back. Give her room and him a minute to find his equilibrium again. "It's fine."

"We can go away for now and try this later." She shrugged. "Maybe get a burger. I'm sure someone serves them for breakfast."

She was trying to make this easier on him. He got that. Tension thrummed off her. The part of her that needed to be here kicked as hard as the part of him that wanted to flee. For her, for her sister, he'd get through this. Face the demons he'd pretended no longer existed.

He squeezed her hand then let it drop. "We're here for Shauna. I can block everything else out."

"Oh, Damon." She rolled her eyes. "You're allowed to ask for help."

"I'm good."

Her fingers skimmed over his bare arm as if she sensed she should keep the lifeline between them open. "This whole I-can-do-it-alone attitude of yours might work in movies but as a characteristic in real-life men . . ." She made the same face she did when he told her he ate a burger every day. "It's not that great. Kind of awful, actually. And, worse, it's not real. Human beings need other human beings. I'd be lost without the three friends I trust to tell me that my skirt is tucked into my underwear."

The comments and the gentle way she delivered them ground his guilt to a fine point. Sleeping with her, touching her, listening to those enticing little sounds she made as she came . . . he didn't deserve that. He never should have taken any of it.

She looked at him, talked to him, like she would look and talk to any other person. Without even knowing, through her words and smiles, she reached out to make a connection. In her head, she likely thought they had. It would explain her climbing on his lap and letting him take off her clothes. But it didn't exist. He couldn't reach across to her and if she kept trying eventually he'd snap. "There's one thing you need to know before we go any further."

"About this place?"

He wanted to step back, break the physical tie between them. Maybe less touching would make it easier, only his feet refused to move. "About us being together."

A frown wrinkled her forehead. "Okay . . ."

"I know this is fake and what happened last night was probably adrenaline and—"

"Damon, just say it."

"The things that happened behind these gates, it burned every feeling, every emotion, right out of me. What you see in front of you is all that's left. A shell." He shook his head and repeated the words that had been echoing in his brain since he started the car this morning. "I've said pieces of this to you before, but I don't want to play you or lead you to a place I can't follow."

She snorted. "You're telling me you're dead inside?"

He would have appreciated her skipping the sound effects, but . . . "Yes."

"That's what this is about?"

"I . . . wait." He couldn't force a decent sentence out over the stammering.

"We'll talk about that later."

Maybe she needed more eye contact or something. He was about to try again when the deep voice that haunted his dreams called out.

"You came." The words cut out just as the ten-foot-tall black metal gates rolled open.

The man in the guardhouse sat twenty feet away and didn't get up to greet them. People milled around in the distance, walking around the Sullivan grounds. But coming at them, just a man and a woman. *The* man. Steven Sullivan, tall and slim and not yet sixty. He'd held on to his youth and could easily pass for forty-something. He walked at a fast clip down the gentle slope of the driveway. The move showed off his athletic build. The sun highlighted the salt-and-pepper in his once dark brown hair.

The mouth. The eyes. All so familiar. The only wild card here was the woman with him. Young, blonde and pretty. Petite and holding a notebook. Dressed in a short skirt and casual top in a look Damon guessed would fit in on any campus.

But this was not *any* campus and he was not just any man. This was the man Damon once called Dad and now didn't call at all.

The man's gaze hesitated on Damon before he turned to Cate and held out his hand. "I'm Steven Sullivan. Welcome."

She took it. Damon could only guess what that cost her. Here was the man she blamed for her sister's death dressed as if they were going to play golf and smiling as if they were old friends.

He gestured for them to come through the gate. "There's no need to wait out here. Come inside."

"We're good here." Those were the first words Damon had spoken to his father in a decade. Damon couldn't believe he got them out without choking.

His father frowned and the disappointed expression, so familiar, set off an ache deep in Damon's chest. In light of what happened here, the law enforcement involvement and all the rumors, growing up in this place should have been a horror. It wasn't. Some of Damon's memories were good. The group dinners. The football games on the open field near the food greenhouses. Carefree and loving . . . until he turned sixteen.

"I invited you as soon as I heard you were nearby. I'd like you to come in and see that things are different here now." Steven swept his arm around him, showing off what looked like newly built cabins and the various people standing on ladders fixing up what used to be the main meeting hall.

On the outside, all shiny. Damon knew the inside was what mattered. "You still lock the gates."

"You can understand how the security doesn't exactly make people want to walk in." Cate shrugged. "You know, because they actually can't."

"The security is here for *our* protection." The woman Damon didn't recognize started talking, clearly comfortable to take the floor from Steven. "You'd be surprised how many tourists want to take photos, how many amateur journalists come here looking for a story."

Steven smiled as he stepped away from the woman standing next to him. It was a subtle move, just a shift of his feet, but it happened. "This is Liza Henderson, my assistant."

That was new. "Assistant?"

His father's eyes narrowed. "Only that, Damon."

"Do you remember Damon?" Cate asked.

"A version of him, yes." Steven's smile came back as he talked. This time it looked like it might be genuine, or at least well practiced.

Damon gave him credit for that. No part of Damon felt light or amused or even comfortable. He had to fight off the urge to move around. To take Cate's hand and get out of there.

"Why don't you come in and see for yourself." Steven moved to the side and gestured toward the long driveway behind him. Then he pinned Damon with his intense gaze. "A lot of things are different from the last time you were here."

The road might be paved now but Damon knew exactly where that driveway led. It wound around buildings, connecting one end of the expansive acreage of full trees and thick grass to the back part of the property. That's where the water tower stood. The stream ran through and a hill running up the far side made it difficult for anyone to sneak over the fortified fence enclosing the land and get to the main buildings without being seen.

The guards might not be as obvious as they once were, but Damon sensed eyes on him. He scanned the open area in front of him. The guardhouse. The two men standing back about fifty feet pretending to hold a conversation. Damon guessed he could pick out every armed spy all over the property. Maybe no longer perched high on buildings, but still present.

"The lack of gunfire is a nice change." But he could still hear it. Every fucking shot from that day fifteen years ago.

His father ignored that. "We use the old academic buildings for classes and—"

"Wait." Maybe Cate noticed he was reeling or maybe she just had a line of questions ready, but she shifted her body slightly, moving just an inch in front of Damon and focused on the man in front of her. "What kind of classes? Is this a school again?"

"Farming, mathematics, writing, crafts. Many of the same things we taught before but now in a much less formal environment."

Steven Sullivan had not lost one ounce of his old

charm. He dove into selling the place like he used to. Smiled and moved a bit of heat into his voice, wooing in a nonsexual way. Getting people to listen to him, to trust him without ever earning it.

Damon knew better. "Where are the guns?"

Liza's hand tightened on her notebook. "I don't think that's appropriate."

"It's fine." Steven waved off her concerns with a fatherly calm while keeping his gaze locked on Damon. "The shooting range is in the same place. The weapons are locked in a vault and the vault is monitored by security both of the human and electronic kind. We've upgraded everything, bring the buildings in line with modern times."

Cate cleared her throat, gaining everyone's attention. "What do guns have to do with crafts?"

"Everyone who lives here acquires skills. They have to be productive and do chores," Steven continued in his smooth voice. "Some hunt."

"You're talking about for food and not humans, right?" Cate asked.

Liza made a strangled sound. "Of course."

As Steven grew calmer, Liza got more jumpy. Her movements were jerky and her responses terse. Damon found the differences in their styles interesting, but he had no idea what it all meant, not even the big family welcome scene playing out right now.

He decided to test them one more time. "That would mean they shoot vegetables . . . or is meat allowed here now?"

"Most things are allowed. We live by simple rules. Everyone does their share. No one steals." Steven seemed to stand up straighter. "No violence—ever."

There was no way he could sell that line. Damon almost laughed that he tried. "That's new, too, I guess."

"We're not a spa or a place to learn yoga." There was a strained tightness to Liza's voice as she talked now. "The goal is for members to become successful metallurgists and wood-carvers, midwives and farmers. Everyone chips in. The food and lodging are provided so long as people work and sell. Most of the share of proceeds from any sale goes to Sullivan to offset the expense of keeping the lights on."

Like the weapons sales. She left that part unsaid but Damon picked up on it.

Steven hadn't surrendered in his informal staring contest with his son. "Damon is well aware of what we do here."

"You're damn right." He relived it far too often in his nightmares to pretend he could forget it.

Liza shook her head. "There's no reason to—"

"What about you?" Steven asked as he turned to Cate. "Most people come to Sullivan looking for something or trying to break out of who they were before. Which are you?"

So smooth.

Such a fucking liar.

Damon broke in, trying to save Cate from having to be civilized while a warm breeze blew over them and people walked around enjoying the sunshine.

"Is this the part where you pretend not to know her name?"

Steven's perfect façade slipped. "Meaning?"

Damon knew he faced off against an expert game player, which made him grab the advantage wherever he could. "Vincent already welcomed us to town."

"Interesting word choice." Cate laughed but there was nothing light in her tone. "If you define 'welcome' by, basically, insisting we leave."

Damon nodded. "Yeah, that."

Steven and Liza exchanged confused glances but he was the one who spoke. "What are you talking about?"

Nice try. "The threats from Vincent at the diner. Then there's the guy who attacked us at the motel last night. Are you pretending none of that was you?" When his father continued to stare with a blank expression, Damon kept on going. "I see that hasn't changed. Practiced incompetence. It sure must make your life easier."

I didn't know about the weapon stockpiles and all those early morning practices. You have to believe me.

Lying then, lying now.

"Despite what you think, I would never hurt you." Steven shook his head. "I've been trying for years to get you to come home, to see for yourself."

Damon had changed his phone number so many times that comment might even be true. "See what?"

"That everything has changed." Anger vibrated in Steven's voice now. He turned to Liza. "Find Vincent. Tell him I want to talk with him. Now."

She hesitated for a second then grabbed the cell out of her back pocket. "Yes, sir."

Damon watched her scurry away. The phone was a surprise. He didn't guess many cults handed those out. "Gotta say, it's a good act. Much improved from your old one."

"You've never been good at trust."

He had to be kidding. "I wonder why."

Steven turned to Cate. "I missed your name and why you two are together."

"Cate Pendleton."

It didn't take long to get a reaction. The color drained from Steven's face and his body swayed. "Really?"

"I guess that means you recognize my name." She smiled, clearly pleased that she had launched the surprise with such ease.

"You've made numerous requests for a meeting."

Damon forced his body to move. He slipped an arm around Cate's waist in a gesture he hoped looked loving. He was still so out of it, so on edge and expecting battle, that he couldn't tell. "We're together. Dating."

Cate shot him a side-eye when he stumbled. Even he could hear the lack of emotion in his voice.

Steven's skin slipped from pale to deathly white. "Excuse me?"

"When I couldn't get your attention, I went looking for people who once lived here and found Damon." She glanced up at him and completely nailed the fake adoration thing, complete with a warm smile and this weird dancing light in her eyes.

Damon made a mental note to work through the flash of awe and panic that moved through him when he realized just how good she was at lying.

"But you kept asking about your sister." Steven shook his head. "I don't understand how this fits together with the two of you."

Because it didn't, but Damon didn't add that part.

"We met, fought, argued, I tried to ignore her and eventually we . . ." Man, what did he say after that?

"Fell for each other." She moved closer. Fit right in that space under his arm. "The one problem between us is this place. He won't talk about it but his life at Sullivan is separate from what happened to my sister."

"So, I agreed to come here. Not right here at first, but you found us." Which made Damon wonder just how far Sullivan's communications reach extended.

Steven sighed. "Then we have a common goal. You want to prove something to your girlfriend and I want to prove something to you." He looked from Cate to Damon. "Go anywhere, look at anything. You'll see that this is the place I always wanted it to be."

There it was. His father handed them the exact kind of access they needed. That made Damon even more skeptical.

"A lot of people paid a high price for this newfound legitimacy." The ultimate one, including his mother, but Damon didn't say her name. He didn't have to.

But Steven didn't blink. "Including me."

"You wouldn't know that to look at you." His father seemed like a man fully in control and enjoying life. Damon hated that the most. He never wanted to know that life just marched on for his dad.

"You don't know me anymore."

"Is that right?" But the old man had a point. It had been years. Steven managed to stay out of the public eye. He never went to jail. He looked the same, slightly older but not beat up by life like he should be.

Steven waved his hand in the air. "Bob at the diner told me you were in town. Word quickly got back to me that you were at a motel. Check out and sleep here. Stay as long as you'd like."

Damon's head almost exploded. Plan or not, this was his nightmare, getting trapped back here. This time paying the ultimate price for being born with the last name Sullivan.

"Your old suite is—"

"No." He could not be in that room. That was asking too much.

Steven looked at Cate, who had remained quiet through most of the exchange. Listening, looking around, likely assessing every move.

"One of the newer cabins, then." Steven followed Damon's gaze. "Maybe you can convince him, Cate. You need answers and this place is his birthright."

Shit. Damon heard the word and rushed to talk over it. "I don't want it."

"Birthright?" She pressed the back of her hand

against Damon's chest as she stared Steven down. "Isn't that an overstatement?"

Of course she heard the phrase. Damon wasn't lucky enough for her to have missed such a big comment. His father had dropped it perfectly.

Steven smiled. "No. As my son, everything you see is rightfully his."

The words hung there, polluting everything.

"We'll see." That's all Damon could get out with Cate's elbow digging into his side.

That eye sparkling thing she did was long gone.

"Yes," she repeated as a roughness moved into her voice. "We'll see."

CHAPTER 11

A thundering rattle muted everything else. Cate could hear it rumble, blocking other sounds, even the steady thump of her out-of-control heartbeat. A burning heat rose inside her. Every muscle itched to lash out.

This is what fury felt like.

Damon stepped in front of her, obscuring her view to the driveway and the tops of the buildings she could see in the distance. "I know that you have questions."

She ground her back teeth together to keep from screaming at him. When that didn't work, she counted to ten. Twice. None of those calming skills prevented the shake she heard in her voice when she finally spoke. "You're lucky there's a new no-violence policy at Sullivan, but once we are off the property, you should run."

He had the nerve to snort. "You really believe the violence thing?"

Another ten count and the fury still spun inside her, begging to get out. "Well, see, since you lie *all the time* I don't know what to believe about anything."

"I left one fact out." He held up a finger. "Just one."

She thought about snapping that finger off and feeding it to him. "Did you get that ability to rationalize from your *dad*? Because you sound like him right now. Evading, trying to put me on the defensive . . . lying your butt off."

It actually hurt to say that word—*dad*. Damon and Steven. Related. She'd spent so many years of her life planning for the moment when she could get access to this property and force Steven to talk, and now this.

"I know you're—"

"Stop talking." Because if he said the wrong thing she would lunge for him. Put all those self-defense classes to good use.

He rocked back on his heels. "I'll wait until you've cooled off."

What the hell? He would not stop talking, which was the exact wrong response. "Give me a year."

Her initial reaction to Damon had been raw and explosive, not businesslike at all. But she'd ignored her misgivings and doubts. She trusted Garrett and Wren because the senator told her to and Cate admired the senator more than anyone else in power. And, boy, did she buy in to the senator's sales pitch. She believed in all the whispers about Wren being this big-time fixer and getting the impossible done.

Then she got stuck with Damon, the son and heir. Implicating anyone at Sullivan meant Damon would have to implicate himself. He'd have to turn on his family and all the people he grew up with, and she could not expect that to happen. Ever.

She stood there, staring at him and hating her wrong left turn in decision-making. She never let the hot guy derail her . . . except this one time.

This would teach her not to listen. Her friends begged her not to waste her sixty-day vacation on her sister's case. They sympathized and listened to her rant, asked all the right questions and offered to help, never discounted her pain. But they were clear that they worried about her choices.

They'd all met for a wine-and-television-show-marathoning party two nights before she left town. One by one they went around the room. Each said she hoped Cate could find a way to move on and build her own life. They loved her mom and insisted she wouldn't want both of them to wallow in grief of Shauna for a second decade.

Go off to Paris, hook up with some guy and eat a lot of bread, they said. Now she wished she'd followed the advice, except for the guy part. That guy part seemed to be ruining everything for her right now. She could handle her needs just fine without one.

"Just one request." Damon held up both hands as if he was trying to surrender to her or beg for mercy. "I'll explain, but not while we're here. Not on this property."

She still debated making a scene. Not a small one either. No, the kind that people talked about for years. "A convenient excuse to put this off."

"You think any part of this assignment, being here, is convenient for me?"

Those eyes and the hitch in his voice. So tempting . . .

Nope. She would not give in and excuse his actions because of his pain.

"You should have told me about this. The whole fake relationship thing? It didn't dawn on you to tell me then?" She shook her head. "Like, after you introduced yourself, you should have said, *there's this thing you need to know first*. That early. Not even after you felt me up. Way before that, Damon."

"Background intel wasn't my job."

It was as if he wanted her to start yelling. "Oh, please."

"You never would have trusted me if you knew my last name really was Sullivan." He put his hands on her arms and gave her a little squeeze.

She shrugged out of his hold. "That was the first honest thing you've said all morning. You admit you were a big chicken." He started to say something and she heard the growl work up her throat as her anger spiraled again. Through pure willpower she bit it back. "I want to kick you right now."

"Join the club. For the record, seeing you here is the exact opposite of you leaving the area." Trevor stepped up beside them. He wore a fake smile and shook their hands, likely to throw off anyone who might be watching and make them think this was an initial meet and greet.

Cate decided it was fine to be pissed at Trevor, too. "Apparently you knew the truth about him being a Sullivan and related to this place. You're clearly the reason he talked about how we should leave here and let things cool down."

Trevor's eyebrow lifted. "But your argument was more persuasive, I see."

That tone kept her anger level on high. It spiked off the charts. "If you're thinking about mentioning the condoms, don't."

"You already broke those out?" Trevor's gaze switched to Damon. "I take back everything I've ever said about straight people being lame."

"Are you done?" And by that she really meant *do you want to die today*.

Trevor swallowed his smile. "Yes, ma'am."

"His father asked us to stay. At Sullivan. In a cabin or suite or something." That offer still made her dizzy though she wasn't sure why she bothered to mention it other than she now assumed everyone had the information in advance except for her.

"Sounds like you guys have been busy learning about each other." Trevor looked back and forth between Cate and Damon before settling on his friend. "And you. What's with spilling secrets you never tell anyone?"

Damon swore under his breath. "My father didn't give me much of a choice."

"You had to know this would come up when you accepted his invitation." Trevor's mouth still hung open. Nothing about his stunned expression had cleared.

Damon shrugged. "I wasn't ready. This is not the

kind of thing you just drop. And I thought Cate would immediately bolt. I wanted her to trust me a bit before she figured it out."

"Trust?" He really didn't know when to stop or how to make this better. In any other situation, she might feel sorry for him, but not today. Not on this.

"I would have told you . . . eventually. I knew the reckoning was coming. I just thought I could push it off a bit longer."

He actually gave her a look that said *duh*, as if she was the one being unreasonable here. "Do you have any idea how big of a fight we're going to have over this?"

Trevor winced. "Epic."

"Understatement." She didn't break eye contact with Damon. "And then your dear dad invited us to stay—which is the mother lode in terms of our ability to collect information, and the whole point of this silly fake relationship plan—and you said no."

"I said no to staying in my old room, because come on. Right there, in his house?" Damon shook his head. "We're not exactly a close family even without the gunfire."

Oh. My. God. "That doesn't matter. You're still not forgiven, so . . ."

When she hesitated, Trevor jumped back into the conversation. "Before you come up with an ending to that sentence, please go back to the part where you were invited to stay. Because the word went out that you were coming back for an extended visit and the order was for everyone to be welcoming and stay out of your way. The clear message was that you had free reign."

Damon shook his head. "Steven will never really allow that to happen."

He refused to get it and that frustrated her more than anything else. She decided to give her argument one more time. That's it.

"I get that this is hard for you and your brain is all scrambled, but pretend you're me for a second. I've been fighting this fight about my sister's death and running into walls and tripping over annoying men in power who treat me like a mindless little girl." When Trevor opened his mouth, she lifted one finger and that was enough to make him stop. "I've watched my mother fold in on herself at the mention of my sister's name."

Cate lowered her voice to a harsh whisper when a group of older teens walked by, bouncing a basketball on their way out of the property. "Over time, it got better, she cried less, but she still hesitates when she passes my sister's photo. Still refers to her in the present tense."

Some of the anger left Damon's face. "Cate."

But she wasn't done. There was so much more inside her itching to get out. "Then I run into someone who was here back then, a person who may be tied to what happened to Shauna, and he inadvertently offered me a chance to dig into it. To finally get answers." She put a hand on his chest. Let it rest there. "If you were me—even with the danger, uncertainty and risks—wouldn't you kick open every door? Wouldn't you take your dad's offer?"

"Of course."

"Then stop holding back information and help me."

Trevor shook his head. "Buddy, you're so screwed."

Damon's shoulders fell as the tension visibly ran out of him. "Fuck."

"Look, I'm not asking you to make up with your dad or forget your pain, but you are my way into Sullivan. I can't imagine how hard this is for you, but I've never been this close. We have to figure out a way through this."

Trevor glanced around. "What if the intel you gather leads you back to his dad as the reason for Shauna's death?"

"Will it?" She had to ask because if this was one more secret, she deserved to know the answer now and not later.

"I don't know." Damon shook his head. "I honestly don't."

Then she had her answer. "We need to find out."

DAMON STAYED QUIET on their way back to the car because he wasn't a complete dumbass. That speech she gave still rang in his ears. Unlike his father's old ramblings, hers came from the heart. She wasn't giving a sermon or trying to play on his emotions. She opened up and told him the truth. Let him see the path she walked every single day. And he got it.

He screwed up by not being honest with her about why he was the one on the mission with her. At the time it made sense. He'd compartmentalized his life during and after Sullivan and never let the sides meet. With her, the sides collided.

He'd held back information to protect himself when his job was to protect her. He knew Cate planned to yell at him. He planned to take it because this time he, not his father or anyone at Sullivan, messed up.

They stepped into the gravel square filled with eight or so cars. It appeared to operate as a makeshift parking lot for Sullivan. There was actually a sign that said GUEST PARKING. Damon didn't know if he should laugh or punch it.

He pressed the fob and the door locks disengaged with a beep. He'd barely put his hand on the door handle when a red pickup skidded into the lot behind him. He recognized Vincent and the man sitting next to him. "This day keeps getting better and better."

Cate's head popped up and she stopped typing on her cell. "What?"

Vincent parked next to them . . . because of course he did. He jumped down and slammed the door shut behind him. "Welcome back to Sullivan."

He delivered the welcome with all the excitement of reading a menu.

"That's not what you said at the diner." Cate then turned to the other man walking along the front of the truck toward them. "And I have no idea who you are."

"Roger, and I admit I'm a bit confused by this conversation."

Damon filled in the blank. "Vincent's brother, and this is my girlfriend, Cate."

The words came out easier that time but still sounded odd to him. Not as odd as the brothers in front of him. They were two years apart and as different as two people could be, always were. Roger smiled and volunteered to help out. Vincent sulked. Watching them now, Damon could see they carried that streak into adulthood.

Roger reached over and shook Damon's hand. "Good to see you. It's been a long time."

He actually sounded like he meant it. Damon had no idea what to make of that.

"Clearly the friendly brother," Cate muttered half under her breath.

Vincent shot her a quick unreadable glance before talking to Damon. "I'm sorry about the heavy-handed routine at the diner. I was trying to save all of us a lot of grief by getting Damon to leave. His presence is going to make some people uncomfortable. He made accusations back then that . . . well, let's just say it's a problem."

The lying. Damon was sick of all of it. "Is that code for my father told you to try to scare me away?"

Roger frowned. "What?"

"Nah, man." Vincent balanced his boot on the rental car's bumper. "That was all me. I was told you were back in town and panicked about how some people would react."

"Like who?" Cate asked.

Vincent hesitated a few more seconds before finishing his thought. "When you left before it was rough on people. Especially on your dad. He becomes useless after he talks about you." Vincent shrugged. "Our parents are gone. He's always been good to us and I didn't want him hassled."

"Are you taking him up on the offer to stay?" Roger folded his arms in front of him as he sat on the hood of the car.

Cate looked at the brothers then to Damon. "There really was a property-wide announcement about this, wasn't there?"

"Literally." For the first time since he'd popped up at the diner, Vincent smiled. "We got a text."

"Cults that text." Cate shook her head. "Go figure."

"This isn't a cult," Vincent shot back.

Debatable, but Damon wasn't about to get into that with two believers who were born here, grew up here and likely would die here.

"We're going to talk the offer over." Damon knew from Cate's earlier speech that they were coming back but he thought being hesitant played better for their cover. No one would believe he wanted to rush in and make up after all this time because of a woman.

"Give it a chance, M—" Vincent clamped his mouth shut before he could finish.

At the near-slip, Cate's eyes lit up. "Were you about to say his real name?"

"This seems like a good time for us to go." Roger slid off the car and smacked the back of his hand against Vincent's chest. "We've got a meeting with Steven, which I'm now thinking is your fault."

"Despite what happened, I hope you stick around for a few days," Vincent said in a smaller than usual voice.

Cate's smile grew wider. "We will."

"Good." Roger winked at her. "See you soon then."

Damon waited until the brothers headed out of the parking lot and started up the hill. Same color hair and broad shoulders. It was hard to tell them apart from the back.

But Damon had to face the person in front of him. He eyed Cate but she was watching the brothers. Not just looking but assessing.

"What are you thinking right now?" It was a dangerous question, but he'd been around her enough to know something was going off in that big, beautiful brain of hers.

"The scent."

He froze as he reached for the button to unlock the car again. "What?"

"I smelled the same aftershave or whatever it was in my apartment just now." She spun around to face Damon. Energy bounced off her. "On Vincent."

Damon shook his head. "But you didn't smell it before."

"I did this time. Faint, but it was there. It's a distinct scent." She stopped moving around and stared at him. "Did you really not pick up on it?"

The woman had a pretty intense sense of smell. He picked up the scent of freshly mowed grass and that was about it. "Maybe he skipped wearing it at the diner but didn't expect to see you today, so he felt comfortable putting it on again."

She made a face. "It's weird, right?"

Damon couldn't really argue with that. "Everything around here is. But we're going to be extra careful around him from now on. I'll also have Trevor sneak around, try to see if he can find anything unexpected in Vincent's room."

The weird part was an understatement, but he needed her to know they had to be on guard, assume they were being watched and followed. Another unprovoked attack seemed less likely. If Vincent had taken his threats from the diner to the motel, he'd pull back now. There was too much attention on him. Hell, even Steven wanted to see him. But they would stay vigilant.

"And you know what else we're going to do?" She leaned against the side of the car.

"I'm afraid to answer."

"You also seem to forget that I'm still ticked off at you for the whole hidden dad thing." She glared at him over the top of the car. "Get ready for it."

Man, she did not forget a thing. And suddenly the truth hit him. She wouldn't forget it if she learned this last horrible piece from anyone but him.

He inhaled, working up the courage to share a piece of his past he'd kept buried from almost everyone. "Ryan."

She froze with her hand on the door handle. "What?"

He swallowed, knowing once he turned this corner he couldn't go back. She would see him in a different light. A dark and cloudy one, but maybe that was a good thing. A wake-up call might make her forget about the condoms and her claims that he had these emotions he was denying.

If he told her the truth, she would care about what he did. There was no way she couldn't.

"Ryan Michael Sullivan. I went by Michael." A huge ball of shame lodged in his throat. "You wanted to know my real name. That's it."

She didn't move. "But Michael was the name of . . ."

He took a deep breath to try to ease the strain of his hammering heart then took the final plunge. "Of the Sullivan who shot the FBI agent fourteen years ago on this property. Yeah, that was me."

CHAPTER 12

Damon sure knew how to dominate a conversation. With a few lines, he shook her and left her with a hollow sensation in her stomach.

They'd driven back to the motel with her in stunned silence. As the mile markers whizzed by, she tried to remember the facts behind the first shooting at Sullivan. Everything she knew came from secondhand sources and articles. So much had happened there that her sister's death became a footnote.

Some said the first run-in with law enforcement should have been a sign. Others blamed the ATF and FBI. She wanted to hear the truth from him.

They'd been back in the motel for almost an hour now. Neither of them had eaten. The bags he talked about packing sat empty on the floor. As soon as they stepped inside, he'd walked into his bedroom through the open connecting door and slipped out of sight.

At first, she heard the water run in the bathroom. Then she thought she heard the bed. A battle waged inside of her. Go in or not. Talk to him or let him start when he was ready, which might mean never.

She'd promised him a fight—and he sure as hell deserved one for leaving out the detail about who his father was—but all the anger had seeped out of her. Confusion moved into its place. It took all of her strength not to turn on her phone and look up every article about that original shoot-out at Sullivan. Maybe it would prepare her for what was to come, to the extent anything could.

She heard a noise and looked up to find Damon leaning against the doorframe between their rooms. He'd changed into a black T-shirt and the ends of his hair were damp. It looked like he'd washed his face but he couldn't wash away everything. The guilt still lingered there.

She saw it all now. That rough exterior, the jokes. They hid a mix of pain and darkness. He didn't think there was any emotion left inside him because he believed he deserved to suffer. Not that he used those words. He didn't have to. She knew from experience how guilt could seep into everything, make it shrivel and warp.

Even now, his gaze traveled around the room, not landing on her. Skipping over the table to the window to her right. Everywhere but her face.

She didn't know how to start but she dove in. The silence chipped away at her nerves until she felt like she could get the words out. But who knew if they were the right words?

"When my sister left for Sullivan I pretended to be happy for her." She could no longer hear Shauna's voice in her head. The way she lifted her voice at the end of a sentence as if she were asking a question when she really wasn't. But she remembered Shauna's infectious excitement when she got the Sullivan acceptance. It practically radiated off her.

Damon didn't move but he was looking at her now. She took that as a sign that she should continue.

"We didn't have money for extras growing up. Some weeks we didn't have money for food, but my mom never gave up. She put herself through college. She got a teaching job that provided the important things I didn't know or care about as a kid, like health insurance. Some sense of financial stability for all of us." She stopped and breathed in nice and deep. Worked up the nerve to talk about what came next.

The more she talked, the more Damon's expression changed. Fully engaged, he watched every move she made from shuffling her feet to rubbing her hands together. He didn't stop her and for that she was grateful.

"Sullivan was the opportunity Shauna never expected to get. College at no cost. No loans. No trying to repay loans. She loved being around people and learning new things but strict classes and weekly tests weren't her thing, so the Sullivan match made sense." Cate sat down on the end of her bed. "This is where my pretending started. See, when she left for Sullivan, she left me. We were this threesome, the two of us plus Mom. We fought over stupid sisterly stuff like borrowing clothes but we protected each other. We leaned on each other and backed each other up with Mom. When Shauna left, I was alone. Lost. Angry with her for having fun without me."

This time she waited for him to say something. He must have picked up on the vibe or saw it on her face because he stepped away from the doorframe and sat on the table, just a few feet away from her. Balanced his feet on the chair in front of him but didn't touch her.

"My brother died when I was really young. I don't actually remember him at all." Damon stared at his hands for a few seconds before meeting her gaze again. "Acute myelogenous leukemia. It has better survival rates now, but not back then. My parents tried everything. Took him to clinics but the treatments didn't take hold." He shrugged. "That was my experience with a sibling. Hospital beds and faint memories of seeing my mother rock back and forth weeping. But then the other kids came to Sullivan. Not many. Most were kids of teachers or people who worked there. I hated when their parents moved and took them away."

She moved forward until her knees touched the back of the chair he balanced his feet on. "I still feel guilty because in my late teen angsty moments, I would refuse to talk with Shauna when she did call. Mom visited here once, but I stayed with a friend. I was trying to make Shauna pay and then she died and those were my last memories of her. My awful behavior."

"You were just a kid."

Not a little kid. Old enough to know better and not

be so selfish, but those traits came with age for her. She earned them the hard way. "How old were you?"

At first she didn't think he would answer the unspoken part of her question. He put one leg down until his foot touched the floor then raised it again. She could almost hear his internal debate. Guilt seemed to flush through him.

"Believe it or not, my childhood was pretty great. The father I knew spent time with me. Explained things, went on walks. His discipline was to talk me to death." Damon's smile came and went. "When I turned sixteen, my uncle, who was my dad's partner in Sullivan, the one with all the money, insisted that I spend time training with him."

Her stomach went into free fall. "The guns."

Damon nodded. "Dad wanted to talk books and theories. Uncle Dan was a work-the-land guy." Damon stopped as he rubbed his hands up and down his thighs. "He listened to fringe radio programs and got spun up. He truly believed the government was out of control and taking people's land by killing them then covering the whole thing up."

"He's in prison." She remembered that much, but that happened much later. She could only assume he unraveled even further at some point.

"Where he should be." Damon's chest rose and fell on a harsh breath. "He started this passive-aggressive letter writing campaign with the FBI. He wasn't really involved in the school but that's not the impression the FBI got. Eventually, agents came in with guns ready.

They scaled the fence at the back side of the property, which was higher back then, and moved in on Dan."

"The shoot-out fourteen years ago." It made her sick that she needed to talk about more than one shooting at Sullivan. This initial one was bad enough. The final one shut the school down and ended in arrests and more body bags.

"I was about twenty. We were at the shooting range." Damon shook his head as his eyes became clouded.

He looked as if he were locked in the memory. She leaned forward thinking to reach out, provide some comfort, but she pulled back at the last sentence. This was the poison that raced through him and colored how he viewed his place in the world.

"The firing started and I shot back. It's what I had been trained to do and . . ." He gulped in air. "I didn't know who was aiming at us. Not at first."

Damon stood up then and started pacing. "There was so much noise. All this screaming and someone yelling into a megaphone and issuing orders that I couldn't make out. It all blurred in my head." He laughed but there was no amusement in the sound. "My uncle made these illogical leaps all the time, would go into these paranoid ramblings, but here these shooters were, on our land without warning. The government had moved in. It's where my mind went and all I could think of and there were these innocent kids running around and my mom, who was also at the range."

Cate's heart ached for him. She'd experienced so

much loss. It's what fueled her. She needed to get close enough to the heart of the chaos because she thought if she did she'd find answers. He didn't get that choice. He was thrown into danger and had to fight his way out.

Without a sound, he went to the window and pulled the curtain back, staring into the parking lot. "When the shooting stopped my mom was dead. The FBI agent who had been sparring with my uncle via email was also gone . . ." He let the curtain drop. "Because of me."

"You were arrested at Sullivan." She tried to sound matter-of-fact, thinking it would help him tell the story, but she really didn't know if that was true or not.

He shrugged without looking at her. "I didn't even know my mom had died from her wounds until my attorney told me."

Cate knew the rest of this piece of the story. Politicians stepped in. The school fought back. Higher-ups in the FBI hung the whole thing on a rogue operation by a rogue employee and the ATF was happy to pass the blame. Back then it made sense and no one mentioned Dan. She had to assume Damon's dad provided cover.

"I was arrested and locked up for four months before the charges were dropped. But the threats that I could be arrested again lingered and it took years for me to be fully cleared. Uncle Dan spent a few more months than I did in jail that time. The official line was that I was a collateral victim in an unfortunate incident." He looked at her then. "That's the actual phrase they used."

Just like her sister's death was called an unfortunate accident. She hated the word *unfortunate* almost as much as she hated the false impression using the word *accident* gave off.

"I got out all pissed off and feeling like I'd been lied to about everything," Damon said, continuing the explanation.

"And your dad?"

"He was lost, in mourning and not much of a help to me. When he did visit—one time in four months—he insisted he didn't know what Dan was teaching us or how he'd pushed the FBI into the fight."

"That really wasn't even a question in the press." Not that she remembered reading. "Everyone sided with Sullivan and no one mentioned your uncle being . . . off."

Damon sat down next to her. Not right on top of her. Their bodies didn't touch, but he was there. "I left and spiraled into a pretty big mess. Quint found me when his friend caught me stealing. I broke into this poor guy's house and by the time I hit the driveway on the way out, Quint was standing there, gun strapped to his side."

She really wanted to meet this guy. To thank him. "He saved you."

"Yep." Damon nodded. "He asked me if I wanted to die and when I didn't immediately answer he dragged me to his car, threw me in and took me to get dinner."

"Let me guess. A burger?"

"Of course." He shot her one of those sexy little smiles of his. "My first one ever."

"I take it Dan got worse from there."

"He spun out of control after that, insisting he'd been right about everything. Made more plans. From what I was told later, he picked up the pace on storing weapons and getting everyone out on the range."

"I remember my mom talking to Shauna about the news but there was so much support for the school that they figured it was fine. In fact, I think it won some sort of award *after* the initial shooting."

"More than one. Politicians and the police chief publicly apologized to everyone at Sullivan. People at the FBI retired early to get out from under the scandal." Damon stood up again, as if the energy in his body refused to let him sit still. "The second shoot-out came years later. That time there were weapons and the student body had dwindled and those left there took on Dan's ideology. I was long gone for that one."

"I've read the stories about that."

"I heard the facts from Wren. You can imagine the file he's collected on Sullivan." Damon stuck his hands in his back pockets then pulled them out again, letting them hang loose by his sides. "You know, in case I ever needed it."

"He tried to save you, too."

Damon nodded. "He did. All five of them and Quint. Later, Garrett."

She didn't understand why he couldn't see the

truth. These things happened to him—things out of his control—and he reacted. A man was dead at Damon's hands and she didn't minimize that. It was clear he didn't either. That kind of horror should stick with a person, change them and maybe make them more grateful or careful, but Damon didn't actually let it define him even though he thought it did.

She stepped up behind him. Debated about doing more than offer support from a distance then took the risk. Her arms slid around his waist and she sighed in relief when he grabbed on and pulled her in closer.

She kissed his shoulder through the soft T-shirt then rested her cheek there. "A man who is dead inside wouldn't care that he killed someone who was stalking him."

The stiffness of his muscles made her hold on tighter. She kissed the side of his neck, hoping to soothe some of the chaos she felt exploding inside him. "You wear this mistake like a protective blanket."

"He's dead, Cate. He had a son and that son doesn't have a father." His hand kept brushing over the back of hers. "That's on me. No one else."

Tension pressed in on them, choking off some of the air in the small room. "You were trying to save yourself and the people around you."

"It's not an excuse."

"It actually is."

He broke out of her hold then. Went over to the dresser and picked up his keys. "I'm going to go get us some food."

She wanted to scream. Not at him this time, at the situation. At all the unfairness. At how broken they both were because of things that happened years ago.

Even knowing it was a dead end right now, that he couldn't really hear her, she tried again. She'd expected to come to Sullivan and focus solely on Shauna. She didn't want to care about the people there or think of them as anything other than a way to collect information.

Those days were long gone. Shauna still stayed at the forefront of her mind all the time, but she made room for Damon there, too. After a few short days thrown together in this frenetic environment she needed to save him as much as she needed to save herself.

"You care about Wren and Trevor and Garrett. About all your friends." The right word was *love* but he looked ready to bolt, so she kept the words more neutral. "Those are emotions, Damon. Real feelings of a guy with a beating heart."

The keys jangled in his hand. "Is a burger okay with you?"

She'd lost him. More talk, trying to reason with him, none of it would work. She wasn't an expert on men, but she was starting to understand this one. "With fries. I'm not an onion ring fan."

He winked at her. "I'll get extra so you don't steal mine."

The light tone had returned. He wore a smile that didn't meet his eyes. She recognized all of it as fake now. This was the Damon mask he wore when the conversation dove too deep. The guy who joked and kept things shallow. Still sexy and funny but just a shell of who he really was.

"Perfect." She said the word to his back because he was already at the door. When it closed behind him, she rushed over to it. Lifted up on tiptoes and peeked outside. The blurry image didn't tell her much except that he stood next to the car with his hand on the roof and the door still shut.

He could deny it but she knew the truth—Damon Knox or Ryan Michael Sullivan or whatever he wanted to call himself felt everything.

HOURS LATER, AFTER they'd eaten and watched hours of bad television together, they both headed to bed. Separate beds. No touching. No real conversation that slipped past joking about what was happening on the screen in front of them. No talk of leaving either. Damon didn't have the energy. Not tonight.

He flipped from his side to his back for what felt like the tenth time. The sheets started off as soft with the right room temperature. Now he couldn't find a comfortable position and he flipped from sweating to chilled every few minutes.

He wanted to blame his father, Sullivan, the weather. He knew this jumpiness rose up from inside of him. He'd struggled with sleeping for more than a decade. He didn't see that changing any time soon.

"Damon?" Cate's soft whisper moved through the quiet room.

He lifted his head then pushed up until he balanced on his elbows behind him. The curtains had plunged the room into darkness except for the tiny sliver of outside light he couldn't figure out how to block. It cast her in shadows but he could make out her long legs and shorts.

"You okay?" Because he wouldn't blame her if she wanted to run from him. Now that she knew who she'd tied herself to, it had to panic her.

"May I sleep with you?"

He must have heard that wrong. "What?"

"No condom usage, just sharing a bed."

"Did something happen?"

"Yeah, I met you and now want to share a bed with you."

He meant a nightmare but that answer was so much better. Scary as shit and confusing, but pretty damn great.

Rather than respond, he lifted the sheet and comforter, inviting her in. Her footsteps thudded against the floor as she practically jogged over to the bed. She slid in, fitting her body close to his. By the time he pulled the covers over them she'd scooted back until her back rested against his front. Her legs curled around his.

His heartbeat stuttered in reaction. Every muscle sparked to life, all signs of exhaustion and fighting with the sheets gone.

He inhaled, taking in the scent of her shampoo and

the smell of flowers on the back of her neck. He had no idea where that came from but he liked it enough to lean in and take another whiff. But that was as close as he planned to get. Already he was looking at a long hot night. Touching her set off a firestorm inside him and it took all of his energy to tamp it down again.

She reached back and grabbed his hand, pulling it over her hip and resting it on the subtle curve of her stomach.

This was going to be pure torture.

"Cate?" He pressed a soft kiss in her hair. "What exactly are we doing right now?"

"Cuddling."

The laughter came out before he could stop it. "Are you kidding?"

Her body stayed soft and welcoming. Nothing about his reaction seemed to bother her. "It's a real thing. Get used to it."

That sobered him up. "You think we're going to sleep like this often?"

"I'm not sleeping alone at the commune or cult or whatever we're calling it."

The sigh escaped him right behind the laugh. "We're supposed to be dating, which includes sleeping together."

"I need answers. You need to deal with your father and his legacy and everything that happened to you back then."

"I already have."

She snorted. "For a smart man, you're talking silly."

"Most people think I'm pretty solid."

"Rock solid." She slipped her fingers through his. "But also a bit of a mess, but a cute mess."

"Thanks . . . I think."

"Take it as a compliment because what I said makes you flawed but very human." She settled all of her weight against him now. "And don't think I forgot that I owe you a huge fight with lots of yelling."

He smiled because she was not wrong. "I was hoping you were ignoring that. Maybe giving me a freebie."

That earned him a second snort. "Hardly."

"I'm sorry I didn't tell you the truth about my family sooner." He wasn't sure when would have been the right time but he never meant to hurt her, so he did feel like shit about it.

"You're going to make it up to me by packing up tomorrow and relocating to the school with me without whining or giving me the silent treatment. I'm not a fan of either of those, by the way."

Since he knew that was coming he didn't fight it. "You're taking away all of my best guy moves."

"I have faith you'll come up with others."

"If I do all these things I'm forgiven?"

She lifted their joined hands and kissed the back of his. "Until you do something else that ticks me off."

"You sound pretty sure I will."

She returned their hands to her stomach. "I know

you think you're all broody and complex and hard to read, but you're really not."

"I'm not sure how I feel about your ability to read me." It felt kind of good and that made him a bit shaky.

"Get used to that, too."

CHAPTER 13

Cate didn't know where they were emotionally but it felt like they had scaled a huge mountain and managed to survive it. That gave her hope they'd find some answers at Sullivan. Since they'd been invited, at least they might not get attacked again. That would be a nice change.

But before the packing and the anxiety about whether they were making the right decision and getting through what she assumed would be some of the worst father-son reconnecting moments ever, she needed something else. Damon.

She stood next to the dresser in her pajama shorts and matching T-shirt. They were pink-and-white checked and her favorites . . . and she was ready to take them off. Better yet, have him take them off.

She needed touching and closeness. They'd spent all night wrapped around each other, with his face pressed into her neck. The rhythmic sound of his soft breathing lulled her to sleep. The heat rolling off his body woke her up twice, but she'd just snuggled in closer and held on.

It was sweet and intimate and a total surprise, but now she wanted more. She needed to feel something other than frustration and sadness over her sister. They'd shared so many feelings and secrets from the past, but a part of her was desperate to know if he could connect with her on a deeper physical level. She had no idea why it mattered so much—maybe she needed that test to clear some hurdle she'd set up in her mind—but it did.

She'd gotten up ten minutes before. All the shifting on the mattress seemed to wake him because when she came out of the bathroom, he went in. Now she waited, looking at the closed door as a tiny bit of light filtered through the dark curtains. Not a lot, but enough to brighten the room and signal morning.

On cue, the bathroom door opened with a click. His gaze went to the empty bed then zoomed around the room. A smile lit up his face as he spied her. Then he yawned and started frowning.

"Why are you up at . . ." He squinted at the alarm clock next to the bed before he fell back into it. "Is it really only six in the morning?"

He sounded appalled by that realization. He sent her a have-you-lost-your-mind look before grumbling about women messing with his sleep.

"It's actually six-o-three." But who was counting?

"You were moving around, so I got up thinking it was later in the day. Even brushed my teeth." He closed his eyes as his arm fell over his head on his pillow. "What a waste of toothpaste."

The poor thing. "I think we can put all your hard work to good use."

He opened one eye and peeked at her. "Tricking a man with the wrong time of the morning is not okay."

He certainly liked to complain about weird things. If he'd stop talking for a few seconds, she was pretty sure she could turn his mood around.

Deciding that standing a few feet away from him wouldn't get the job done, she went to the bed. Crawled right up there and straddled his hips with a leg on either side of him. "I'm betting I can make it up to you."

Both eyes opened now. "I'm listening."

She saw the spark, the moment it hit him that he was getting a special kind of wake-up call. "Good."

The corner of his mouth kicked up in a smile. "That tone sounds dangerous."

"It is. Risky, dangerous and maybe a little stupid." She rested a hand on his chest, learning the sharp lines of his muscles through his thin T-shirt.

"It's like you're describing my personality."

She lifted her lower half a bit then settled back down against him again. "No arguments there."

A strangled sound rose up from inside him. "So, tell me what's happening right now."

But he knew. How could he not know? She was practically riding him. "We have one thing to do before we relocate."

"Eat?"

She reached into the elastic waistband of her shorts and took out the condom she'd pocketed a few minutes earlier. Held it up with two fingers, daring him to act confused now. "This."

"That's a condom."

The guy was not so quick in the morning. "Yes, it is."

"You know that's a really bad idea, right?" But his hands went to her waist and he eased her upper body down until her face hovered just above his.

She rested both hands on his shoulders now. She pretended it was for balance but she really just liked touching him. "Totally agree."

"We exchanged crappy stories last night. I'm still shaky about my dad. You're still trying to figure out how much of a detriment my being a Sullivan really is."

"All good points." Not that they mattered to her right now. This—them—was not about work or the past. It was about the heat bouncing off them and the spark that ignited during their early banter. The spark that never died out.

"Then why?"

She flicked her thumb over his bottom lip and smiled when he opened his mouth to give her better access. "Are you really asking that?"

One of his hands slipped around to her back. Those fingers explored and caressed. "The hotness, yes. I see you and my eyes cross and my dick gets hard. No one is debating that."

She could feel him right now. Those boxer briefs would be no match against his growing bulge in a few minutes. "So romantic."

"I'm not a romance guy."

If true, he was doing a fine job of pretending. "You curled up with me to sleep last night."

He winced. "About that. No mentioning the cuddling thing to Trevor."

"I'm not promising." If he said one thing that ticked her off she might tell everyone at Sullivan. Ruin his tough guy reputation without a thought.

"I will never hear the end of it."

"You're not helping your argument about why I should stay quiet." She held the condom up right in front of his face. "But back to this."

His hand slipped lower on her back. Those fingertips dipped under the waistband of her shorts, past the top of her underwear, to massage her bare skin. "You're still holding it."

"I can throw it away." She could hardly breathe with his fingers doing that. She had no idea how she got the comment out without panting all over him. "You're not really going to make me talk you into this, are you?"

"The idea has possibilities. Kind of sounds like hearing you beg."

She waved the condom back and forth. "I don't beg or force. If you don't want to . . ."

He covered her hand with his and slipped the condom out of her fingers while doing it. "Don't you dare."

Smooth. "That's a yes?"

"Every warning I gave you before still applies."

She rolled her eyes because come on. Only he

would issue a remember-I'm-dead-inside warning before sex. "No emotions. This means nothing. Got it."

He froze. "I never said it wouldn't mean anything."

From the guy who claimed not to have emotions . . . right. "Now, that *is* kind of romantic."

"I'm trying to be clear." He sighed. "And failing, apparently."

She leaned down until her elbows hit the pillow on either side of his head. The move put her mouth right above his. "You do have a bit of a problem with mixed messages."

"Let me be dead honest about one thing—I want you." He pressed a soft kiss on her lips. "Have since I first saw you and you were trying to fire me or exchange me for Garrett."

"I like Garrett."

The second kiss lingered as he palmed her ass and started a gentle massage of the skin there. "Do you like me?"

Her head fell a bit until her forehead rested against his nose. She blamed his fingers. The touch of skin to skin had every muscle inside her tightened. "Are you fishing for compliments?"

"Just asking." He pushed her shorts down, had those and the underwear over and off her butt cheeks.

"I do." Her fingers slipped through his hair, holding him still for a kiss that she felt the whole way to her knees. When she lifted her head again he looked as dazed as she felt. "You ground me."

"Is that good?" His hands started moving again. They slipped up her sides, skimming over the outer part of her breasts and dragging her T-shirt with them. With one tug, he had the shirt up and off.

She pressed back down again, loving the feel of her chest against the soft cotton of his shirt. For now, she'd tolerate his clothes, but not for long. "Very."

"But—"

"You're dead inside. Yeah, I get it." The next kiss started slow, a seduction of her tongue licking over his bottom lip.

When his hand plowed through her hair to hold her steady, the mood shifted. Tension bounced around them. The good kind. The kind that revved up the energy. Need caught like wildfire and spread through her. The kiss possessed and promised and left her gasping when he pulled back again.

He continued to nibble at the corner of her mouth. Then kissed along her cheek to that sensitive space below her ear. "I sense you're not taking my warning seriously."

"Because I think you're wrong." She shoved at his shirt, desperate to be with him with nothing between them. "But this is just sex, so I won't prove it now. There's no need for us to mix up one with the other."

"Uh-huh." He sat up, taking her with him. His arms lifted long enough for her to push the shirt off and throw it on the floor. "Then explain why I feel like I'm being set up."

"You can say no." But she shifted her weight, sitting on his lap with nothing but a strip of her rolled-down underwear and his boxer briefs between them.

His heated gaze wandered over her, stopping on her breasts. Her skin flushed from the attention. She was about to say something when he lowered his head. He traced his tongue around her nipple. Round and round until a shiver ran through her.

"I only want to say yes." He lifted his head just long enough to talk then his mouth was on her again. Sucking and licking and generally driving every clear thought from her head except the ones about him.

She somehow found the air to get another sentence out. "Then do it."

"Done." With an arm wrapped around her waist, he flipped her over. Swung her until her back hit the bed. "This is temporary because I really liked the feel of you on top."

"That makes two of us."

In one quick move, he stepped off the bed and dropped the briefs. Then he was back, over her, his fingers tugging off her shorts and underwear. Her mind blanked out as she took in the sleek muscle running down his leg and his growing erection.

Everything about this man was impressive.

They spun again and he tucked his body in a pile of stacked pillows. He sat with his back against the headboard and his legs sprawled in front of him. She had no idea where the condom had gone. She sort of depended on him to keep track of it as she climbed on top of him again.

This time their bodies met without the distraction of clothes and material. The gentle friction of skin against skin had her heartbeat hammering in her ears. Need flooded her when his hand skated between them, over her curves to her heat. A single finger slipped over her, teasing her. He brushed once then twice and her hips tipped forward with the need to get closer.

"Damon, now." She whispered the words right before she bit down on his shoulder. Her tongue darted out to smooth over the nip. But when his body trembled in response, she did it again.

Her body begged for more. Her back arched, bringing her chest tight against his. She ran her fingers through his hair. Still, he waited, that finger barely skimming over her.

Unable to take one more second, she dropped her hand until it covered his. She didn't force. She'd hoped he would get the hint.

"Show me." He pressed a line of kisses down her throat. "Guide me."

That deep sexy voice was back. The one that scraped over her nerve endings, leaving her raw and shaken.

She took his hand and pressed it hard against her. At first, he didn't move. She eased the pressure then so did he, which was not what she wanted at all.

"Damon." She licked her tongue around his earlobe. "I need you inside me."

That's all it took. His hand slipped out of her hold and his finger slid inside her. He rubbed back and forth, plunging in and out as she said his name on a harsh gasp. His speed picked up then. Two fingers pumped inside her while another fingertip rubbed right on that spot that made her hips buck.

The room blanked out on her as his hands worked. She was wet and ready and he had to feel it. She couldn't ask again. She needed him to sense her need and respond to it.

Then one of his hands left her and she heard a rip. The condom. She'd never loved that sound more. He guided her with his hands on her hips. Lifted her up, just a bit, until she fit over his tip.

Glancing down between their bodies she saw her nipples press against his chest and his length wedged between them. He'd gotten the condom on and now she watched it disappear inside her, inch by slow inch. As his body eased into hers those tiny inner muscles ached and stretched, taking him in and clamping over him in a tight fist.

"Fuck." His forehead rested against hers as he looked down. "I need you to move."

She wanted to hold back and savor, but she welcomed the delicious sensation of him pressing inside her. But his plea echoed in her ears then through her body. She lifted up and settled back down. Let the rhythm in her head take over as her hips moved without a signal from her brain.

His hands wandered over her back. His mouth caressed her breasts, sucking and that hot mouth so inviting. They curled around each other, touched each other, kissed each other. There wasn't an inch of her body that didn't feel worshipped by his tongue and fingers. Through it all, she rode him. Fast then slow, bringing them both to the brink then biting her bottom lip while she pulled them back again.

Time blended and their soft moans filled the room. She was lost. On the edge and fighting off the end when his hand slipped between them again. Over her while his body pressed into her. The combination made the need inside her twist and tighten. She felt the start of her orgasm and tried to push it away, steal a few more minutes, but her body shook and her breath hitched. A second later she came on a rush of shifting and moaning.

Beneath her, his body stiffened. She could feel him holding back, waiting for her. But then his legs tightened against her. His hands held her still as he lifted his hips and pressed deeper inside her. His body shook as he came. His hands clenching and unclenching against her back and waist.

Waves of pleasure crashed into her and time drifted away. When she came up for air again, opened her eyes and floated back to reality, the tiny pulses continued inside her. She felt boneless and beautiful, powerful and free. He gave her that. They'd carved out this time to forget everything else except what they needed. No embarrassment or regret.

"Cate." He whispered her name as his head fell back, exposing that amazing length of kissable throat. She gave in and pressed her mouth against it.

As time ticked by, she wanted to say something

profound. She settled for snuggling against him. She let him take her weight as her face slipped into the crook between his neck and shoulder.

She inhaled and a mix of sweat and soap played on his skin. "You smell so good."

"I doubt that."

His body vibrated against hers. Every part of her body touched his. There was no reaction he could have that wouldn't run through her.

She yawned. "You're right. It's too early to be up."

"Then we should rest."

She had no idea how much time passed. The air conditioner hadn't clicked on and heat rose in the room. She opened her eyes and stared at the ceiling. The room fell into shadows due to the curtains but she could make out the checkered pattern above her. She concentrated on that while she tried to remember how to breathe again.

Being with him was as good as she thought it would be. Better because he was more attuned to her, giving and not selfish. He may not think he possessed emotions but he had to know he had skills. And when the heat cooled the sweetness set in. Even now he lay beside her, shoulders touching, and held her hand. The gesture was so touching that she couldn't stop smiling.

"Remind me to thank Trevor," he said without opening his eyes.

For whatever reason that struck her as hilarious. She laughed as she turned her head to look at him. At that strong side view with that firm chin. "Why, did he teach you how to do that?"

Damon snorted but his eyes stayed closed. "For the condoms."

"I would but I think his ego would be unbearable."

"Good point." He slowly turned his eyes and his gaze met hers. "We could stay in bed all day."

For the hundredth time, she was struck by the bright green of his eyes. How clear they were now. The guilt and worry clouding them yesterday had eased. But all that prettiness was not going to get him out of what came next. "We can stay here until noon, checkout time. I called the manager and asked."

He groaned. "Clever."

"You might want to remember that."

"As if I could forget." He curled onto his side and watched her. His fingers swept her hair off her face.

That's all it took. The intense look, the slip of his leg over hers. The memories of the last hour flooded back and she wanted it again. "But we do have hours to kill."

His eyebrow lifted. "Are you familiar with the concept of recovery time?"

She was willing to bet he could go from zero to a hundred pretty quickly. "You have hands and a mouth, don't you?"

There was no mistaking his grin now. He shifted, moving his body over hers. He stared down at her. "Cate Pendleton, I like your style."

This man made her heart flip inside out. No one

had ever captured her attention like this. To be fair, she never let it happen before. She enjoyed dates but stayed focused on the bigger goal. Put her private life off until later. With him, her defenses dropped. She heard about his past and it only made her want to know more, to show him how the man he was differed from the kid he used to be.

She wrapped her arms around his neck and pulled him down, just inches from kissing him. "Show me."

CHAPTER 14

Damon had no idea how he let Cate talk him into taking a tour of the place where he grew up. Well, he had some idea. The sex had been pretty fucking great, but still. Following Liza around as she half spoke and half lectured made him want to heckle her.

She talked with the certainty that only a young twenty-something completely entrenched in the idea they understood *everything* could possess. She also clearly hated him. Liza looked at Cate and smiled. Liza glanced in his direction and her jaw tightened.

"We're thrilled you decided to stay here." Liza topped off her tour of the new flower beds by handing Cate a brochure about the fruit and plants they sold at markets.

"Are you?" he asked then swallowed a groan when Cate elbowed him.

But Liza's sunny smile didn't slip that time. She kept right on talking, winding them along the path by the greenhouses toward the plant nursery where they'd started this bit of exercise. "Of course."

Cate cut off Damon's smart-ass reply with a glare before she turned back to Liza. "How long have you lived here, Liza? Did you grow up here or—"

"Three years."

"How old are you?" Because the fact she looked about eighteen was starting to make him feel old.

Cate cleared her throat. "Damon."

If Liza noticed the byplay, she didn't let on. She was too busy waving to a group of people walking into the greenhouse. "Twenty-three."

"May I ask you another question?"

Liza stopped and looked at Cate. Liza's fingers curled around the edge of her notebook as she nodded. "Steven told us to be welcoming."

A completely logical answer. Damon didn't even try to come up with a response. Instead, he let his head drop back and the sun hit his face. Maybe if he ignored the tour it would end faster.

"I'll take that as a yes," Cate said. "What made you come here?"

"Probably the same thing that motivated your sister."

Damon slowly lowered his head again. The admission opened up a whole new line of questions. Liza didn't pretend not to know about the past and why Cate might be here. Being that open surprised Damon. So much of what was happening at Sullivan and with the people they talked to did.

Cate studied Liza for a few extra beats before sighing. "You know about her?"

"Of course." Liza brought her notebook tight against her body, wrapping her arms around it like it was the most precious thing in the world. "The accident is part of the school's history and we take it seriously. There's a plaque for her and a cabin dedicated to her memory."

Cate's mouth dropped open twice before she got a word out. "A plaque."

"But to answer your question, look around you and you'll get it." Liza opened her arms and gestured toward a tomato plant.

Cate didn't break eye contact with Liza. "Grass, trees. Yeah."

"Freedom."

Yeah, she actually said it. Freedom. Damon decided Liza didn't need a brochure because she was the human equivalent of one. "Maybe be more specific?"

"I'm not stupid. I know what happened here, how off-track Steven's brother took the school. But now, with him gone, it can be something else. Bigger and better than it ever was."

Off-track? Damon had heard a lot of shit in his time, but that was big. She had to know people were killed here. That others ran away in horror. And through it all, his father sat there, pretending not to know anything about any of it.

His refusal to own up to the chaos that exploded all around him was one of the failures that hit Damon the hardest. He'd been in mourning for his wife, yes. He'd also been in charge and he never took responsibility for one piece of the destruction that he let happen in his drive to obtain his dream.

Cate frowned. "What exactly do you think this can be?"

"A place to nurture talent."

Liza had the unique skill of being able to string words together and make them sound reasonable without *really* saying anything. Damon really hated that. "Are you being specific yet?"

"People can come here and take the time to write the book they've always dreamed of writing, or paint or create." Liza sounded as if she were in awe of her own words. "Philosophers, writers, artists, scientists."

"You sound like my dad." She clearly bought into his dream. Damon didn't understand how she failed to realize his father always had this same dream and that it never panned out.

"Because he's brilliant." Without any hesitation, Liza slipped right back into lecturing mode.

She could use whatever tone she wanted but he could not handle the blind hero worship. "He's had some missteps, Liza. There's a reason he lost everything."

Her head snapped back and she wore an expression that suggested she thought everything he just said amounted to garbage. "What did he lose? He has this place and people who are loyal to him."

Anger welled inside Damon. "My mom."

She shook her head as if she didn't understand what he was saying. "What?"

"His mother died here," Cate said, rushing the words out.

But Liza didn't get the point. "I know. I told you I'm familiar with your uncle and everything that happened on his watch."

Damon fought back the urge to yell. Liza's memory was almost as selective as his father's. Of all the things that ticked him off over the last few days, this hit him the hardest. Despite the history and all the pain that happened on this property, his father still wallowed in denial. He focused on the intangible, ignoring the price real people paid for his desire to be some sort of benevolent academic figure.

"Not to hit you with the truth, but—" He lowered his voice and forced his nerves to settle when Cate sent another glare his way and a couple walking by openly stared. "My dad was here when the killing happened. He was Uncle Dan's business partner."

Liza scoffed. "You can't believe he knew about the weapons and Dan's secret plans."

So that was the line of crap being spewed now. Revisionist history at its worst. Damon didn't even know how to respond to it without lecturing every person living there.

"Speaking of which . . ." Cate put her hand against his chest and shifted so she stood slightly in front of him in the least subtle hint ever. "Why so many guns?"

"So people can hone their skills." Liza drew out the answer as if she were talking to a child. "Protection."

"Now you sound like my Uncle Dan."

Liza's mouth clamped shut and her mouth fell into a thin line. "You'll have to excuse me. I have a meeting."

Sure, she did. "All of a sudden. Imagine that."

"I'm sure you know your way around, you being a Sullivan and all." There was nothing open and inviting in her tone now. She had flipped into full-on disapproving.

That made two of them. "Formerly. My name is Damon Knox now."

She shook her head. "You'd give up all of this and walk away?"

This time Cate grabbed a fistful of his shirt and took a bit of his chest hair with it. "He already did."

The answer didn't stop Liza from leaving. She stomped off, pushing past a gardener without stopping to say hello.

"I think I ticked her off." He knew he should feel bad about the passive-aggressive battle. He didn't make it a habit of fighting with twenty-somethings about history, but this was *his* history and her trying to slap a bucket of sunny paint on it made his head pound.

"You could be less jerky." Cate eyed him with a be-better expression as she smoothed out his shirt. "Next time try harder to stay in control."

It was fair, but still . . . "She was ridiculous."

"She's young." Cate sighed. "And she hates you."

"Was it the fact she almost ripped her notebook

in half every time I opened my mouth that gave it away?"

"That was a hint, yeah." They started walking again, doubling back to the area Liza had seemingly avoided. The part with the guns. "But I have to admit she does seem kind of . . ."

"There's no way I'm finishing your sentence for you and risking being yelled at for being an asshole."

"Smart." Cate stepped closer to him, until their arms rubbed against each other. "But the hero-worship-of-your-dad thing?"

"Now imagine an entire school like that and you have what it was like around here when I was growing up." Damon remembered what else sat at the back of the property and slowed down. The top of the water tower could be seen all over the campus but he wasn't sure she was ready to walk right up to it and deal with the reality of what happened there.

She ran her hand over the fold of the brochure Liza handed her. "If everyone was so loyal to him and loved him and loved this place, why didn't anyone see what your uncle was doing?"

That was the question that played over and over in Damon's mind. He feared he knew the answer and it was life-shattering. The final step in dealing with the fact his father may have played an active role in the demise of so much.

Damon tried to keep the answer neutral but he felt anything but. "Hard to imagine they didn't."

"She worked with him, you know. Shauna did."

He stopped. "My dad?"

The wind blew her hair across her face and she slipped it back behind her ear. "Your uncle."

That didn't make sense. Nothing he'd read in Wren's file talked about that. No one ever mentioned it. "What?"

"Shauna had an interest in botany and agriculture. She wanted to open what would now be considered a natural food market." Cate twisted the brochure in her hands as she talked. "I found some paperwork in the notebooks the school returned to my mom, memos from your uncle. Lists of books she should read. Provided by him."

"That doesn't mean that—"

"She wrote some papers and she must have had him read them because there were handwritten notes from him about them, but nothing in the official school paperwork suggested she took any sort of class by him."

Damon ran through every possibility, every reason for Dan and Shauna to deal so closely with each other, and had a hard time coming up with an option that didn't put his uncle in the middle of the questions about her death. "You're thinking she got close to him and realized something was wrong and then . . . what, he killed her to keep her quiet?"

"Is it that absurd?" She stepped in closer, resting her hands against his chest. "I trust your opinion, so please tell me."

"At one point in my life I would have said there was

no way. Now, who knows." Which led him to an awful option he promised he would never do. "Shit."

"What?"

He refused to lie to her. In a short time, they had opened up about so many things from their pasts. He didn't want to close the door again. "That's my reaction to the idea of having to go to prison and talk to my uncle."

Her fingers skimmed along the underside of his chin. "You would do that?"

"If you needed me to." And that was the truth. For her, he would. They were kindred souls in that way, both needed to settle the past once and for all.

"You're a good man."

His knee-jerk reaction was to deny but for just a little while he'd let her think that. He'd pretend he believed it. "You wouldn't say that if you knew the wild arguments I'm coming up with in my head *not* to see my uncle."

"There are other ways we could try. We follow through with the plan to use us, this fake love affair, as cover as we talk with people and get into buildings." She grimaced like she knew what she was about to say was provocative. "And at some point we need to talk to your dad."

"I knew you were going to say that."

"Liza did say everyone is supposed to be extra nice to the returning prince." Cate leaned in and dropped a quick kiss on his mouth.

"Do you see me frowning at you?"

She took his hand and started walking again. "Let's go find some people and be charming."

"That's my least favorite thing ever."

"You'll survive."

CHAPTER 15

The water tower soared over the back half of the property. It was the focal point in the middle of the open fields. For Cate, it served as a flashing beacon. The last place Shauna ever stood.

She tried to block that out as they headed for the gun range. The targets came into view. They ran in a straight line across, about twenty feet away. A few people wore headphones as they concentrated on firing, with what looked like instructors by their sides.

Vincent and Roger stood by tables set up under a canopy and out of the sun. Open gun cases were spread out in front of them. They talked as they manned the bullets, keeping what looked like a watchful eye over everything around them.

Roger was the first to see them. He smiled as his gaze flicked to their joined hands then back up again. "You're here."

At least his tone was more welcoming than Liza's had been near the end. Cate figured that could change at any minute. "Everyone seems really happy about that."

"Do you shoot, Cate?" He seemed ready to hear a denial.

That only made it more fun to give him the real answer. "I've been to the range."

Damon glanced at her. "Really?"

"I have hidden skills."

"Apparently." He winked at her before dropping her hand and walking around to Vincent's side of the table.

"Shouldn't you know that about your girlfriend?" Vincent asked.

Damon shrugged. "We're in the learning-about-each-other stage."

She loved that about him. His ability to maneuver his way through difficult and sometimes unexpected conversations. As a skill, it came in handy while they hunted down information.

Vincent held out a weapon in front of Damon. "You want to try it out?"

At the offer, Roger's eyes bulged. "Vincent, maybe that's not—"

Damon waved off the concern. "It's fine."

His tone sounded sure but Cate didn't know if this was a guy thing, bluster or real. With his history, it would be understandable if he didn't want to handle a gun here, on the property where something so awful happened. He'd put hers in the motel safe, but that was different from holding a loaded one on the Sullivan grounds and firing with purpose.

She watched the conversation with all the nervousness of a first-time mother sending her baby to school for the first day. She wanted to rush in and fix this, turn the conversation to something else. But she need not have worried. Damon handled the gun and the magazine like a pro. Checked the chamber and adjusted his grip as he walked up to the line. Not a surprise in light of the kind of work she suspected he did now.

With headphones on and his body locked in a stance that showed off that cute butt of his, he took a shot. The muscles across his shoulders bunched as he unloaded four shots. Each one hitting the target with deadly accuracy.

Of course he could shoot. She'd yet to find much he couldn't do except keep a healthy diet.

"Huh." Vincent took off his baseball hat and scratched his head. "You still can shoot. Guess some skills never go away or get rusty."

That suggested the brothers had no idea that Damon's odd jobs dealt with danger. They might know when he rode into town, but they didn't appear to know anything that mattered about who he was now.

Damon held off on responding until they returned to the canopy and he went through his gun safety mental checklist again. Then he handed the weapon back to Vincent. "Did you think I would be afraid of a weapon?"

"Wouldn't be that weird for you to be spooked after . . ." Vincent swallowed the end of his sentence. "You know."

Cate decided that was enough of this conversation.

She wanted to run through history with the brothers, but not Damon's history. She looked at Roger and gestured at the array of weapons laid out in front of her. "Speaking of which, this kind of display, so out in the open, doesn't worry you?"

He shook his head. "It's safe here and it's good for people to keep in practice."

"If I open that door will I see a stockpile of your more lethal weapons?" Damon turned and pointed at the set of double doors going into a building that was built into the side of a hill. Beside the left one was a square pad and a guard stood next to that.

Vincent shrugged. "Yes."

"No," Roger said at the same time.

Cate was starting to see why Damon had trust issues. Anyone hoping to survive would have run so far and so fast away from this place. Despite the greenery and leafy surroundings, nothing struck her as genuine. "Want to try again, guys?"

"There are locks and protocols," Roger explained.

Damon made a humming sound. "You wouldn't need those if you kept fewer weapons here."

"You know the answer to that." Vincent shut the case in front of him with a hard thud. "This is hunting country."

"What are you hunting?" Damon asked without missing a beat.

"Come on." Vincent fiddled with the lock on the case, ignoring the clanking noise it made. "Nobody likes pests."

Roger stared at his brother with a blank expression before flashing her another smile. "Bet you're happy to be here."

She wasn't sure what he was getting at but she answered honestly. She'd spent years trying to gain this access to this land, sure that it would be sold and she'd lose her chance forever at some point. Only by pure luck, and maybe the strong will of Damon's dad, that didn't happen.

She'd waited even longer for someone she could trust to walk with through every detail. Now she had that in Damon. "I actually am."

Roger frowned. "That's not what I expected you to say."

"My sister was here, back when it was a school."

"And now you're with Damon." Vincent snorted. "Coincidence?"

"Her sister died here, but I'm sure you both know that." Damon cut off the sentence there but it sounded like he wanted to add the word *dumbass* at the end. "Shauna Pendleton."

"I hear there's a lovely plaque in her honor around here somewhere." She didn't know if she'd ever get over that answer and the fact Liza thought it was a good enough tribute. "Did you know her?"

The second the words left her mouth, the men started squirming. She met Damon's gaze and saw his eyebrow rise, which suggested he picked up on the sudden air of desperation as well.

"Uh, sure." Vincent took off his hat again and folded the brim in his big hand.

Roger nodded. "Yeah."

"That's not very specific." But it was telling. She wished she had a camera to capture this moment and the stunned looks on their faces. These gentlemen knew something and were fighting not to share it.

Roger sat on the table next to the closed case. "She was sweet and funny. Loved to dance."

Cate's mind went blank for a second before rebooting again. "Dance?"

"We used to have these outside gatherings around the firepit on Friday nights." Roger smiled as he described the memory. "People would play music and some would sing. Others danced. Your sister danced."

Vincent smiled. "She was really good."

"Were you here when she died?" Damon dropped the question and had the other two men looking at him.

Roger shrugged. "A lot of us were. It was on a weekday with classes the next day."

"But she was out by the water tower." The structure Cate was trying so hard to ignore even though it seemed to hover right over them.

"Well . . . that's not . . ." Vincent winced as his voice trailed off.

Roger sighed. "Students went there."

Damon looked from one brother to the other. "What are you trying not to say?"

"To have sex. To smoke." Vincent's wince grew

more pronounced as he spoke, as if he thought he was spilling some big secret.

Damon's eyes widened. "On the water tower? You mean under it, right?"

"Sure," Roger said. "But people would fool around and climb the ladder. It was stupid and no one does it now. There's a locked gate around the entire structure."

"Does the plaque tell you not to go inside the fence?" Cate couldn't hold back the sarcasm. The whole story made no sense when she added in the very real fact her sister couldn't get on a stepladder without getting weepy.

Vincent stared at her. "What?"

"One of the professors found her." Roger hesitated for a second then continued. "Connelly. The math guy. He's at a think tank now."

Cate knew that much. The poor man had been repeatedly questioned. Turned out he had the unfortunate luck to walk his dog by the water tower early that morning, as he did every morning. The security cameras set up around the academic buildings showed him heading out. The image cut off by the tower because, of course, there were no cameras there, but picked back up shortly after. Everyone who analyzed the footage of him coming in and out agreed he only had time to walk the dog. And no motive. He was in the wrong place at the wrong time and paid for it.

"So, you think she was partying by herself and fell?" Damon asked Roger, clearly thinking he was the brother with the intel.

"Some students talked about partying out there earlier that evening after a test. My guess is she went back or she forgot something or she was meeting someone."

This was new. No one ever mentioned a party before. There was no reference to it in all the notes and interviews she'd read. "Who?"

Roger shook his head. "I have no idea."

"She didn't date anyone seriously."

Damon laughed. "That was a quick fill-in answer, Vincent."

"We were questioned back then and a few years later when the prosecutor reopened the case to take another look." Vincent looked from Damon to Cate. "Both investigations said it was an accident."

"But you're here to prove that wrong." Roger began to swing his leg back and forth. "We heard about how you two met when discussing this case."

Damon made an odd sound. "Sounds like my dad has been chatty."

She had a bigger response ready. One based on the truth. It was the other reason she wanted in those gates. "I just needed to feel close to her, walk where she walked."

Vincent nodded. "Makes sense."

"We should let you get back to your practice." Damon slipped around the table and hooked an arm around her shoulders.

"Dinner tonight?" Roger asked. "The four of us."

She spit out the first answer that came to her even

though she absolutely didn't mean it. She'd need time to decompress after this. Maybe some wine. "Sure."

Damon guided them away from the tower and the gun range. They walked in silence, nodding to the few people who passed them. It wasn't until they were back on the main path and headed for the living quarters that Damon glanced at her and smiled. "Walk where she walked?"

"It's no less absurd than the idea of her hanging out at the water tower by herself." The more the scenario played in her head the less compelling she found it.

"Was she a loner?"

That was an easy question. "Never."

Damon gave her shoulder a squeeze. "Then I think we know how realistic the story is."

She sure did. "Not at all." She made a mental reminder to tell him one more thing and did that now. "No scent this time."

"Wait, you didn't smell the aftershave or whatever on Vincent?"

"Not even a hint." And she'd strained and hung close, thinking she'd find a concrete piece of evidence.

He shook his head. "I wonder what that means."

"That makes two of us."

CHAPTER 16

Damon and Cate made it through a quick dinner, begging off after about thirty minutes claiming to be tired. The first night in the cabin had been just about as rocky. The inside of the log structure was an open and airy space. The ceiling soared above the studio layout.

After everything that happened and all the tension he'd held inside all day, they'd spent the night actually sleeping. Between being back and the very real sense that someone might be watching, he'd taken sex off the table. And she didn't offer. That left cuddling and after two times he thought he was getting kind of good at it.

But this was a new day and he'd been summoned. Not to his father or the diner. This rendezvous spot, a restaurant, took him out of town and through the woods to a structure that looked like an abandoned railway car. The sign said it served food, and that was good enough for Damon.

Cate decided to stay back, preferring to spend time

looking into some of those classes Liza described. She said something about trying to get on Liza's good side to make up for his appalling behavior. What he did and said seemed to sound worse every new time she described the situation. He remembered being a little rude. Cate insisted he rolled his eyes every time Liza spoke. Though he'd been tempted, he knew that wasn't true. Cate was trying to make a point—that they were there to make friends and get people talking—and she made it.

But Damon was pretty sure whatever Cate used to woo Liza wouldn't work. Liza had a job, maybe self-imposed, but she acted as the marketing team for Sullivan. None of the real stories about the place would interest her, but Damon applauded Cate for trying.

Since Trevor was there, watching over her from a safe distance, Damon had felt relatively secure making the drive. That was before he sat down across from Garrett, who he expected, and Wren, who he did not. No one ever expected Wren to show up anywhere.

"Both of you? This seems bad." Damon balanced the menu against the salt and pepper shakers on the end of the table. He sensed Wren wasn't there for more than the coffee anyway.

"It's always nice to see you."

Uh-huh. As if he would have bought that even if Garrett weren't the one saying it. "What are you doing in Pennsylvania?"

Wren shrugged. "Sightseeing."

"I hear the pie is good here," Garrett added.

It was as if they practiced this routine. Maybe they did. Who knew what they did behind those desks all day. "You're both hysterical."

Garrett raised two fingers. "I'm funnier."

Wren snorted. "Not really."

"Guys, business." Because he knew they were setting him up for the delivery of bad news. That's what they did. They double-teamed and used humor to lighten the mood. Damon didn't find any of it calming right now. "Here's a list of people I need you to run in-depth traces on. There's intel in the file, but not what we need. Find the serious background, skeleton-in-the-closets stuff."

Garrett grabbed the folded piece of paper and shoved it in his shirt pocket without looking at it. "Oh, good. I was looking for more work this week."

"Take it up with your boss." Damon was doing his part. The rest was up to them.

"The main reason we're here." Wren leaned back in the booth and stretched his legs out, knocking his foot against the side of Damon's before moving it again. "We're thinking you taking on this assignment was the wrong call."

"That's convenient since you're the one who sent me here." Damon shook his head. "I specifically remember refusing you and you ignoring me."

"To talk with people in town, get into Sullivan and look around. Reconnect and get people talking." Wren flipped a spoon end over end as he talked. "I never thought you'd move in."

Damon loved the guy but no fucking way was he letting Wren wiggle out of this. "The point was to get close. Now we'll all be living together. It's as close as I can get without moving specifically into my dad's house, which I refuse to do."

"Call it a miscalculation but I assumed you'd keep a bit of distance. I also didn't think an attacker would take a run at you the first night you stepped into the county. The speed with which your father, or someone at Sullivan, figured out your location makes me want to get a look at Sullivan's communication infrastructure."

Garrett frowned at Wren. "Who talks like that?"

"Professional people," Wren shot back.

"With a stick up their ass. Give me this." Damon reached over and grabbed the spoon before Wren banged it on the table one more time. "But, and I want to be clear here, you're admitting you made a mistake."

"I never said that." Wren shot him a never-going-to-happen look. "The point is someone at Sullivan, possibly your own father, has the ability to mobilize a trained attacker, and that guy got by you."

Damon didn't like that comment one bit. "He didn't."

"You were stabbed," Wren shot back.

Damon lifted his shirt to show the small cut that was already healing. "It's nothing."

"Is Cate okay?" Garrett asked.

"She's tougher than I am." And Damon meant that. He'd watched her walk right by the water tower and not shake. He knew it had to scramble her insides, but she held it together, which was just about the sexiest thing he'd ever seen. "Back to the money."

"We traced it." Garrett snuck a peek at Wren before continuing. "Found every thread and spent days tracking it all."

"Gun sales." Damon couldn't think of another explanation. It wouldn't be a stretch for the place either but as a result of some of the restrictions placed on the property after the second shooting, selling weapons was supposed to be a restricted activity.

"No." Wren took out his phone and after pushing a few buttons, flipped it around for Damon to see the screen. "When your mother died the government paid your dad a settlement."

"What?" The words blurred in front of Damon. He glanced up at Wren, waiting for an explanation.

"Private, quiet but big. It's why your father never sued over the FBI mess." Wren looked at the phone but didn't take it back. "That and the fact he needed to hide the truth your Uncle Dan really was trying to build a private army to destroy the legitimate one just as the FBI suspected."

Garrett lowered his coffee cup. "Bet he was fun at Thanksgiving."

"Your father lives off that money. It's in a trust and he draws from it. It's steady. The financial planning was pretty impressive, actually. One of his professors helped him set it up." Wren being Wren, he walked through the information in a clear and concise way.

A payoff made sense but the fact his father managed to hide it . . . Damon should have seen that
coming. "There are new buildings and fancy security
equipment. Lots of weapons."

"The school, even with significantly fewer people
there and less money coming in, is self-sustaining.
For now. There appear to be plans to blow it bigger,
and I'm not sure the income it produces, alone, can
support that." Wren reached over and swiped his finger across the cell screen and the pages of whatever
document he was referencing flipped. "But for now
they grow what they need. Sell all sorts of items.
They no longer pay full-time educators and your dad
doesn't take a salary."

"He's managed to go legitimate." Damon would
never have said it was possible. Not when his father
never admitted that his grand experiment had gone
deadly wrong in the first place.

"He would argue he always was. But, honestly, you
should get out of there. You can find closure another
way." Wren genuinely sounded concerned.

Damon wasn't sure how to react to that. Jokes he
could handle. Some weird guy talk in a railway car
was way out of his comfort zone. "I have closure."

Garrett shook his head. "Maybe you don't know
what the word means."

They were concerned. Damon got that. He didn't
like it because the idea of friends worrying about
him made him squirm, but there was a bigger problem
here. "Look, even if I wanted to go, Cate won't leave.

She thinks this is her last chance, and I don't think she's wrong. For the first time, she will have front row access to Sullivan. My dad insists everything is open for her to review. She won't leave until that happens or he breaks his promise."

Wren sat up straight again. "And if your dad was involved with what happened to Shauna, at least in a cover-up of her death, what do you do then?"

"Have him arrested."

"Easy to say." Wren grabbed his phone and turned it off before slipping it off the table. "I've been through this. When Emery found out about her dad . . . let's just say she's still trying to deal with the emotional fallout. She will always wrestle with it."

Emery, the love of Wren's life and the daughter of a man sitting in prison. A man Wren and Emery put there. Damon saw the parallels. "But you're handling it. So, it can be handled."

"We're together. She has full support from me and her friends. We're going to get married, if I can ever get her to say yes."

"Amateur." Garrett pointed at his shiny new wedding band. "I can give you some tips to get it done."

Wren kept his focus on Damon. "Are you offering to be there for Cate, to go through the fallout with her? She's your fake girlfriend, Damon, not your real one."

Damn, he didn't want to think about any of that. It all sounded so . . . big. "I have to see this investigative part through."

"Fine, but lean on Trevor," Wren said. "But know he has orders to pull you out if this goes sideways."

"How exactly will he do that?" But Damon could imagine Trevor trying. His friend would enjoy every minute of that struggle.

Garrett got the waitress's attention and held up his now empty mug. "My money is on Trevor."

"Thanks for the vote of confidence." The phone in Damon's pocket buzzed. At this point he welcomed the interruption. Or he did until he saw the screen. "Shit."

Garrett frowned. "What is it?"

But Damon was already sliding out of the booth. Every instinct told him to rush. "Cate."

DAMON HAD LEFT on his errand a half hour ago. He managed to do it without lecturing her about safety, but she guessed that cost him something.

The second he pulled out of the parking lot, Trevor started popping up. Everywhere. She appreciated the concern but she didn't need a babysitter or a bodyguard. Well, she probably did, but she also needed just a few minutes of privacy.

She had a demon to wrestle. A place she needed to visit, to pay homage, even if it was for a short time and the only result was for her to cry until she fell down.

For this errand, she didn't have to sneak to get there. She walked right across campus, in front of everyone. Said hello, even stopped when a few people introduced themselves.

If they were going to hurt her it wouldn't happen out in the open. Probably not in daylight. Probably not at all after Steven made a show of welcoming them to Sullivan and insisting they could look around without worry. That had to send a message to the person who tried to attack them . . . unless it was Steven, but that didn't make sense to her. She saw the spark of hope in his eyes when Damon didn't immediately refuse the offer to stay. It wouldn't make sense to invite them in only to try to run them off again.

A few more turns and she landed at the right spot, or near it. She could never bring herself to look at the photos of her sister after she fell. She'd reviewed the autopsy reports and read every horrible word. The photos were too much. She knew she'd never be able to un-see them.

The path ended at the locked gate. It was only about six feet high and looked easy to climb, but she didn't try. Instead, she walked around the outside, letting her fingers trail against the metal. After she completed a full circle, she stood there and stared. There was no talking and no groups of people here. This place could only be described as secluded, probably on purpose since the tower loomed over a pretty big section of land.

Inside the fence stood a small structure no bigger than a shed. Everything looked new and shiny. There were no signs of disrepair.

She slipped her fingers through the fence holes and rested her forehead against the metal. It felt cool on her skin. Closing her eyes, she tried to imagine Shauna walking here. There wasn't a fence back then, but the remainder of the area looked about the same.

When she opened her eyes again her gaze traveled up the structure, over the ladder hooked to the side of the catwalk and railing near the top. She didn't have a problem with heights and she never would have made the climb. The idea made her dizzy.

She pushed away from the fence, thinking there really was nothing to find here other than pain. She couldn't hear the sounds of students partying or imagine anyone enjoying the spot. It was quiet and cold. The breeze swept over the open space and the shade of the trees didn't reach here.

Loneliness. That's the sensation that hit her. Dragging loneliness, the kind that pulled a person under and held them there.

She sighed, ready to leave and go hunt for Damon. For the first time in a long time, when the sadness swamped her, she wanted to talk to someone other than a therapist. She wanted him. Letting him in was new and not exactly comfortable, but that's what her brain and body called out for her to do.

She started to turn when she heard the footsteps. She shifted, expecting to be hit with another warm welcome . . . just as Steven ordered.

Hands grabbed her. She felt the tug on the back of her shirt then her body slammed into the fence. The metal wires dug into the side of her face. She called out but her voice sounded small as it spread out over the land.

She kicked back just as something hard slammed against her shoulder. She reached out toward the pain when her legs buckled beneath her. Something smelled off, weird. She shook her head but a cloth pressed tighter against her mouth. She inhaled and the dizziness turned to nausea.

The world started to blank out on her as her body crashed to the hard ground. Her muscles refused to move and something dark covered her face. She called out as she tried to steady her legs enough to get up on her hands and knees. As soon as she made it, she fell to the side again. Then the rattling started. Keys or chains—she couldn't make it out. Couldn't see anything.

She called out but her voice sounded small in her ears. Then she started to slide. It took her a second to figure out she was being dragged. Caught in a desperate gnawing frenzy, her hands smacked against the ground to stop the move, but she couldn't get her grip. Her fingers refused to curl. Every order from her brain went ignored.

But the ground kept moving. The disorientation and the drugs, whatever covered her face, had her catching quick blinks of light but nothing more. Her back hurt and her arm felt as if it were being wretched out of its socket as the warm sun poured over her.

The dragging seemed to go on forever. Her legs

slammed against the ground. Her hand hit on something hard. She could make out shuffling and heavy breathing. Not hers. She called out, trying to get her attacker to say something but she only managed to make a croaking sound.

Her back lifted off the grass . . . that's what she smelled. The scent broke through the blankness. She tried to inhale, to bring fresh air into her body and clear her head, but whatever was wrapped around her head made that impossible.

Her head clunked against something hard. She heard a thunk and thought it sounded like a shoe. None of it made sense until something cool rubbed against her shoulder.

The water tower. Someone was trying to drag her up the ladder even though her muscles refused to work.

She started to struggle harder then. Used every ounce of energy, knowing she'd only have a short burst or two with whatever was fogging her brain. She reached out and her fingers brushed against what felt like denim. Must be jeans. She grabbed for a handful, digging her fingernails as hard as she could with limited strength. The move earned her a kick. Then another.

Suddenly her body dropped to the grass again. All the pressure tugging and dragging her stopped. She heard the thunder of footsteps on the grass . . . getting farther away, which didn't make any sense.

After a few seconds of quiet, she strained to sit up,

to call out. All she could manage was to prop her body against what felt like the rung of a ladder. She tried to think but her breathing came too fast now and she started gulping in air. Panic overwhelmed her and her heart rate kicked up even higher.

She would not die this way.

"Hey!"

A voice broke through the darkness. She couldn't identify it through the waves of anxiety washing through her. Then the cloth came off and the light blinded her. She blinked, trying to make out the figure standing in front of her with a face obscured by the sun.

"Cate." A hand swept over her hair and across her cheek. It was a gentle touch performed with a shaking hand.

She knew him. She could feel his concern and the shock pulsing off him as he crouched down in front of her.

Roger.

He looked around the area and then back to her. "What happened?"

She could only put a few bits and pieces together. The crap in her system still clouded her brain. The surprise hit and the cloth. Being blindfolded in a way and dragged around like a forgotten doll. The aches and pains hit her all at once and she nearly cried out.

"Cate, can you talk?"

This close she could see his hair was damp and his eyes wide and concerned. She inhaled, forcing her mind to focus as her body teetered on the edge of panic. She thought about the sound of his running footsteps. A new scent hit her, this one mint, like from gum. She hadn't picked that up before, which meant one thing. Not the same person.

Roger was a pretty big guy. He would have been able to drag her without trouble. That didn't mean he wasn't there and in on it, but she tucked that possibility away because thinking about it would lead to kicking and screaming and she wasn't sure she had the strength for either right now.

"Someone attacked me." She rushed out the words, not wanting to give away every detail in case they mattered later. Not wanting to be here on this grass, under the shadow of this tower.

"Damn it." Roger jumped to his feet but stayed low, almost face-to-face with her. "We should get you up."

"There was a cloth and . . ."

"Okay, we need to get you help." He put his hand under her arm and then moved it back again, as if he wasn't sure if and where he could touch her. "Cate, work with me here."

"I need Damon." A fact had never been so clear to her. His presence calmed her.

She wanted to tell him, to walk through every detail with him. Then she wanted to forget it all. Wrap her arms around him and drift off to sleep.

Roger stood up and tried to take her with him. "Let me lift you—"

"I can't." Her legs would never hold her. She could

barely feel her feet and exhaustion still weighed down her muscles.

She forced her hand to move. Tried to reach into her front pants pocket but her fingers refused to co-operate.

"Here, let me." He must have understood because he grabbed for her phone and held it.

She put her hand over his. "Please find Damon."

CHAPTER 17

Damon would have sworn his heart stopped three times in his rush to get to her. He blew out of the restaurant parking lot, ignoring the concerned yells and looks from Wren and Garrett. They could get the details from Trevor, because he needed to get to Cate.

Now, a good twenty minutes and a harrowing drive filled with honking horns and lots of swearing later, he kneeled in front of her. She sat in an overstuffed leather chair in an office he didn't recognize. This was one of the new buildings, but none of that mattered. He didn't have time to analyze it or even look on the walls. His entire focus stayed on her.

He took her hands in his and nearly jumped from the icy cold of her touch. "What happened?"

He heard a version from Roger. Some of it made sense. Most of it didn't.

"I don't . . ." She shook her head as her teeth clicked together.

Aftermath. Damon had seen it before, experienced it several times. It could hit like the flu and sweep through your entire body. The adrenaline burn-off had begun and whatever had been in her system—Roger mentioned a cloth and a drug when he called Damon with details during the drive—wasn't making it easier for her body to regain control.

Damon reached up and wrapped the blanket tighter over her shoulders. It was a warm day and the room had a musty, unused smell but the coolness radiated off her. She needed a warm shower and some of that tea she liked to drink that smelled like tree bark.

After a few attempts, she finally opened her mouth and started talking. "It's okay. I didn't fall."

"Is that the point?" Anger flooded him. Not fury at her. At himself and everyone else who failed today.

He left her alone. Trevor failed to watch her. His father, once again, provided a place where violence was the norm. There was so much hate to go around.

"She slipped on the ladder, though why she was on it or in a restricted area is unclear." His father made the comment from where he stood by the fireplace at the far end of the room.

She shook her head. "Not the ladder."

Of course not. She never would have ventured up there, not after Shauna. And Roger had made that clear. That's not where he found her. Damon knew because he questioned Roger, making him repeat his story three times.

But Damon picked up on something else. A subtle shift in the way she held her body and an almost pleading look in her eyes. It was as if she wanted to keep the details spare in front of his father. Damon didn't blame her. He didn't trust anyone at Sullivan, including the man who raised him, and she shouldn't trust them either.

At least Roger had been there. Why was a little fuzzy for Damon. Roger swore the talk about the water tower with Cate the day before tickled a memory. He went there, hoping something might come to him that would help her. Then he saw the open gate and opened lock abandoned on the ground. He thought he spied a pile of something by the base of one of the legs of the tower.

That was Cate.

With no one else around, he ran to help her. He was the one who texted Damon. He was the one who later called Damon to let him know Cate was shaken but okay. That she was asking for him, because that didn't grip his heart and shatter it into a million pieces.

But by the time Damon got there, his father had taken charge. The man who liked to sit back and act like he didn't know what was happening around him had no trouble rallying in time to send Roger away. Damon wasn't sure what to make of that.

"I thought there was a fence and all this security. What happened to those protections?" Damon asked without looking in his father's direction. He was not the concern right now. She was.

"That was my fault." She dug her fingers into the edges of the blanket as her expression changed. Sadness moved into her eyes. "I went there alone."

"You what?" He wanted to yell at her. Shake her

then hold her. He hated that she'd taken a risk, though he had to admit he would have done the same thing in her place.

She reached out to him then. Her fingers brushed down the front of his shirt and he grabbed for her hand, desperate to touch her. Even now the steady thrum of panic moved through him. Seeing her, smoothing a hand over her face, was not enough to convince the racing in his brain to slow down again.

"I wanted to see where she died."

Damon closed his eyes when he heard the pain in her whisper. Of course she did. She was here on a mission. It was no wonder she tried to complete it with or without him by her side.

He glanced over at his father. Saw the usual pressed dress pants and button-down shirt. He looked every inch the professor today. The only sign of worry came in the lines around his mouth and the way he stood so stiff with his hand fisted against his mouth.

Seeing him touched off a new wave of anger in Damon. "Where were you? Where were your people? You have security cameras here, right?"

"They were on the property, doing their work."

What a nonsense answer. His father ignored half of what he said. "And the cameras?"

"I reviewed the feed. There's nothing on them."

He reviewed them. Him. He didn't even blink when he gave that response. Damon felt his control falter. "How could that be?"

Steven shrugged. "They didn't record. It happens.

It's not a big deal. We've had the company out twice to look into the issue."

All too convenient. All a load of shit. "It was a big deal for her. Look at her."

"Are you suggesting someone who lives here did this to Cate?" Steven's eyes narrowed as he talked.

The campus had a locked gate but his father wanted to blame an outsider. Typical.

"Maybe what was good for one sister is good for the other."

His father stepped away from the fireplace and came closer to where she sat. "Cate, you can't believe that—"

"Someone hit me . . . or something." She winced. "I don't remember."

The newest attack started another alarm ringing in his head. He thought no one would come after her at Sullivan. Not since his father was the one who insisted they stay and made that clear to everyone. Now Damon didn't know what to think.

He would figure that part out later and the best way to keep her safe. For now, he had a message of his own to deliver—to his dad. Because this bullshit was over. "This happened on your watch by one of your people."

Steven kept looking at Cate, as if trying to convince her the truth she knew had to be wrong. "I figured you were climbing, like your sister."

More lying. Roger had to have explained what he saw and knew, yet his father latched on to some random piece of information and decided this was an accident. Another accident.

Not this time.

Damon stood up and faced the man who once meant everything to him. "That never happened."

Steven frowned. "What?"

"Shauna was afraid of heights, Dad. She wouldn't have been on that water tower. It wasn't an accident. Her death deserves more than a damn plaque. It should be solved."

Steven shook his head as the blood drained from his face. "There was an investigation and . . . and the police. We were all questioned. Forensics."

The old man put on a good show. Either that or he really believed what he said. Damon wasn't sure which was the right answer but neither absolved him. His father had been running from the truth for years. He took the easy way out, regardless of who else paid the price. "All your friends. They covered for you to keep this sham of a place running."

"What are you saying?"

Damon never wanted to have this conversation. He knew once they did he could never call it back. With the words left unspoken he could let a tiny spark of hope stay alive inside him. Not that he intended to act on it, but he could fool himself, now and then when he needed to believe his gene pool didn't suck, that his father honestly was as clueless as he pretended to be despite being as smart as he was.

"You were in charge." The words tumbled out of

Damon. "You either knew what happened or you purposely stayed ignorant then allowed people to lie about it."

Shock moved over his father's face and showed in every line of his stiff body. "What kind of man do you think I am?"

Not a good one, and it killed Damon to even think that. This was more than a stained gene pool. This was about having the first man he ever believed in destroy his trust. "I don't know. That's the point. I really don't know you at all."

Steven lifted his hands as if he was going to launch into one of his usual lectures, complete with gestures. Then his arms fell motionless to his sides. "I built a school. Your uncle was the one who lost control."

He sounded so fucking sincere. "You don't get to sit back and take in the money but avoid all of the responsibility."

Damon felt a tug on his pants and looked down to see Cate reaching out to him. He slipped his fingers through hers, trying to warm her up. She nodded, as if giving her approval for the road he was about to take. He didn't know he needed it until she offered it. Her supporting him, not just his usual friends. It was a new sensation. A welcome one.

He turned back to his father. "You weren't an academic sitting in a room, never talking to people. You are a brilliant man. You lobbied politicians. You made friends with powerful people. You worked the PR.

The only thing—the only damn thing—you didn't do was control Dan."

Color flushed Steven's face again. "You were the one who was with him all the time."

Damon heard the anger ring in his father's voice. His whole body vibrated with it. The calm, unflustered man who built a school then helped knock it down by his inaction, fought to hold on to his control.

Screw him.

To come out firing by blaming a sixteen-year-old boy? No fucking way. "Because those were the rules. Your rules, Dad. You turned me over to him for classes and training, ignoring how Dan was getting more secretive and holding private instruction. Mom begged you to talk with Dan and not send me to him, but you did it anyway. You said Dan could teach me skills you couldn't. Those were your words."

Cate stood up. The move was shaky, but she rose and leaned against him. Kept her hand linked with his and stared his father down.

"But you didn't stop him."

For a second Damon questioned what he heard. When confronted, his father doubled down, casting more blame. Putting it all on him. A kid who got sucked under Dan's skewed influence. Scared and barely out of his teens, confused as he tried to protect his family.

"I pay for that every fucking day." He felt Cate's hand squeeze his as he spoke. She barely had the strength to sit up when he arrived and now she helped him form a wall of fury in front of his father. Her support was exactly the kick he needed to keep going. "That's the difference. You disassociate yourself from Dan and what happened back then. You play the victim and move on. I live with it."

Steven's gaze switched to her and his shoulders fell. "You're upset about Cate and lashing out at me. I get it. That's how you operate."

Her being hurt made Damon sick and this was the second time. On his watch, someone grabbed her. And who knows what would have happened if he hadn't gotten to the attacker at the motel first. But that's not what this confrontation was about.

A part of him knew his father's concern for her was real. He wasn't an animal. That was the point. He would never physically hurt someone himself. But that was a pretty low bar. "You don't get it."

His dad pointed at Cate. "She should rest."

"I'm fine." Her voice sounded stronger now.

Still, Damon knew his father wasn't wrong on this one topic. Damon was desperate to hold her and apologize for everything that happened to her since they met. That meant cutting this short, which he was fine to do. Standing there sucked the life out of him.

He spared his father one more second of his time. "More denial. That's all you do."

When his father started to respond, Cate jumped in. She tugged on Damon's arm until he looked at her. "We should go."

Steven held up a hand, as if trying to stop them from moving. "Are you afraid he'll say something he'll regret? I doubt he truly regrets any of the choices he's made with regard to leaving this family. The only question is why it took him this long to unload on me."

The answer was so easy. Even thinking the words started an ache in Damon's chest that he feared would never subside. "Because I knew what you'd say."

"Then I guess for once I didn't let you down."

This man he loved for so long but never really understood. The disappointment and frustration. After everything that happened, he still didn't get it.

Damon looked his father straight in the eye, just as he'd always done. "You're exactly wrong."

CHAPTER 18

"Please don't make me repeat the story again." Cate sat curled up on the couch in their assigned cabin. Damon had tucked a blanket around her and made her a steaming cup of tea. She held it now but hadn't sipped from it yet, preferring to let the warmth soak into her skin.

"The fifth time was probably overkill. I can see that now." He sat next to her on the couch, facing her with his arm stretched over the top of the cushions behind her head.

The lightness she loved so much had moved back into his voice. The shoulders that were bunched with tension back when he argued with his father had fallen back down to a normal level. His hand lay open on his lap. No clenched fist or tightening across his jaw.

This Damon seemed healthier, calmer. But she wasn't fully convinced what she saw was real. She guessed he put on a show to ease the anxiety still flowing through her. She appreciated the effort but she wanted him. The actual him, anger and all.

She held the mug against her chest, letting the heat

wind up around her face. "I kept hoping I would re-member something new. It's just all so hazy."

"The last two times you added a fact you hadn't before." He slipped his fingers into her hair and played with the strands resting on her shoulder. "Nothing big, but new pieces."

She slowly lowered the mug. "I did?"

"The part about the attacker breathing heavy. The way the footsteps sounded light and under strain."

"But that's nonsense stuff."

"Maybe not." He shifted until his leg touched hers. "Remember how you knew the attacker at the mo-tel couldn't be Vincent because of his scent? Then later he did smell like the person who broke into your house? Now we know Vincent is not what he seems." He waited until she nodded to continue. "It's like that. Tiny details that can add up to a picture. You're good with picking up on those things others miss and that nose of yours could win an award."

His voice was so much softer than usual, his tone much more patient than before. The change mirrored his concern, which made the shift pretty sweet. It also freaked her out. She depended on him to be *him*. After a week of knowing each other, counted on it. Sarcas-tic, ready to eat and wanting to be anywhere but at Sullivan. He talked big but unlike a lot of people she knew, he backed it up with action. That's the Damon she'd come to expect. The one she now thought about all the time, even when they were only separated for a few minutes. Because that wasn't pathetic at all.

This subdued version started a revving in her gut. It brought fear bubbling up to the surface. The one thing—maybe the only thing—that could make this day worse would be to watch the life drain out of him. She'd seen hints of that as he argued with his father. Times when it sounded as if he'd given up hope. Brief moments when he really did sound like the hollow empty shell he claimed to be.

She knew that wasn't the true him. They might not have known each other long but desperation clawed at her at the idea of him turning into a different kind of man. Not when she'd come to depend on him being this way. Not in a victim-needing-rescuing kind of way. In an enjoy-the-sparring-and-loving-the-intimacy way.

If her friends could see her now. Her, the one who lectured about romance being fun but overrated. The one who insisted she was fine dating now and then and not getting into a big relationship thing. She'd talked about not having time and being torn in a bunch of directions because of this open question with her sister. Now she knew why the women in her life who loved her so much just shoved wine at her and rolled their eyes.

Attraction didn't always hit in big ways. Sometimes it snuck in and surprised. It gave her hope on a grand scale when previously she didn't have much at all.

She reached out and slipped her fingers through his, needing to re-establish the connection and loving that such a simple gesture could do it. "Today was unbelievable. I never thought I'd be in that sort of position, so vulnerable and unable to properly fight back."

Being at someone else's mercy was her nightmare. She took self-defense classes and armed herself with information. She didn't take risks. She'd even picked a career that everyone insisted was a good one without wondering if she might like it.

She'd made every decision, programmed every aspect of her life, to erase or at least limit the panic and confusion she knew as a kid. To stay away from the carefree life that led to her sister's death. Yet, here she was. In danger but still desperate to see this through.

Damon grounded her. He made her feel strong. Right now she needed that strength because if she stopped and analyzed all that had happened in the last few days she feared she'd crumble. Run away, back to safety.

"You could have been seriously hurt," he said as he brushed the hair off her face.

They were having two different conversations. She needed to focus on him because if she thought about what happened to her and how awful the ending could have been—with her helpless and clinging to any hope not to fall off that water tower—her body would shake and her stomach would start that nauseating rolling sensation.

Inhaling, pushing out the memories of the grass and the water tower, she tried to nudge the conversation back in his direction. "I meant for you. Are you okay?"

"No one tried to hurt me today."

She beat back the trembling that raced through her. "The talk with your dad."

"What, you think that scene was odd? Struck me as the usual family drama aired for all to see. No big deal."

The way he shrugged sliced through her. He compared the emotional tug-of-war to an everyday argument about the correct way to squeeze the toothpaste.

There was nothing healthy about that kind of denial and she funneled all her energy, all the anxiety bombarding her, into trying to help him see that. "It sounded big and painful. Like, maybe you'd been holding back and finally let go."

"Possibly." He nodded. "Some of the words had been stuck inside for a while. They needed to come and now they have. Done."

He made it sound so unimportant. The sadness in his eyes suggested otherwise.

"Damon." She rubbed her thumb over the back of his hand. "You don't have to fake your way through this. Not with me."

"There's nothing to talk about."

"I was sitting in that room, Damon." Just listening to the accusations they lobbed at each other had been painful. She couldn't imagine living through those days and that estrangement. She never would have survived losing Shauna if her mom hadn't been there for support.

"It's over. Let's focus on other things." His fingertips grazed her neck. "Like you."

"I'm fine." She could almost say the words automatically now.

"Drink your tea."

The soothing touch ran through her, relaxing her. The combination of concern for him and his sweet gestures had her heart flipping. After a brutal verbal battle, he still put his worries about her first. He was *that* guy.

She debated cajoling and even insisting that he talk with her about what he was really feeling, but there had been so much talking today. After rounds and rounds it ceased being productive. Especially when Damon clearly had shut off any willingness to relive the discussion.

Hours had passed since the showdown. The people who lived and worked at Sullivan would be meeting to start dinner preparations soon. But that was out *there*. In here she could hide and snuggle in her blanket and not have to face anything that happened or whatever could in the future.

After a few more sips of tea her energy rebounded. His closeness likely helped that along. She wouldn't be running a marathon anytime soon, but she never had before either. The aches and pains had started to subside. She'd skipped offers of heavy medication and stuck to over-the-counter pain relievers, letting the cloudiness hovering in her brain clear. She wasn't about to forfeit any more control.

"I'm going to let you get away with this. This time only." She peeked at him over the top of her mug.

"Should I know what that means?"

Their joined hands rested on his leg, right above his knee. She stared at them, trying to remember when she'd stopped caring about such a perfect touch. At twenty-four or twenty-five? The months rolled by after that and now she thought maybe she'd missed something important.

"The temptation is to poke and bug you and get you to admit how much today sucked for you." She chalked that up to her competitive spirit and need to solve problems. But she didn't have to be an expert in probabilities to know how well that would work.

He ran his fingers over hers, paying each one special attention. "Getting that text saying you were in an accident sure as hell sucked. I still can't believe someone tried to hurt you. Are you sure you're okay? There's probably an urgent care nearby and we could—"

"There you go, changing the subject." Taking it away from where she wanted it—on him.

"Are we fighting?"

She bit back a laugh. "You can't tell if we are or not?"

"You don't sound pissed but I thought I should check. Just in case."

"I'm just letting you know I'm on to you." She leaned over and set the mug down on the coffee table.

The move had her dropping his hand for a second but she picked it right back up again. "These tricks you do, where you pivot off a touchy subject then act like things don't matter? Not buying it."

He sighed at her. "Today should be about you. Someone drugged you."

The conversation kept circling back to the place she didn't want it to go.

"I don't want to think about what happened and how close it was to being so much worse, Damon." She'd tried everything else, so now she tried begging. "Please."

He gave her fingers a gentle squeeze. "I want to argue with you."

"Of course you do. That's who you are. We argued about potato salad on the drive to Pennsylvania."

"It's still an unnecessary side dish."

She had to smile at his stubborn insistence on that point. "Then let me win this one. Talking about what happened at the water tower will just make me relive it, and right now I need to tuck it away. We can analyze later."

His gaze searched her face for a few more seconds before he nodded. "Fine, but it's no use discussing my dad. We've talked about this."

"The dead-inside thing?" She rolled her eyes because there was no way to hold it back. "I got it."

"You think you know me so well." His delivery stayed even. All the anger of earlier today had disappeared.

She had the sense he was treading carefully through their talk, trying to avoid trouble and desperate to prevent them from going too deep. "I didn't actually say that."

His head fell slightly to one side. "What am I thinking right now?"

Pushing could lead to fighting and she had no interest in that. "Probably dreaming about burgers."

The exhaustion had eased from her bones. Revived and gaining strength, her needs shifted from comfort to something else. She wanted to feel something. To not think or worry or investigate. For a little while, she wanted to be Cate the woman and not Cate the sister.

A smile stretched across his mouth. "I could eat."

"Shocking."

"But I was thinking you should rest." His palm slipped over the blanket to squeeze her knee underneath. "Sprawl across the bed. I'll drive and pick up food a little later."

Not tempting at all. She didn't want to be alone. Didn't want him to leave, even though she knew she'd be hungry soon. Her ideal next few hours included him and a bed and so much touching. She'd avoided a disaster today. After that violence, she needed softness. He might not think he could provide it, but she knew better.

Time to clue him in on her preferences for the evening. "Hmmm."

His smile didn't waver. "What's that noise about?"

"Napping is not what I had in mind. Not right now."

"Napping plus food. Did you miss that last part?" He sounded so serious, as if he were describing sacred activities.

"Sounds interesting." She nodded, pretending to think about his offer.

"Do I need to sweeten the deal?"

Now he was getting it . . . sort of. "Shower."

"Oh." His eyes widened. "Sure, right. You should take one of—"

Since that answer took them a step backwards she sped up the game. "Together."

"Us?"

He was extra cute when he got confused. She was starting to wonder if that stammering would always be his reaction when she took the lead on their bedroom activities. "And then we climb into bed and a few hours from now after we're both satisfied and starving, you go and get food."

His hand stopped rubbing soft circles against her leg. "But you were injured today."

The chivalrous response wasn't a surprise but she was not having it. "I'm not delirious. It's not adrenaline."

"Are you sure?"

"I need to feel something." She knew that with absolute certainty. She lifted their joined hands and kissed his fingers. "With you." Her mouth slipped down to his wrist and she licked a gentle line along his pulse.

"I . . . we should . . ."

She smiled against his skin. "Don't worry, I won't expect you to feel anything."

His fingertips below her chin, he lifted her head to meet his gaze. "Am I allowed to like it?"

The sound of his deep voice spun through her. He might sound amused but the intensity in his eyes was very serious. Very sexy.

She fought for breath. "I can probably let that happen."

Without another word, he slipped his hands under her thighs and shifted her until she sat on his lap. Facing him, she wrapped her arms around his neck and let her legs fall close to either side of his hips.

The intimate position provided her with a front row seat to the emotions passing through him—worry, need, determination. He morphed from one to the other. By the time he landed on the last his hands tightened against her thighs.

Sitting there, not kissing him, became impossible. She leaned in and pressed her mouth to his, at first light then not. As it had every time before, the kiss tumbled through her. The touch of his lips started the world spinning. Heat flushed through her and her muscles trembled.

The kiss had her moving in closer, slipping her hands down his back. Need pounded on her. The kiss stole her breath. Snapped her common sense in half. Then the world started spinning as he stood up, taking her with him. The air rushed under her and his strong hands clamped against her thighs. She hooked her ankles around his hips and held on.

A few lunging steps and they crossed into the bedroom area. She heard a thump as his elbow hit the switch. The soft yellow light above the bed clicked on. Her back hit the mattress a second later.

Watching him crawl over her filled her with a revving excitement. She knew what came next. Those long legs. The strong hands. How he could use that mouth to make her chant his name. The whisper of naughty words as he slipped inside her. Having already been with him, she needed all of it again.

He balanced his weight on his elbows and looked down at her. "Be sure."

The words didn't sound like a question but she knew it was. He didn't move or touch her, didn't lean down and kiss her. He wanted permission after the long, hard day.

Of course he did, because that's what good guys did.

She slipped her fingers over his bottom lip, trailed them along his mouth. "Yes."

CHAPTER 19

The word echoed in Damon's head. Her clear eyes sent a burst of relief spiraling through him. The sound of her voice, all scratchy and sexy had him wanting more. He'd held back because of the day and the horrors she'd been subjected to. Until she mentioned the shower he'd been worried about her and thinking they could rest. But he was wide awake now.

Shower. He was more than ready to try that fantasy.

He lifted up to his knees and dragged her to a sitting position then to her feet. Her eyes widened but she didn't say anything. The only sound he heard was the distinct humming in his ears that told him he wanted her. Bed, couch, shower . . . it didn't matter where. He needed their bodies together and his hands on her.

Walking backwards, he guided them toward the bathroom. He kicked his sneakers off as he walked, fumbling and shuffling. Kissing her through smiling and laughter. A lightness that was so different from every other minute that day.

The white tile felt cool against his socks. Half out

of balance, he put his foot on the toe of the other and pulled his leg back. The move stripped the socks off as he pulled his shirt up and over his head.

They were a mass of jerky movements and hands tearing at clothes. Her sweatshirt landed on the edge of the sink. She flicked her purple slippers off with two quick kicks. He didn't bother to see where those fell. He was too busy skating the glass door on its tracks. A second later he reached for the handle and a stream of water pounded against the empty shower walls.

Before he turned fully around to face her, she'd dropped down to sit on the toilet and went to work on his zipper. Damon froze. He waited to see what she would do, silently begging her not to toy with him. He needed her hand and her mouth.

She peeked up at him. Those dark eyes filled with wonder. With . . . excitement. He loved how she reacted to him. She didn't hold back. She didn't hide. His body belonged to her and she took full advantage.

Her hand dipped inside the band of his briefs. Her cheek rubbed over his length. He knew then he'd never survive a long round of foreplay. Whatever cool he'd shown would soon expire. Watching her shift from disconnected and not interested when they first met to confident and ready now had his fingers curling in her hair.

Steam filled the room as the rush of water echoed around them. When her lips closed over him, the last of his control expired. A moan rattled up his throat and his hips tipped forward.

Her hot mouth moved up and down on him. From this angle, he could see her flushed face and watch her hand press against him as desire ripped through him.

"Cate, now."

She didn't hesitate. The sexual torture stopped . . . but then it started again when she stood up. She shoved her lounge pants off and stepped past him. After a quick test of the water, she lifted one of those long lean legs and stepped inside. With her eyes closed she faced the spray and let the water run over her. It soaked her hair and dripped down her chest.

He'd never seen anything sexier, so he didn't waste time getting to her. Naked now, he slipped in behind her. His hands skimmed over her damp shoulders to circle her waist. He pulled her back against him, letting the spray douse both of them.

Her hand slid down his hip then over the outside of his thigh. Nails dug into his skin, pinching and exciting him. It only took a slip of an inch for her hand to land on him, to travel up and down his length. The squeeze, the pumping. Every touch made his hips buck.

From the way her mouth dropped open when his hand slipped over her belly and kept going down, to the way she grinded her ass against his erection, everything about her tempted him. She had him whipped up and gasping for breath. The friction of skin against skin sent his need spiking.

Slick from the water, their bodies moved against each other. He kissed the side of her neck then her shoulder. He tormented her with gentle bites then licked her skin to soothe her again. When she spun around to face him, he lost it. His hands traveled over her. From her breasts to her back, cupping her ass, then he started again. Desperate to know all of her, he caressed every inch. Let his finger slide deep inside her.

The slip of his feet stopped him. His hand shot out and it smacked against the glass to hold them steady. Through pure will he kept them on their feet, but one thing was clear—they needed a bed. Any flat surface, or one not slippery from water.

He reached behind her and turned off the spray. His muscles moved on fast-forward now. He whipped out one of those thick white towels and wrapped her in it. Without separating from her, he got them out of the tub. They turned and bumped into the counter. He lifted his head from hers long enough to look for another towel and he stubbed his toe against the bottom of the cabinet.

Enough. They could be wet for this. Even better.

He had them spinning back into the bedroom area. The towel fell to the floor with a whooshing sound. Then she fell back onto the bed with her hands by her head and a sexy smile playing on her lips.

They were wet and a mess . . . and the moment was perfect.

Without breaking eye contact he reached for the nightstand drawer next to the bed. On the first try he missed and heard a thud.

She laughed. "There's a condom *on* the nightstand."

The words refused to translate into anything that made sense in his head. "What?"

"Grab. It."

That order worked. He glanced over long enough to get what he needed then he was on top of her, his body sliding over hers. She opened her thighs and dragged him closer. He could smell her, feel her. She felt so soft, so right, and underneath him.

Before he could blink she took the condom. She had it out and was rolling it on him. Her hand moved between their bodies, causing his hips to buck. Primed and ready, his body took over. His fingers slipped over her, into her, again. He could feel her open for him. When he tried to adjust his position, she grabbed on to his butt and held him tight against her.

The woman wanted what she wanted and he was damn grateful that it was him. The need traveled both ways. It pulsed between them, twisting and tightening. His body ached from wanting to join with hers.

With his hands on her hips, he gave in. His body slid into hers. A slow, demanding press that had them both gasping. For a second, his vision blanked out on him. All thoughts of slowing down or making this last fell away. Deep in her heat with her internal muscles clamping down on him, the world tipped right again. All the pain rushed out of him. In its place, a thundering need.

He moved in and out. His pace picked up and his hands tightened on the back of her knees. He held her open, plunged inside her, while he kissed the length of her neck. There wasn't a part of her body he didn't cherish. He wanted to shower every inch with attention. That was his last thought before the orgasm hit him. He gasped as his body took over.

Swirling his finger over her, he tried to bring her with him. His head fell forward and his mouth rested in that delicious juncture at the base of her neck. He heard her sharp intake of breath and he kept going. Sliding deeper into her, touching her in the place sure to make her body dance and jump. Kept up the sexy double play until her hips arched off the bed.

Her breathing came faster and fell harder. He felt every move she made beneath him. Felt the tremble move through her. And when she started to come, he closed his eyes and gave in.

Minutes passed, maybe longer than that. He didn't really care. He didn't want to open his eyes. All that mattered was Cate laid over him in a sprawl. Her hand rested on his stomach and her cheek against his shoulder. He wasn't even sure when they turned over or how they landed in this position.

The closed curtains plunged this area of the room in shadows. But he didn't need to see her to know she was relaxed. He could feel her breath blow over the bare skin of his chest. She relaxed against him, balancing her weight against his side.

He'd just assumed she'd fallen off to sleep when he heard her yawn. "That was nice."

He knew she was messing with him because he could feel and see her smile, but still . . . "*Nice?* Ice cream is nice. A warm day is nice."

"Ice cream?" She lifted her head and stared down at him. "Cookie dough ice cream is way more than nice."

"I'm not a huge fan."

She shook her head. Even managed to look disappointed. "I will never understand you."

He thought he had been pretty clear about his love for the meat family, but she felt so good resting against him that he didn't bother to point that out. "Likely not."

"But . . ."

With her face all shiny and happy, he couldn't fight off the urge to kiss her. He leaned down, touching their lips together in a lingering touch.

When he lifted his head again, she smiled at him and he had to make a joke. "Any chance you're going to finish your sentence?"

"I think you're going to like it."

He liked her. Too much. That was the potential problem that started to haunt his days. "I'm intrigued."

"I could use a hamburger."

The laugh burst out of him before he could stop it. "See? It's the perfect food."

She snorted. "I don't know about that."

"Don't ruin it. For a second there you were the perfect fake girlfriend."

"I was hoping to win that award."

"I am willing to make a burger run." When she opened her mouth to say something, he rushed to finish his thought. "But you have to admit burgers are nature's perfect food."

She looked over the side of the bed. "I probably have a granola bar I can eat."

Her laughter filled the room as he flipped them both over and hovered above her. "You will not win this food battle."

"Are you sure?" Her stomach picked that minute to rumble. "Traitor."

"Did I mention I'd throw in a few orders of fries?"

Her eyes widened. "Why didn't you say that from the beginning? That's the perfect perk." She pushed against his chest. "Get going."

He groaned as he sat up. "I think you want me for my food."

"Get me food and I'll show you how much I want you."

He was out of bed and in his jeans four seconds later.

She let him get to the door before calling out to him. "If you can find a piece of fruit, maybe buy that, too."

"Do you promise to stay naked while I'm gone?" Because if she did he might wreck the car thinking about it.

She rolled her eyes instead.

"I'm serious." Suddenly, he really was. The idea of her being there, waiting for him. Of them eating then falling back to the bed. It sounded like the perfect night to him.

She sat up with the sheet sliding off her breasts toward her waist, flashing him. "Yes, but you better hurry."

"Challenge accepted."

CHAPTER 20

Cate suddenly hated breakfast. Sitting at a table with Damon and his father in the middle of a room bustling with people going back and forth to the buffet was her new nightmare. It felt as if everyone watched them, even though she knew they were a bit more subtle than that.

So much talking and moving around . . . except for their table. Damon had barely said a word. The few he did were reserved for her and centered on getting food. He'd acknowledged his father with a nod as they sat down. Nothing more.

He spent the rest of the meal stirring the milk in his cereal bowl, probably wishing it was a bowl of ground beef. The thought of kicking him passed through her head more than once. Steven wasn't her family but she'd run through every single bit of mindless chitchat in her repertoire with the guy. Even she couldn't talk about trees and the weather for an hour. And it had only been fifteen minutes of painful silence.

She blamed Damon for the discomfort. His father asked them to join him for breakfast. Again, he did it in the form of a note slipped under their door. Not her favorite way of making a request. Since Damon ripped it up, she guessed he wasn't a fan either. Actually, she didn't need to guess because he spent most of the morning stomping around, not saying a word except for the occasional *I can't believe we're eating with him.*

In hindsight, she probably should have taken that as a no and suggested they go back to the diner. She could be there, eating toast and enjoying an overflow of strawberry jelly without anyone watching, but no.

They were stuck now, in the rectangle room filled with a mix of four- and six-person tables and longer ones flanked by benches. People fell into several obvious groups. Apparently in cult-like communes people still naturally divided into cliques.

The younger people sat together. Those who looked more like professors from back when this place actually was a school congregated at the smaller tables near the coffee setup. She sat across from Steven and watched him section a grapefruit with the precision of a surgeon.

Lucky her.

He must have sensed her staring because he glanced up and smiled. His gaze bounced to Damon then back to her again. "Thank you for joining me."

"We figured your table served the best food," she said, trying to make a joke and failing miserably. "Or at least got the chance to eat first."

Steven lowered his spoon as a frown formed. "Everyone shares here. The food distribution is equal."

She debated explaining the concept of sarcasm to him but went with drinking her tea instead. But for the first time in three minutes—she knew because she was counting—Damon's head lifted. He watched his father. Without saying a word, they stared at each other.

Damon was the first to break. "I'm pretty sure she was kidding."

"Oh." Steven sounded confused by the idea but kept right on talking. "There's someone I want you to meet, if you haven't already."

He motioned to someone behind them. Cate turned, silently hoping not to see Liza standing there. She was nice enough and dedicated but naïve in a way that set Damon off. Cate really wasn't in the mood to referee again this morning.

"Hello." Trevor's deep voice rang out as he came around Damon's side of the table to stand next to his father.

Damon didn't even blink. "We've met. He introduced himself the first day."

Steven's frown disappeared. He looked satisfied, likely because he thought that meant his employee, or whatever Trevor was supposed to be, had listened to orders.

"Good." Steven motioned for Trevor to take the open seat at the table. "Trevor will be helping you."

Damon's eyebrow rose. "Excuse me?"

It was official. She was impressed. She also had no idea how they pulled it off. They clearly had this big *Band of Brothers* bond and a shared past, yet they acted like almost-strangers. She wondered if she should be worried about the ease with which they lied. Truth was kind of a big thing with her and Damon had already tiptoed through her tolerance on that point.

"We kept the older documents," Steven said, launching right into an unexpected topic. The only nod to the importance of their conversation came in the way he lowered his voice, not to a whisper but quiet enough that anyone around them trying to hear would have to strain. "Lists of who lived here, went to school here. Records. Files."

Damon shoved his bowl to the side and leaned on the edge of the table on his elbows. "What exactly are you saying?"

Trevor waited for a nod from Steven before talking. Managed to look every inch of the quiet guy obeying orders. "Before breakfast, your father took me aside and asked me to spend whatever time was needed to guide you through Sullivan's paperwork."

"What?" Okay, she squealed a little but it wasn't her fault. Being undercover was not one of her skills.

Damon stayed calm. "Why you?"

"Trevor didn't live here through any of the . . ." Steven cleared his throat. "Problems."

That word seemed to cover every circumstance around here. Maybe he was trying to be helpful but having people refer to her sister dying as little more than a nuisance made a ball of anxiety start spinning in Cate's stomach. She worried it wouldn't subside until she hit something. "Problems?"

"I thought you might want a neutral eye. Someone to help who didn't also have the burden of living here at the time." Steven stared at his son. "I assumed you would trust that more."

"Maybe it would make sense to talk with people with firsthand knowledge." Damon held up a hand as he glanced at Trevor. "No offense."

He shrugged in response. "None taken."

They still didn't act as if they knew each other as anything more than two guys who said hello for two minutes days ago. Their ability to compartmentalize and play this game fascinated her. She looked for any signs of cracking behind the façade but couldn't see them. Neither acted nervous. Their voices stayed steady. They looked at each other, but not for too short or too long a period of time.

"You are free to talk to anyone." Steven let out a sigh. "I didn't specifically order it, not in those words, but I suggested it would be good for Sullivan if people were open and honest with the two of you. Even if it hurt."

"Okay." She didn't know what else to say, so she went with that.

"Trevor already began gathering what you need this morning." Steven held out his hand and Trevor passed over a file and a zip drive. "I have contact information for some of those who used to live here and will get in touch with them first to let them know I approve of this mission you're on." Steven opened the file and scanned whatever he saw inside. "Roger and Vincent might be good resources."

She couldn't help but wonder what time Trevor got up to get started on this project. And how soon after that he sent all of the information back to Wren and the office to get working on their end.

Damon's attention stayed locked on his father. "Why are you doing this?"

"Despite what you might think, we don't have anything to hide here." Steven picked up his spoon then put it down again. "So much of the history of this place is out in the open, in the public view through investigations and television shows."

"You mean the documentary." Damon shook his head. "It didn't say much."

Steven sighed. "Then hopefully the paperwork will."

The tension ratcheted up as the Sullivan men spoke. She could feel the people sitting at other tables glance over. Their voices hadn't lifted but the body language was all wrong for a friendly breakfast chat. Trevor sat without moving but something in his position, the way he hunched over the edge of the table, ready to pounce, made her think they were on the verge of another verbal battle.

She was not in the mood for a second round. She also wanted to get her hands on the documents, though she doubted they would say anything of importance. "Where is the rest of the material?"

"Our private . . . in the family's rooms. At the house." Steven visibly swallowed.

Even she felt sorry for him in that moment. The man's family had been taken from him, sometimes through his own actions and sometimes not, but there was no debating he was alone.

"You kept those?" Damon said the words nice and slow, leaving a space between each one.

"I had hope."

Damon's eyes narrowed. Just a fraction. "Of what?"

How could he not know? Looking at Steven, even she knew.

"That I'd see you again," he said. "Or did you think the calls and messages through lawyers and attempts to find you even after you changed your name were just for show?"

"You have to be kidding." Damon's voice lifted that time. It carried over the din of the room and even more people glanced their way. "You shut me out while I was in jail."

"You spent a lot of time trying to discredit Sullivan and our mission here. That took a long time to forget." When Damon started to respond, Steven talked over him. "But you are my son."

"I'm very aware of that fact."

"And you're here, aren't you? I guess I should thank Cate for that."

She waved off the compliment since it was based on a lie. "Damon came back to Sullivan for me."

That much was the truth. He could call it a job or his responsibility or pretend his friends forced him, but she knew better. Damon was not the type to do anything he didn't want to do. Him being here meant something. To her, it meant everything.

The chair screeched against the concrete floor as Steven pushed it back without getting up. "I have a file room that's kept locked. Trevor, I temporarily changed the security code to the same one you use for the storage shed. You have complete access to the house, as do they."

Trevor looked at Damon for a few extra seconds before turning to Steven. "Of course. Let us know when we can start."

"Now. I'll move out of the house to temporary accommodations for a few days." Steven stood up then. Pushed in his chair and plastered a blank look on his face. Generally looked as if he hadn't been talking about heart-wrenching topics five seconds ago. "In fact, I need to finalize those arrangements with Liza."

Maybe it was the pain thrumming off him or the brief peek she got into his yearning for a real relationship with Damon. Either way, Cate felt guilty about kicking the guy out of his own bed. "You don't have to move out."

"Yes, I do." Steven shook his head. "Being there is hard enough without opening that door."

He lost her. "What door?"

This time his smile was sad. "You'll see."

AN HOUR LATER, Damon couldn't get comfortable in his chair. He threw that half pillow thing poking into his back on the floor. What were those for, anyway? Then he shifted . . . and did it again. Nothing helped.

Being in this building had him on edge. Just walking up to the stone house set back in a cocoon of trees started a kicking in his gut. He grew up here but hadn't been back for years. Three stories of gray stone with a deep porch with stone pillars and a swing. The porch stretched most of the way around the house. Flowers in a riot of purple and pink sat in pots out front and in boxes under the windows.

He knew the Sullivan horticultural team had something to do with the fresh happy look. But that didn't stop the pain from slashing through him when he remembered the way his mother fussed over the flowers she planted here. Trimming and talking to them. How she asked Dad to build those flower boxes.

Walking inside the double doors hit him just as hard. The large open entry and wooden staircase highlighting the hall. His grandfather built a portion of the building and his father added on. It had been the perfect place for a president of a university to live. Plenty of entertaining space with living space on the top two floors, the upper one belonging to him. It was also a little boy's dream.

He used to run through the yard flying kites or

kicking a soccer ball. When he thought his parents weren't looking, he'd slide down the solid bannister, trying to go from the top of the staircase to the very bottom in one swoosh without falling off.

He strained, trying to remember the sounds of laughter in the history of the house. He had no trouble hearing the crying. His parents when they lost his brother. His father the night of Mom's memorial service. His own in the ten minutes he was given to say goodbye before the police led him away.

He'd lived here, ate here. Had his first kiss in the backyard.

Today, despite the sun shining in from the floor-to-ceiling windows, the air felt dank and stale. The damp smell likely came from *the room*. It sat right off the dining room. A locked office with a solid wooden door that survived from the house's original building in 1896. The locks and electronic panel were new. This being the one room he was never allowed to enter hadn't changed since he could remember . . . until right now.

He heard the thud of boxes as Trevor moved everything that wasn't furniture out of the room, stacking the items on the dining room table and floor around it. He didn't complain, which surprised Damon at first. Then he realized Trevor knew this was the one place on the earth Damon did not want to be. This house held more than ghosts. It sheltered demons.

Trevor wiped his arm across his forehead as he dumped off the last arm full of files. "Here we go."

Cate's hand slid over Damon's as she looked to Trevor. "You manipulated this, right? You being the one to help us is just too convenient."

Trevor smiled at her. "I made sure I hung around. Dropped a hint or two."

The comment had Damon looking up, searching the usual place. "Maybe we should—"

"I did a sweep. There aren't any devices in here." Trevor groaned as he dropped into the nearest chair and started sorting items into piles. "One of us worked all night."

Cate reached for the tea a woman Trevor called Tina had set down in the middle of the table before leaving the house. "You think your father sleeps with cameras aimed at him?"

"I think if he were involved in what happened to your sister that it would make sense for him to allow access then listen in to see what intel you have. To know how close we were getting."

Trevor snorted. "That's not pessimistic at all."

"Interesting coming from you." Damon slid into the seat across from Trevor.

"Are you usually a negative Nancy?" Cate asked, looking amused by the idea.

Trevor put his phone on the table and pointed at it, as if to issue some sort of challenge. "Would I have ninety photos of my boyfriend in my phone if I were?"

Her eyes lit up as she reached for the cell. "Let me see."

For a second, Damon watched them. Their heads

hovered close together as Trevor flipped screens. Every now and then he would point to something or talk about where he and Aaron were when the photos were taken. London. New York City. Chicago. Tokyo. The list turned out to be long, which made Damon smile. Trevor deserved a happy ending after having such a shitty start to life. He'd found it somehow, against all odds, with a guy who got him.

The thought made Damon look at her. She had her long dark hair pulled over her shoulder so it fell across her chest. She smiled and laughed, and when she did some of the tightness in Damon's chest eased.

He hated to break up the moment, to pull them back toward the darkness, but his throat had started to close. The longer he stayed in this house, the more the memories assaulted him. If they didn't focus on something else, he'd have to bolt. Run outside and gulp in air that wasn't tainted with all the wrong that had happened here. "We could work?"

She continued to look at the photos. "Some things are more important."

"Wait, really?" He would have bet money he'd never hear those words come out of her. "Than digging through the Sullivan private papers?"

"He's really cute." She smiled at Trevor before looking back at Damon. "And yes."

"I've tried to tell your pretend boyfriend that his priorities are messed up." Trevor pocketed his phone. "But he prefers to be an island."

She shook her head. "Right? It's annoying."

"I'm right here." But they were off again. Bonding and getting each other, so comfortable. Damon was starting to think she was a people collector. She read them and reeled them in, including two men who thrived on danger and secrecy. That was quite a skill.

"This time I'll be the negative one, but I'm guessing we have access to all of this because he knows there's nothing to find." Cate looked at Trevor's carefully crafted stacks as she talked.

"You give him too much credit," Damon said.

Trevor nodded. "And us too little."

"Meaning?"

When Cate frowned at them, Damon rushed to explain, "Usually what happens is people don't realize they've dropped a clue. More than likely there is one kernel, one tiny thing in here. We have to find it."

Cate let out a little hum. "You two are turning out to be more helpful than I anticipated."

"Now can we talk about the condoms? Maybe discuss how many you have left." Trevor mumbled the question without looking up.

Her frown slipped to a glare. "Only if you want to die."

Since that was the perfect response, Damon didn't try to add to it. He dug in. They all did. A comfortable silence fell over the room as they reviewed files and made notes. A few times someone would ask a question and then they'd all go back to work again.

They'd agreed each file—every single piece of paper and computer note—would get a review by all three of them. It took longer, but this might be their only chance and they weren't going to miss something big due to fatigue or confusion. Especially since Damon knew to his bones this offer would never happen again. From the look of some of the files, including the few with water damage, he wasn't sure anyone, including law enforcement, had seen the contents of these.

Two hours in, Damon found it. The tiny piece of information that might mean nothing but could mean everything. He reread the memo a second time. "Your sense of smell was right all along."

Her head popped up from the inside of a file she'd been studying for ten minutes. "What?"

"What if I told you Vincent had a thing for your sister?" That was an inference, but Damon didn't see how what he was reading could mean anything else.

Trevor took the file and started reading. It only took a second for him to see. It. "There's a note here, in his school file. A professor's note about him being distracted."

He passed the file to Cate who took her time. "My sister's name is in Vincent's file. No comment or bigger statement. Just her name in some guy's handwriting."

But it didn't take a huge leap of logic to know the cause and effect of her name being right there next to the professor's concern. "This is before she died. Five weeks before."

"What about after?" Trevor asked.

Cate went back to scanning. She seemed to read a section then do it again. "He wasn't . . ."

That's where she left it. Just a phrase hanging in the air.

Trevor leaned forward in his chair. "Now is not the time to cut off a sentence."

"Vincent took a leave of absence. Worked but didn't go to class." She slid the file back to Damon.

"Would that have been so weird?" Trevor's gaze traveled between them. "Really though. Someone he knew died. You said that thing he told you about dancing. If he had a crush and she died he'd naturally be upset."

"But he didn't mention a crush, or dating or anything like that." Damon appreciated Trevor was choosing his words carefully and not jumping to conclusions. But they worked half based on instinct and him shutting his down would not help her. Cate was strong and prepared to hear bad news. She didn't need to be shielded, so Damon didn't try. "Imagine how upset he'd be if he watched her—or helped her—fall off a water tower."

"Maybe upset enough to get into my condo and look around, leaving the scent of his aftershave or cologne or whatever that was behind," Cate said.

"Roger, too." Trevor dumped another file on top of the one they were already reading. "It looks as if all the students were given time off to mourn. Counselors were brought in. The police came."

"Sounds like my dad managed to handle something sort of right."

"Roger was offered time off, too. He's described as despondent." Trevor turned the file to show Damon.

Damon flipped through a few pages. He knew he should feel dirty peeking into something as private as kids' education records but he didn't have a choice. He also didn't have a warrant, so his options were limited.

"You're right. The school called in mental health professionals, which is pretty routine these days, but some students needed one-on-one time. Here's the list of students and professors sent to the counselor for ongoing treatment." There, folded and hidden in the back of an unrelated file. "No counseling files are in here that I can see."

Cate shifted until she sat on her knees on the hard chair. "Anything from your uncle?"

"No he's . . ." Damon worked his way back to the files dealing with Dan. There weren't many, which made him think the FBI or the prosecutor or someone took those. It's possible his father turned those over in an effort to save the school . . . and himself. Then Damon remembered the odd paragraphs that didn't seem related to anything else. "Wait a second."

"What do you have?"

There in blue ink. A ramble with words scratched out. "A few pages in draft. Maybe for her memorial service. Did they have one?"

"Two—one by my mom back home and one here," Cate said without having to look at anything.

"Her death hit people hard." Damon reached for her hand and enfolded it in his. "Does any of this help?"

"Why would it?" Trevor asked.

"Shauna didn't die alone and unloved." She squeezed

Damon's hand. "It looks like people cared about her. She'd built a life here before whatever happened happened."

Those words, so softly delivered might have sent him to his knees if he'd been standing.

"That matters." Damon got it. He glanced at Trevor and watched the understanding dawn on his face. Yeah, he got it, too.

After nearly a minute of quiet, Trevor stood up. He collected his notes and took the files they'd been talking about. "I'm going to take all of this. I'll give the list of potential witnesses, including the separate one I've made, to Wren. Let him and Garrett start working on contacting the people who aren't here anymore. Maybe one will remember something."

Damon put his free arm behind the back of Cate's chair. "All we need is that one."

"Thank you. This is dangerous." Her voice was soft as her gaze moved back and forth between them. Then it landed on Damon. "For you it's emotionally difficult, even though you won't admit it."

She expected Trevor to joke, but he didn't. "We're here for you."

They were. All of them. This group that started off as supposed lost boys. And because of them, she was ready. "For the first in a long time, I feel like I really can be here for Shauna."

CHAPTER 21

Trevor left the investigation hours ago to get something to eat and report in with Garrett who was skulking around the county. Damon debated tagging along. He thought maybe it would do them all some good to get off the property and have a solid meal, by which he was thinking steak.

It might have happened if Cate hadn't gone down a rabbit hole of reading. She told him to go ahead without her and since that wasn't happening, he skipped the nicer dinner in favor of a quick trip to the main dining room for a takeout container. With that polished off, he was ready to end for the night. Work anyway.

He turned to tell her that but stopped before he got a word out. She sat on the oversized leather chair in the library with her feet propped up on the ottoman. With one hand she flipped pages of the file on her lap. With the other, she toyed with the end of her hair.

So graceful and sexy. So utterly feminine. If just watching someone could provide comfort, this scene would do it.

They'd agreed to give up at dark and get out of there

for the rest of the night. That happened a half hour ago and she still sat there, turning those pages. He'd barely been able to get her to try some soup for dinner before she returned to the boxes by her feet.

At least his nerves had calmed down. The urge to jump out of his skin had subsided. Not that it would ever be easy to walk around the creaky hardwood floors of his family home. Memories bombarded him, both good and bad. But the longer he stood there, the more those worth remembering took over.

He chalked up any positive thoughts he still had about the place to his mom. She used to wake him up by shaking the mattress and making these funny sounds. Then there was the bread recipe she got from one of the nutrition students. She made two loaves every week, sometimes more, because he insisted on using it for a sandwich every day.

He hadn't thought of those times in years. Hadn't let the images in. Now they flowed through him and he couldn't figure out how to slam the gate shut again.

"We don't have to do all of this in one day." He made the observation while standing at the window facing into the yard.

At the sound of his voice her head popped up. It took another few seconds for her eyes to clear. "It's weird, right? All this stuff has been sitting here, with no one paying attention to it. Now that we have the chance I feel this churning need to race through and not miss a thing."

"You think there are more clues in there to find?"

"Not really." She let her feet drop to the floor and sat up a little straighter. "It's as if reading through this preserves it somehow."

"It?"

"The school."

He almost groaned because he wasn't convinced keeping that memory alive was a good thing. "There are some who believe the only answer is to banish any mention of the school."

"But people built lives here, learned things." She made a face as if she were searching for the right words and not finding them. "They had this community, and for all the awful things that happened later, there was a point when the idea of it and what it could be was pure and the dreams were a possibility."

"Now you're the one who sounds like the school brochure."

"I know and it makes me a little nervous." She shut the file and dropped it on the stack on the floor. "But that's not all I'm feeling."

"Panicked. Anxious." A whole list of emotions ran through his head. "Do those work?"

"More like excited."

His guesses weren't even close. He never would have picked that word. "What?"

"Like a burning need to plow forward."

"Maybe you hit your head harder than we thought at the water tower." But he recognized the gleam in her eyes. He knew from experience there was nothing more intoxicating than being on the verge of breaking a case open.

Nothing they'd found today pointed in that direction for him. He felt like he was trudging through the weeds. For whatever reason—the house, his father, his growing feelings for her—he couldn't think straight. Thoughts kept spinning on him. Every step forward seemed to lead him right back to where he started.

Maybe the student files would get them there. They had new intel but they were running out of energy. At least he was. She looked ready to run a mile.

"Any chance I could beg you to leave and come back to the cabin with me." He held up a hand. "Just until tomorrow. I promise."

She watched him for a second. More like studied him. Her gaze moved over his face. When she finally stopped, she stood up and stretched. Winced as she started to move, but she got to him. Stopped right in front of him.

"You are the only reason I'd leave." She wound her arms around his neck. "That face of yours is the perfect reason for a break."

"Ms. Pendleton, are you making a pass?"

"I've been sitting in the same position for hours." She dropped a quick kiss on his mouth before lifting her head again. "My muscles need a good workout."

The words pumped life into his lower half. Having her in his arms sent his temperature spiking. That's how it worked with her. She touched him, turned that sexy voice on him, and he lost the ability to do anything but babble.

Only one problem . . . "Not in this house, right?"

That struck him as a bad idea. And pretty wrong.

She threw him a you've-got-to-be-kidding look of horror. "God, no."

"Good woman."

He started walking her backwards, stopping long enough for her to scoop up the strap of her bag and for him to grab his car keys and wallet off his father's oversized desk. They got as far as the door before he had to kiss her again. He shoved her up against it, careful not to jar her or her new bruises.

Her back thudded against the wood and his palms landed on either side of her head. He brushed his mouth over hers, lifting only long enough to tease her before kissing her again. "You are so fucking sexy."

The way she challenged him, intrigued him, kept his brain firing and his dick hard. She broke through his defenses. That scared the shit out of him but also left him in awe. He doubted it could have happened a year ago. He hadn't been ready or willing back then. She made him both now.

When he pulled back, their heavy breathing mixed. Her fingers tapped against his chin and started traveling. They slid down his chest and flattened on his stomach. Didn't stop until they reached the top of his belt.

"Yeah, time to go." He reached around her for the doorknob. It rattled in his hand.

She laughed. "What exactly are you doing back there?"

"It's stuck." He waited until she stepped to the side to try again. "Not unusual. Things are always misfiring and breaking in an old house."

With better leverage, he turned it and pulled. The door shook on its hinges but didn't open. "What the hell?"

"Damon."

The sudden shakiness of her voice had him glancing at her. "What's wrong?"

Instead of answering, she looked down. He saw it then. The thin curl of smoke snaking under the door. For a second it didn't make sense. Smoke meant . . . "Fire."

"Is the door hot?" She leaned in closer as if she were trying to listen for noises in the hallway.

The sharp scent hit him then. He could smell the distinct edge of fire. Heard a strange whistling sound and a cracking. The realization got him moving. "We need to get out of here."

With a hand around her elbow, he headed for the window. After a few steps, her arm slipped out of his grasp and he stopped. She stood frozen by the door with smoke winding around her feet.

"Cate!" He went back to her and took her hand. Gave her a little tug. "We need to move."

Waves of anxiety crashed through him with a flood of adrenaline right behind. With his heart racing and his gut aching with the need to run, he got them going.

They only had two choices out—one was blocked by fire and the other sat a floor off the ground.

He went for the drop to the ground.

His body buzzed with energy now. His muscles moved as if on autopilot. He picked up the chair on the way to the window. "Watch out."

She ducked as he lifted the chair. It smacked into the glass with a deafening crash. The window shattered and shards scattered across the floor with a pinging sound. The noise mixed with the roaring in his ears. He couldn't tell if it came from the far edges of panic or from the raging fire. He didn't see flames but he sensed they were close. He could imagine orange eating through wood and peeling the paint off the walls.

He could worry about all of that once he had her on the ground and safe.

When he turned to her she'd already slipped off her sweater, leaving her wearing a white tank top. She had the material rolled around her arm as she knocked the jagged glass out of the window and spread the material out in the windowsill for added cover.

She peeked outside. "That is so high."

"One floor." He could make out the slanted roof of the porch below. "Less than that."

She looked at him with eyes filled with terror. "What are you looking at?"

"We're going to the overhang roof then down to the ground."

She shifted her weight and balled her hands into fists. Fear seemed to have her in its grip but she didn't fold or give up. She practically bounced on the balls of her feet, as if trying to work up the nerve to go out there.

Not that she had a choice. Gray smoke billowed toward them now. He saw a flash and watched as flames licked around the doorframe.

He wanted to give her a minute to adjust but they no longer had that. "Time's up."

He hoisted her up and into the window. She tucked her feet and slipped them through to the outside. Glass crunched under her and around his feet. He tried to ignore all of it. Cuts and bruises beat being burned alive. No question there.

She slid down the gentle slight slope then stopped. A thundering yell stuck in his throat but that's not what she needed. Calm and reassurance would get her to safety. He inhaled, thinking to clear his head but heat filled his lungs. The air burned and coughing felt like getting hit with a hammer. He doubled over, trying to get it out but every time he opened his mouth the burning sensation intensified.

"Damon!" She leaned in, caught the hem of his sleeve and started pulling him closer.

The move was enough to snap him back to the room and the fire. He swallowed back the pain and nearly dove out the window. They sat on the porch roof with him behind her and began to slide down. Embers flew twisted in the air around them. He could hear voices and yelling but didn't see anyone. Still, relief soared through him. People were coming.

Her legs shook as she shimmied down on her ass. "We're going to be fine."

Over and over she said the words until they played in his head like a mantra. Soon, he was believing it. This was an easy drop for him, but he wasn't thinking about him. His mind was on her . . . and whatever they were going to find when they got on the ground.

They reached the edge of the roof. He was about to drop over and hope all those practice landing drills Quint made them do years ago still sat somewhere in his memory when he heard a new sound.

"Damon!" He looked down over the ledge and saw Roger and two other men standing on the ground.

His body flipped into fight-or-flight mode. He refused to trust what he was seeing. Everything about this seemed wrong but with Cate grabbing on to the back of his shirt and the smoke clogging his brain, all he could think about was getting her down.

"You have to catch her."

"No!" The scream came from Cate.

But it was too late. Damon slipped his hands under her arms and brought her to the edge of the roof. She flailed and reached back for him, but he didn't give her a choice. "I'm going to hand you down to them."

"We've got you, Cate." Roger called out orders to his friends as they crowded closer to grab her.

The truth flashed in Damon's brain. All he needed to do was lower her and they would grab her feet. She would be fine. They could do this . . . then his brain grew fuzzy. The dizziness hit him out of nowhere.

Somehow, he managed to help her turn around and pushed one of her legs off the roof.

She held his arms in a death grip. "You have to come with me."

"I'll be right after you." But the world was spinning on him now. A wall of heat crashed into him. Taking a quick look behind him, he could see the flames devour the library.

"Damon, let go!"

He heard Roger's voice and obeyed on instinct. Cate gasped as her body slipped farther over the edge. Fear made her eyes huge and glassy but she didn't scream as her body went into free fall. Then she jerked to a stop as the men on the ground caught her.

Success. "Yes." Damon dropped down on his side on the roof. He could rest now. As soon as he closed his eyes he heard the shouting. It broke through the sudden exhaustion.

Cate screamed his name.

"Damon, do not make me come up there."

Trevor. Damon didn't know how much time had passed but he would know that voice anywhere. Trevor sounded pissed. The thought made Damon smile until he remembered his friend's yelled demand and scrambled to sit up again.

Shit, he'd been dozing off. Sleeping now meant death and Damon was not about to die at Sullivan. The thought of that had him pushing up on his shoulder. In a long and painful slog that seemed to last forever, he crawled to the edge. His muscles weighed a ton and it was hard to move but he kept going. He didn't have a choice because fire sped up the outside wall of the house.

He had to get down. He had to fight this fire.

He kept repeating those two comments in his head. Focused on them as he dropped first one then another leg over the roofline. His feet swung in the air. Then a hand clamped down on his ankle, which didn't seem possible but he was being dragged. His hands scraped against the roof before his body took flight. The journey didn't last long. Strong hands caught him and guided him down.

His back hit the grass as he fought to drag in clean air. When he opened his eyes, Cate kneeled on one side of him and Trevor glared at him from the other.

"Stupid dick." Trevor's voice didn't rise above the frenzy around them.

Fire crackled and sirens wailed in the distance. The house seemed to shift and moan as flames shot out of windows.

"We need to get you medical help," Cate said as she tried to hold him down when he tried to get up.

Trevor nodded. "He inhaled too much smoke."

Footsteps thundered around them. Vincent joined the group. Then others. People had gathered. They switched from looking at the house to looking at him laid out on the ground.

"We need to get this fire out." With Cate safe, that was the only thought on Damon's mind. No one else was in the house. People should be safe, but if this spread that might not be the case.

He struggled to stand up, ignoring Cate's pleas to stay down and Trevor's mumbled profanity. They were right. His body fought him even as adrenaline tried to surge. That didn't stop him from issuing orders. "The hoses. We need to hit the house and get this under control."

Roger nodded. "You heard him."

"Is the front gate open?" Trevor asked. "We have to let the fire trucks in."

"I can get it," Roger said, shouting to be heard over the sudden swell of noise around them.

Trevor and Roger working together eased some of the pressure in Damon's chest. He could concentrate on the flames. For that, they needed water and lots of it. He started to follow the group Roger had sent off to the landscaping sheds, thinking that's where they'd find most of what they need, but his knees gave out. Without Trevor's firm hand, Damon would have gone down.

"You should stay here." Vincent put a hand in front of Damon's chest. "We have enough trouble."

Cate frowned at him. "What does that mean?"

"The place has been in an uproar since you got here." Vincent aimed his response at Damon. "Now this."

But Damon didn't have time for bullshit. So many questions filled his brain—why was Roger there? How did Vincent get to the house so quickly? Or had he already been there to set the fire? All things Damon vowed to worry about later.

"Get out of my way." Those were the last words Damon spoke as he stumbled away from Vincent.

Damon forced his legs to work, concentrated on putting one foot in front of the other as his head started to clear. By the time he met up with the group dragging the hoses, adrenaline fueled him. Energy coursed through him as he carried the hoses back to the worst of the fire.

The sirens screamed now. The trucks were close but it could be too late for the house if they waited much longer. He was about to yell new orders when Trevor took over. He maneuvered and managed the people. He had Cate standing back but still engaged by holding one of the hoses.

Voices called out. People ran around. Water shot from the hoses and hit the fire with a hiss. Smoke clogged the air and orange-and-red flames shot up, as if refusing to give in to the water. They fought and shouted back and forth. Damon's hands locked over the hose and he planted his feet to keep from getting shoved around. They made progress but not much. Enough to stop the spread but not enough to put it out. Not even close.

People poured into the area. A fire truck slammed to a halt near them and firefighters seemed to multiply. Someone draped a blanket over his shoulders. Slowly, the nonexperts were pulled off the fire and checked. They sat around on the ground and huddled in groups. He heard crying over the thumping and thudding of the now dying fire.

He turned to look for Cate. Panic swamped him when she wasn't standing where he'd last seen her. Then he felt her slide her hand through his.

"This way." She pulled him over to the ambulance he hadn't even noticed until right then. Before he could say anything a first responder slammed an oxygen mask on him and started checking his vitals.

Trevor appeared behind Cate. They both wore expressions filled with fear, though Trevor also managed to look worried and pissed.

"You're lucky I didn't chuck you into that fire." He shook his head. "Really lucky."

"I'm fine." Damon pushed the mask down and reached for Cate's hand again, not sure when he lost hold of it. "All that matters is that you are."

"Because of you." She glanced away for a second before looking at him again. "You could have been killed."

"He's too much of a stubborn jackass for that." Trevor's voice sounded harsh but he reached in and cuffed Damon's shoulder. "I'll check on everyone then you're going to a hospital."

Cate nodded. "Definitely."

They were losing it. No way was he spending hours in an emergency room. "Absolutely not."

Trevor put the oxygen mask back on Damon's face. "It wasn't a question."

Trevor took off then. He headed for Roger. They switched from talking to looking at the now charred side of the house.

Damon had a fleeting thought about his father and where he might be. He shoved the mask off a second time. "Dad is—"

"Fine. Trevor said he was talking with people near the back of the house—apparently it's worse there."

Damon thought he knew why. "Did this start on the second floor?"

She frowned. "I guess. Maybe."

The room and all that previously locked-up information sat near the center of the fire. It was too much of a coincidence for the fire to start right after they finally got a look inside. But Damon didn't mention that. There would be time for theories later. Right now, all he wanted to do was hold her hand and look at her.

That seemed to make her worry more. Her frown deepened. "Are you okay?"

He was about to answer with some comment about how he hated seeing her in danger. Watching her slip over the edge of the roof even knowing a rescue waited below . . . damn, that was too much.

She didn't give him a chance to get any of that out. "The hose? What were you thinking? You weren't in any condition to play fireman."

Any other time, with any other woman, he would have made a joke about how he thought women loved firemen. "I spent my entire adult life running away from this place but at the thought of losing it, I had to save it."

The anger seemed to seep right out of her. Her body slumped. "Oh, Damon."

"It surprised me, too." He nodded to the medic as he gestured toward someone sitting on the ground and moved on.

"Not every memory you have of your family and this house is bad." She tightened her hold on his hand. "Don't let your father, this fire or the FBI or anyone else steal those from you."

A good argument, but he wasn't ready to delve in too deep. Not yet. "I didn't intend on being here this late."

She smoothed her hand over the side of his face. "What are you talking about?"

"I planned for us to leave the house earlier tonight."

She snorted. "We should have."

"I was thinking the opposite." He watched the firefighters work together on the hoses. "Thanks to being here, we might have saved the place."

"Well, now it's time to work on you."

"That sounds good." Unfortunately his body was willing but not able. He still felt shaky. But in an hour or two, hell yes.

"Nice try, stud." She sat next to him and cuddled into his side. "You've already played the role of hero tonight. Now it's time for me to help you."

He slipped an arm around her shoulders and tried to ignore how much energy that simple move drained from him. "I like the sound of that."

"You know what word is really sexy?" She pulled his oxygen mask back up to cover his nose and mouth. *"Hospital."*

"No." The mask blocked most of the sound of his voice.

"The sooner you get the okay from the doctors, the sooner we can shower and crawl into bed together."

He groaned but didn't protest.

"I told Trevor that would work." She stood up and held a hand out to him. "Time to go."

CHAPTER 22

They got stuck in the emergency room for five hours. The small local hospital was not equipped to handle the influx of people from the Sullivan fire. Doctors were called in. People ran around in a frenzy of activity. Cate thought the word *chaos* fit.

By the fifth hour, she'd grown weary of listening to Damon's grumbling. The man complained nonstop. Like, just keep talking and insisting he was fine. Of course, he managed to ruin that speech several times by falling into a hacking cough that knocked him breathless. She refrained from saying *told you so* but just barely.

But it was kind of hard to be ticked off as she sat on the side of his bed, holding his hand and watching him drift in and out of a fitful sleep. That move on the roof, staying up there too long to make sure she got down without incident, almost cost him everything. She flipped between wanting to hug him and wanting to hit him for being so reckless.

Alarms sounded and the constant beeping echoed in her brain. A curtain partially hid them from the bustle of the room, giving them a bit of privacy. Not enough for her to crawl up on that bed with him, though she thought about it.

The curtain rattled on the bar. Metal screeched against metal as it slipped around and Damon's father stepped into the open space with Trevor right behind him.

Steven's gaze wandered over Damon's still form. He glanced at the beeping machines and focused on the cuff automatically taking his blood pressure. Cate guessed he was trying to gain his composure and she gave him a few seconds to do it. The man had an ego, after all.

He nodded in Damon's direction. "How is he?"

"Ornery and belligerent."

She saw Trevor smile at her answer. He didn't say anything but the tension seemed to run out of him at her comment.

Steven shook his head. "I'm serious."

"Yeah, so was I." She thought about standing up and giving Steven some privacy with his son. Thought then discarded. Exhaustion tugged at her muscles, keeping her right where she was. "But the doctor said his lungs look better than expected. She wants to keep him here for observation, so we're waiting for a bed."

"He agreed to stay overnight?" Trevor asked, sounding as stunned as she felt.

"I didn't exactly give him a choice." She glanced at Steven again. He hadn't moved and his gaze stayed locked on Damon's face. "I promise you, sir. He's okay."

Steven shook his head. "I don't . . . what?"

"The doctor said he's going to be fine." She thought about reaching out for the older man's hand and immediately decided against it. Nothing about him said touchy-feely. He looked like he was stumbling around, not quite his usual in-control self. The decent thing to do would be to comfort him, try to find the right words to make it bearable for him to see one more family member in this position. With more sleep, she hoped they'd come to her.

"We have a few injured here." Steven shook his head. "That fire. Who could have predicted that?"

Everyone? That's the first thought that popped into her head and she almost said it.

"We'll get to the bottom of it," Trevor said as he shot her a look around Steven's shoulder.

His expression promised revenge. After knowing him a short time, she sensed Trevor would not handle an intentional fire being set on his watch very well. Neither would Damon, which was why she didn't balk when the doctor talked about sedating him so he could rest. Keeping him down might be impossible otherwise.

"Faulty wiring." Steven's voice sounded distant, almost hollow.

Trevor's eyebrow rose. "Is that what someone is saying was the cause of this?"

No way. If so it was the most convenient excuse ever. Cate didn't want to be *that* person, but there was a limit to how much coincidence she could accept. "I'm sure we'll know the truth soon."

"An old room with faulty wiring." Steven glanced over his shoulder at Trevor. "I should have warned you before sending you in." Steven shook his head again. "This could have been so much worse."

"As one of the two people trapped in the house when it happened, I'd agree."

Steven's gaze zoomed right back to her. "What are you saying?"

She was trying *not* to say it, hoping he'd come to the conclusion on his own, but he didn't. Now she got why Damon found dealing with his dad so frustrating. It was like a purposeful refusal to see the obvious. She had no idea how anyone could move through life like that.

Steven blinked a few times. It looked as if he were snapping out of the trance he'd fallen into at seeing Damon in the bed. "We lost so much."

"Hmmm?" He could be talking about almost anything, so she kept her response neutral.

"All the documents." Steven looked from her to Trevor as some of the color moved back into his cheeks. "We've lost all those years of paperwork."

Now that would have been convenient . . . for someone. But as luck would have it they had most of what they needed. All day they'd been scanning material with their phones and taking pictures. When Trevor left for his meeting with Wren and Garrett he'd taken the relevant files and notes with him.

No, Steven had opened the door for them to look around and they didn't wait. If someone had been counting on them to take weeks to complete the work, they'd messed up.

"We have what we need." She had no idea if that was true but it sounded good to say it.

Steven frowned. "How can that be?"

"We're going to solve my sister's case." Certainty flowed through her for the first time ever when it came to Shauna. There must have been something in her tone or the words she used, because she had Steven's full attention now. "A fire is not going to stop me."

"It was an accident."

She didn't know how he could believe that. "Which incident are you talking about?"

Steven stared at her for a few seconds. He stood there, tall and unwavering with an unreadable expression on his face. She couldn't tell if that was confusion or concern. Either way, she'd made her point. This was one accident too many. This mirrored the unwanted visits to her house, which she assumed was Vincent from the scent she recognized on him, only this time strayed into much more violent territory. An unseen hand snooping around, cutting off access. Stoking fear without ever being seen.

Well, she would not be scared this time. She wasn't going anywhere. If this was Vincent, he should buckle in for a fight.

"I need to check on some of the others." Without another word, Steven pivoted and left the room.

Trevor watched him go. "That is an odd man."

Understatement.

Cate could think of so many other words that fit, and none of them were all that flattering. "He blocks off reality like no one I've ever seen."

Trevor reached up and grabbed the end of the curtain. He pulled it around tight until they were enclosed in the suffocating private space again. Just the three of them and a bunch of beeping machines. "Which is why I'm convinced Damon is adopted. He's the most practical, look-at-the-facts guy I know."

Cate heard the sound buried under the joke. That tiny tremble in Trevor's voice. The way he picked his comment to joke but there was a depth of concern underlying the words. "He really is going to be okay."

"Of course he is." Trevor rubbed his thumb against the inside of his other palm. "The dumb bastard. I thought I was going to have to drag him off that roof."

She watched the hand gesture, hypnotized. She didn't remember seeing him locked in a nervous gesture since they'd met. He didn't strike her as the type. Neither had Damon, but he insisted he was quite capable of panicking. Well, neither one of them could top her in that department. "He clearly wanted attention."

Trevor smiled, clearly happy to play along. "It's obvious, right?"

"Both of you shut up."

Cate almost jumped off the bed at the sound of Damon's gravelly voice.

"Sleeping Beauty awakens," Trevor said.

"Were you awake this whole time?" It wouldn't surprise her but it might make her grumpy. Hiding in bed and making her deal with his father was the kind of thing he would get away with exactly one time. Next round, he was up.

"I drifted in and out." He grimaced as he pulled the sheets up higher on his body. "The smell in here bugs me."

Trevor shook his head. "Because things smell clean?"

Damon's eyes popped open. "Shouldn't you be up-dating Garrett and Wren?"

"Do you know what it took to keep them from rushing in here?" Trevor snorted. "Be forewarned, they want you out." He shot her a side look. "Both of you. As far as they're concerned, your fake relationship has flamed out without a proposal."

She understood and appreciated the concern but she wasn't here on vacation. She knew from the beginning the trip carried risks. Serious risks. She'd lost her sister here, so she was completely clear on what Sullivan followers were capable of, though she had to admit they were more obvious in their attacks than she'd expected.

"But we feel close." Right at the edge of something big. "Isn't that why someone really set the fire?"

Trevor sighed at her. "We don't want you to be a target, Cate. The idea is to limit the risk to you, not actively invite more."

"I came here expecting trouble." More like being kicked off the property than burned out of a building, but the point was she knew there were risks and took them.

Trevor threw up his hands. "You're as stubborn as he is."

"She's worse." Damon looked at her then. "You know the proper authorities are going to come back with a bogus faulty wiring story. They'll back Dad up. Talk about how the room has been closed off and something sparked."

She hated that he was right. This one time, she wanted him to assess something the wrong way and misstep. But she knew the truth. The whole incident, the loss of property and potential loss of lives, was going to disappear in a pile of paperwork.

"Total bullshit." Trevor crossed his arms in front of him. "It's interesting though."

Damon shook his head as the blood pressure cuff started to automatically clamp down on his arm again. "No part of this trip has been interesting."

She had to agree with that . . . well, almost. "Except meeting me."

Damon winked at her. "That goes without saying."

"The fire wasn't set outside the library. We already have photos from the house including from the air," Trevor said, picking up the conversation again.

"Someone snuck in and took them in the dark?"

Trevor waved off the concern. "Wren wouldn't let a little thing like nighttime beat him. But my point is if someone really wanted to burn you two out it would have been easy. This was aimed at a room you weren't actually in."

"My guess is someone thought it would take us a long time to look through the paperwork, days probably, but then realized you were moving fast." Damon made a grumbling sound. "That's what you get for skipping meals, by the way."

She decided to ignore the newest round of whining. More than likely she'd have to listen to more back at the cabin tomorrow. Damon might reluctantly agree under pressure to stay until morning. That didn't mean he'd be quiet about it or concede to staying much past sunrise. "The good news is you can ignore a few of your lists of potential suspects . . . although I guess they're still witnesses."

Trevor frowned at her. "Meaning?"

Before she could answer, Damon jumped in. "Not to sound ungrateful for the rescue assist, but Roger and Vincent sure got there fast."

"Right." Trevor nodded. "I'll ask around, figure out where they were all day and try again to get a close-up view of their cabins. I failed the last time because someone was always around, but I'll do it this time. See if I can find anything."

Damon whistled. "Dangerous."

"But necessary," Trevor said. "We can't have people going around burning down buildings with people in them."

"Even if it's not them or one of their crowd, the person we're looking for has to be at Sullivan, not some former student or professor living far away. The property is still locked-down. Only us and people with access have gotten in. So, unless you've seen someone new wandering around, we have a finite pool of suspects." Her mind went to the one person she didn't see through the smoke and yelling. "Speaking of which, where was Liza?"

"Working with Damon's dad." When Cate started to ask questions, Trevor held up a hand. "I checked, so yes, we believe her."

That's not the answer she wanted but she guessed it was good for them to disqualify people as the killer as well. "So, nothing has changed. The rule here is simple—don't believe anyone associated with Sullivan."

Trevor smiled at Damon. "Including you?"

Cate answered a different question. The one about how dangerous Damon was to her on a very different level. "Especially him."

DAMON HAD BEEN out of the hospital for a day. Even being inside that amount of time had been too long inside for his taste. He hated being confined. He didn't do all that well with being told what to do either. But this he could do without complaint or trouble.

"Yes . . ."

Cate's rough voice, all deep and hot, skated across his nerves. She was begging now, which meant she was almost ready. Almost.

He lowered his head again, licking her, opening her with two fingers as she squirmed on the bed. He'd been wanting to touch her like this from the beginning. So many times she'd taken the lead . . . and he loved it.

This afternoon, he was in charge.

He'd waited until they arrived back at the cabin to say a word. He'd let her think he was tired. He'd even mentioned taking a bath. He figured the last time he'd done that had been twenty years ago. He was an in and out guy, except when it came to her. He wanted to savor her and right now he was.

Her back arched off the bed and her hands slipped into his hair. She was close now. After an hour of foreplay, touching and tasting her, she hovered on the brink. He'd spun her up then brought her back down several times now. Now her body begged for completion.

"Damon, finish this!"

She'd moved from begging to ordering. He liked the change.

Her legs dropped open even wider, giving him all the access he needed. Those hands guided his face closer to the very heat of her. His tongue never stopped working. It brushed over her, circled her. With each swipe her breathing grew more labored.

Her hand tugged against the back of his head,

bringing him in closer. Those fingernails dug into his hair, his shoulders—anywhere they touched. She made a satisfied sound, half sigh and half huff as she touched him.

He could feel her leg muscles tremble as control slipped away from her. That was just the sexiest thing ever.

With one last pump of his finger, one final circle over the spot guaranteed to make her body buck, her body let go. Her chest heaved from the force of her harsh breaths. Her hands slipped out of his hair to grab on to the sheets for leverage.

As he watched, the orgasm chased and overtook her. Her skin flushed and those thighs clamped harder against the side of his head. Then she went boneless. Her heels slid against the sheets until her legs lay flat.

The whole scene, from beginning to end, fascinated him. The way she handed over control of her body. How much she enjoyed being touched. Half the time he let her guide him because she knew what her body needed more than he did.

With his erection thumping and his jeans suddenly too hot and tight thanks to the constricted space in there, he rolled to his side. Didn't go far, but leaned up on an elbow and stared down at her. Those dark eyes remained closed until he leaned down and placed a chaste kiss on her forehead then her mouth and finally her chin.

"You have to be exhausted and . . ." She dropped

her hand and swept the back of it over his length. "Ah, yes. Not all of you."

His body jumped in response to her soft touch. It happened then was gone. He seriously considered begging her to continue.

"I take it back." The way she threw her arm over her closed eyes made the statement even more dramatic.

"What are we talking about?"

"You can be trusted." She lifted her arm and peeked up at him. "To do this. You are *really* impressive at this."

He would have laughed if he weren't rock hard and afraid of exploding. "I have other skills."

"I should see those to make sure."

"I thought maybe you'd be willing to show off a few of your own first."

A sly smile crept across her face as her hand skimmed down his chest. "You should tell me exactly what you need." She turned over and kept moving until one of her legs rested across his. "Don't leave anything out."

His stomach flipped. "Maybe I'll whisper."

She slid the whole way on top of him then. Her mouth hovered over his. "Talk slowly and use very naughty words."

"You might be the perfect woman." And he meant that. Every word she uttered struck right at the heart of what he wanted.

She kissed him then. "Say that again."

CHAPTER 23

Cate met Trevor at the gun range as planned. Suddenly it was very important to him that she be ready and able to fire a weapon to his satisfaction. Her assurance that she'd taken safety classes was met with a heavy dose of disdain. Clearly, Trevor thought only he could teach this skill, or that she should pass his test first. After a night locked in Damon's arms, with him proving he was very healthy, thank you, she was too exhausted to argue.

Damon's reaction to her need to be prepared mirrored Trevor's. He wanted to be here for the lesson but he had a series of informal meetings with some of the workers who had been on staff when Shauna died. He decided to play it as a long-time-no-see check-in. Informal then go from there. Neither Trevor nor Cate could pull that off, which meant Trevor had babysitting duty. They were smart enough not to call it that, but she knew.

In some ways, it was sweet. They worried. But they could calm down because she wasn't a martyr. They possessed the training. She didn't. If they said to run, she was going to bolt. The only reason she dragged her feet on leaving Sullivan completely was she now knew there was something here to find. Once gone, Steven would never let her back in. Never be this accommodating. This counted as her one—and she expected only—chance.

Problem was, the fire had her shaky. Seeing Damon, so strong and always in control, brought down by the smoke was a wake-up call. These men might be lethal but they weren't immune to the awful things that could happen. She had far less training, which made her even more vulnerable.

She spied Trevor in the tent with an open gun case in front of him. She approached, but not until she made sure he saw her. No need for worries about friendly fire today.

After a quick look around, she noted that they were alone. People usually lined up for practice. She guessed he used some sort of enticement to work on these private lessons. Could be he just invoked Steven's name. Everyone seemed to scurry when he gave an order.

Trevor looked up and smiled. "How's the patient?"

That wasn't the topic she expected. "What?"

"Damon." Trevor's eyebrow lifted. "The guy you're sleeping with."

She was not the type to advertise her private life. The word *private* had a meaning, after all, and she believed in using it. Having her love life broadcasted around Sullivan proved to be an odd sensation. Not totally unwelcome because she found she liked the idea of being linked to him on a personal level. Maybe too much.

Damon took it all in stride, so could she. But the idea of a no-strings arrangement of sorts no longer felt right to her. At some point they had crossed over. The question was how far and how long before Damon panicked.

But Trevor asked about her favorite topic. Too bad he was not being her favorite today. "Fine. And by that I mean he kept insisting we're all overreacting, he never lost control on that roof and that it's perfectly normal to fall down when you try to pick up a hose."

"Sounds like you've had quite the morning with him."

That smile made her wary. Trevor tended to wear that one right before he launched into something borderline inappropriate. "Aren't you chatty today? Did you find anything on Roger or Vincent?"

"Still looking, and nice try at throwing me off topic."

The tactic tended to work for Damon, but clearly not for her. She admitted defeat. "It was worth a shot."

"As if it's hard to tell what's happening between you two." Trevor pulled out a gun and held it. Checked the chamber then did it again.

Yeah, there it was. Trevor wanted to talk relationships but he was pretending otherwise. That stood in sharp contrast to Damon who had never even confirmed they were in a relationship. For all she knew he considered her a pal and thought the sex, the sleeping together every night, meant nothing.

"It's a fake relationship." It actually scratched her throat a bit to say the words this time.

Trevor kept working with the weapon. Handled it like the pro he was. "Is that still the case?"

Good freaking question. Not that she was ready to admit that to him.

"You're kind of nosy. Is this a new thing?" She felt like she should have had a warning about that if so.

Next, he removed the Glock and put that on the table next to the other gun he'd pulled out. "I make it my business to check on Damon."

That sounded serious. As if they were headed for the kind of talk that would have both of them squirming. "He must hate that."

"As if he knows. Please." Trevor snorted as he grabbed the separate boxes of bullets. "I am way more subtle than that."

"That is not a word I would use to describe you." In many ways he reminded her of Damon. In some very significant ways, he didn't. They handled problems differently. Trevor avoided the gruff side of the personality that Damon sometimes showed. Those blips in his temper. So far, she'd only seen Trevor as calm.

"Aaron says that, too." Trevor scoffed as if everyone else was the problem. "None of you understand me."

"Uh-huh." But that brought her back to a topic that had been filling her brain. "Does Aaron know you're here?"

Trevor frowned. "On the shooting range?"

"In Pennsylvania. On this assignment."

"Ah, yes. Of course."

Of course. As if he would never keep a secret from the man he was in love with. She had to wonder if that was really true. "There's no top secret, need-to-know thing happening with this assignment?"

Trevor kept up the fiddling with the weapons and bullets. "I think you're watching too much television."

"I'm just wondering if . . ." How did she ask something so personal? She wanted to know how they managed their relationship. How much truth and trust was involved? Things that were totally not her business.

She had reasons to ask, sure. She'd started sleeping with Damon without thinking any of this through. The danger and worry. But now she felt it. That meant it would always be there but would likely be so much more intense if he were away from her.

She didn't even know if she was supposed to slip into some new role. She also wondered if whatever they had would immediately snap off the second they resolved Shauna's case.

Trevor stood there with wide eyes and a bit of amusement on his face. "What are you trying to ask?"

He had to be making this hard on purpose. "You know."

"I actually don't."

Fine. "Seeing someone who does your type of work—"

"Seeing?"

"Come on. You are purposely making this conversation difficult."

He laughed. "Now I am, yes."

She thought about aiming one of the many empty weapons sitting around at him. Just because. "Want to tell me why?"

The amusement faded from Trevor's face. He leaned against the table with his feet stretched out in front of him. "Damon has been dealt a shitty hand. So many things happened to him that were out of his control. And being locked up? That's the ultimate shitty hand."

She agreed. They saw him the same way. As someone who got roped into a lot of other people's messes. But none of that explained why they were engaged in verbal somersaults. "So? Or if you prefer, therefore . . . ?"

"He doesn't open up, Cate. He lives alone, limits his social life and insists that's all he gets. All he deserves." Trevor glanced down at his hands before looking up again. "That's the part that's always frustrated me. Here we are, the five of us plus Garrett now, all with our varied difficult backgrounds, but Damon thinks he's the only one who hasn't earned any sort of calm."

Something in his tone caught her attention. She knew about Quint and the five friends. Not enough, but some. The men meant everything to Damon. He'd made that much clear. In many ways, they rescued him. But for the first time she thought about how they'd all needed support. That while Damon was getting help, he was helping right back. Something he seemed to be convinced he was incapable of doing these days. "Was it that bad for all of you?"

"You don't end up desperate and on the verge of destruction without something life-defining happening to you." Trevor rubbed his palm with the thumb from his other hand in what was starting to look like his nervous gesture. "But that's the point. We'd all been through the worst but only he decided he hadn't paid enough. Sure, we were all self-destructive but for Damon it wasn't even that. The penance never stops. He thinks he needs to pay forever. That he doesn't get real happiness."

This was another way of talking about Damon's view that he was an island. That no one could get in. All of these issues led her to the same place. But Trevor's tone, fair but concerned, took her to a different question. "Are you worried I'm going to hurt him?"

Trevor's hands dropped to his sides. "I'm stunned he's giving you the chance to potentially do that."

The words moved through her, leaving a warm sensation behind. With all the talk of shutting down, he'd actually opened up to her. She ran through the family stories and tiny pieces he'd dropped. Then it hit her. He talked about not letting anyone in, but she was already there.

Trevor shook his head but he looked the exact opposite of upset. "You should see your face."

She tried to swallow her smile. "What?"

"You like it."

Why fight it? He knew. She knew. Heck, Damon probably knew. "That I might matter to him? Yeah, Trevor. That doesn't suck."

"Now that *is* interesting."

These guys and their cryptic talk. It annoyed her even as it kept her guessing. "What?"

"That you want to matter. What with you being a *fake* girlfriend and all."

She started to say something when she heard a sharp ping. This part of the property was more secluded. No one lived over here. They kept it roped off for safety purposes. Even the weapons and ammunition supply lockers stayed locked up . . . supposedly.

When she heard the second ping, she grabbed Trevor's arm, catching him off balance and dragging him down to the ground with her. She waited for the hard ground to smash into her face but it never happened. When she opened her eyes, the world spun around her. Through some tricky maneuver of his, she'd landed on him. Now he shifted her underneath him. Every step, using his body as a shield without thinking twice.

His voice dropped to a whisper. "Now that we're down here, can you answer one question—why?"

She strained to hear something. Except for a light wind that rustled the leaves of the trees, she couldn't pick up anything. "I thought . . ."

He stared down at her from their tangle on the floor. She finally kicked the word out. "Shot."

"We're on a shooting range."

She hated that he sounded so logical while her voice bobbled and her stomach twirled. "Alone."

He frowned. "Someone taking a shot at you out in the open would be a pretty bold move."

He was right. Coming under fire here, now, didn't make sense. "I really thought someone was shooting at us."

His eyes narrowed for a second before he nodded. "Then let's be careful."

He slid his hand along the edge of the table and grabbed the gun. She didn't see what type it was. He brought it down to his lap and pocketed it. He loaded it while he watched their surroundings. He didn't move but his gaze kept shifting.

The woods were quiet. No gunfire or approaching footsteps. She instinctively knew that didn't mean anything. Someone could lie in wait out there, but she was beginning to doubt her hearing.

"I'm getting sick of feeling so vulnerable." She hadn't meant to say the words out loud. Before she could explain, a whistle sounded and she spun around to find the source. Without thinking, she reached for the other gun Trevor had set out.

He caught her hand right before it touched the metal. "We're okay."

She felt like a deer standing on the highway in the middle of rush hour traffic. "What are you talking about?"

"That's Damon."

They recognized each other by whistle? Well, of

course they did. They had skills and secret calls she
didn't even understand, including this one.

The rustling started again. Ten feet away from the
sound she spotted a blur of blue. That's when she figured out the sound was some sort of subterfuge. Trevor
didn't panic or take aim as the streak ran across to
them. The loud footsteps came first then his face, that
amazing face, came into view.

He ducked down at the last moment, bringing his
body even with theirs on the ground as he slid. He
knocked into the side of her but not hard. An arm
wrapped around her as he nodded to Trevor. That
touch, almost nothing compared to all the others,
calmed her. Some of the tension eased out of her neck
and the tumbling sensation in her stomach stopped.

"What exactly are we doing?" Damon asked without taking his gaze away from the green field in front
of him.

"Honestly?" Trevor winced. "Nothing."

She bit her bottom lip, trying to separate out the
panic screaming in her head from the reality in front
of her. "I thought someone shot at us, but it's pretty
clear I was wrong."

Damon blew out a long breath. "For the record, that
is not the way I intended to spend my Tuesday."

Trevor frowned. "I thought it was Thursday."

"Whatever." Damon leaned in closer to her. "You
okay?"

"Spooked." There was no other word to describe it.
She sat crouched on a cement pad outside a shooting

range on what was, in effect, a large estate. This was not an everyday occurrence for her.

"That's the right response," Damon said.

It didn't feel right. Her eyesight blurred and she was pretty sure if she opened her mouth too wide her heart would pound right out of there. "I wish I were like you."

"Annoying?" Trevor asked from over to their side.

"The whole thing where you don't feel anything." Even though she didn't believe it, she'd love to adopt that skill right now.

Trevor laughed as he looked at Damon. "Are you not feeling anything right now? Because, honestly, you look ready to wet yourself."

"You're lucky you were helpful today," Damon shot back. "Since we're sitting around waiting to possibly get shot at, probably for no reason, go ahead and tell us what you're hearing from the regulars."

"The gossip is still about you being Steven's son." Trevor shook his head and continued to look amused. "Then there's the other thing."

"Is this about me?" Because she was already sick of being gossip fodder.

"That you two are sleeping together. That's not gossip. People totally buy the fake relationship cover . . . if that's what we're still calling it." Trevor shook his head. "No, some folks think Damon started the fire. Getting back at Daddy and all that."

Damon lowered his gun and stared at Trevor. "I'm not ten."

Trevor snorted. "The response to that is too easy."

As much as she enjoyed the boy banter, and right now she really didn't, she wanted to leave this area. "I know you two think I'm hearing things."

"This is a shooting range," Damon said, basically repeating Trevor's response to her.

They both missed the most obvious point. "We're the only ones here and I don't think Trevor tried to shoot me."

Damon frowned at her. "The other range."

She froze. "What?"

"This is the lower range." Damon spoke slowly, as if he sensed she was too far gone to understand him otherwise. "There's a smaller off to the left of this one."

Well, that was annoying. But since she was the one who had them all ducking and hiding, she couldn't exactly fight with Damon on this point.

Trevor glanced at his watch again. "It's been seven minutes and no other noises, so I think we're clear." Without another word, Trevor stood up and the world remained quiet. "Seems like we might be okay."

She stood up next to him then with Trevor in front of her and Damon behind her. They'd flipped into protection mode. She'd overreacted or heard something and assumed it was something else. "I'm sorry."

Damon brushed his hand down her arm. "Never apologize for being safe."

"It's hard to make out sounds with all the echoing." Trevor shrugged. "It's no big deal."

Funny, but it felt like a big deal. She'd taken on their paranoia and she had no idea what to do about that.

CATE WALKED AROUND freely now, but Damon still hadn't regained his ability to swallow. They still hung around the ranges and he couldn't help but feel like a target. "This is getting out of hand."

Shootings, fire, break-in. There was only so much they could take. Every time he thought they had Cate safe, something new unraveled.

"It's about to stop," Trevor said.

"What do you mean?"

"You've been summoned. I think the fire was the last straw for our boss." Trevor waved to Roger and a few of the people with him. "Your old motel room in twenty minutes for a private chat with Garrett."

Reckoning. There was no other way to describe it. Damon knew once he added in the part about the shooting this morning Wren would lose it. He hated putting people in danger. He really hated doing that to an untrained civilian.

"You told them we're fine, right?" Not that it would make a difference. Damon sensed Wren's patience was at the end.

Trevor shook his head. "Sorry, but I'm with them on this one. The attacks have veered from amateur to more targeted and planned out."

"Which means we're close to figuring out the truth." Damon knew he sounded like Cate now.

Speaking of her, he looked around. Made sure he saw her. He couldn't let her wander away.

"Cate is not a professional. There are a lot of innocent people here." Trevor unloaded the weapons and returned them to their cases. "I get the idea of drawing the person out but we need to find another way."

He was right. Hell, Damon had thought the very same thing himself this morning. "So, I've got to go listen to this lecture from Garrett now?"

"Have fun."

Damon started to walk away, then stopped. "And, um—"

"I'll watch her."

DAMON DIDN'T EVEN have a chance to close the door to his motel room before Garrett started talking. "We're done here. It's time to pack up this assignment and move on."

"No." It was a knee-jerk reaction to being ordered to do something. Driving over, he'd decided they needed a sensible draw-out plan that maximized information and intel. Now he was fighting back and he didn't know why. Not really.

"It's not a request." Garrett held a take-out coffee cup and played with the edge of the lid, popping it off then pressing it back down again. "We need to handle this another way. Trevor will plant cameras and work on getting some visuals from outside as well."

"It doesn't matter because as soon as Cate and I

leave, the issues will stop." That's the one thing he felt pretty certain of. The town, the school, had been quiet for years. Then he burst in, pretending to be someone else, and they'd been fighting a menace ever since. But part of him thought the anger, what had this person ticked off, was Cate coming to town. The targeting was too personal for it not to be the problem.

"This whole case began because someone was getting into her house and messing around."

Garrett wasn't wrong often, but he was now. "No, it started because someone killed her sister."

"You're using that word now?"

Damon knew that was the only answer. "Seems obvious."

Garrett nodded. "Wren thinks so, too."

But they had another problem. One who didn't work for Wren or much like taking orders. "She's determined. I'm trying to keep her safe but it's getting harder." *Impossible* was the word he was looking for.

"You still have perspective when it comes to her?"

Damon glanced around the room and saw signs of her everywhere. The sweatshirt she liked to wear at night. They'd somehow missed that when they left to stay at Sullivan. Her handwriting on a note about food, a note he kept for some reason. "Meaning?"

"You're dealing with messed-up family stuff. You're sleeping with her. There's no way to keep it all separate and clean."

Suddenly everyone wanted to talk about his past. He'd gone years without them interfering with who he dated. Now everyone seemed to have an opinion. "Was there an office memo I missed about my private life?"

Garrett frowned, with most of his usual charm in hiding. "The violence isn't going to stop. It's going to increase, ratchet up."

"I know." Because that's how these things worked. Damon had been around long enough, seen enough.

"So . . . ?"

"I'll get her out." That was the only answer left.

"You don't really have a choice. I'm not kidding, Damon. Make it happen."

Easy for him to say. He was happy and in love and thought that meant he had some unique perspective. But Cate was uniquely Cate. "You don't know her like I do."

Garrett looked around and leaned in, as if he were going to share some top secret intel. "Want some female advice?"

Damon almost laughed at the seriousness in his tone. "From you?"

"I'm a married man now."

"You've been married for like ten seconds." When Garrett frowned at him, Damon relented. "Fine, go ahead."

"Don't fuck this up."

That's all he said. A simple sentence that would get him gut punched if he tried to use it on Cate. "How is that helpful?"

Garrett winked at him. "It is. You just don't know it yet."

CHAPTER 24

ate walked around the outside of the burned-out shell that was once the side of the Sullivan family home. Around safety cones and caution tape. Through puddles created by the force of the hoses.

The fire had started in the old locked office, as suspected. It licked and burned its way up the hall, barreling through wood and walls that had survived for more than a hundred years. Now a layer of black soot stained every surface that wasn't charred. The floors, weakened by the flames, bore holes and cracked if you walked close to the fragile edges.

Glancing to her right she watched Trevor roam around the backyard while he talked on the phone with one of Wren's people, a forensic expert specializing in arson cases. In an earlier call, Wren told him that those in charge in Salvation kept mentioning the faulty wiring but the photos Trevor snuck in and took looked more like arson. The localized burning and pour patterns suggested someone used an accelerant to get the job done faster and leave nothing behind.

The answer seemed obvious to Cate. She got too

close and someone literally tried to burn it all down. She tried to imagine Steven torching his own house, the last place that held memories of the family he'd lost. The answer didn't make sense to her, but then desperate people often did unimaginable things.

She heard the sound of footsteps near the now broken and fire-scarred stairs to the front of the house and spun around expecting to see Damon. His father stood on the edge of the grass, feet away from the shell of a porch.

"Have you seen my son?" His voice sounded flat and emotionless.

The tone matched his slumped shoulders. For a man who usually dressed like he was born to work on a college campus, today he looked disheveled. There was a coffee stain on his blue button-down shirt and his hair stuck up in places, like from his fingers running through it.

Every detail seemed just slightly off. She tried to remember if he'd referred to Damon as "son" since they got here. If he referred to Damon at all.

"He had to run an errand." A quick trip to see Garrett. She expected a full press from all of the men helping out on the case when Damon returned. She could feel her time here ticking down.

Steven's eyebrows snapped together. "He left you here?"

She couldn't tell if he meant he wanted her out or if he worried for her safety. More than likely he didn't know. She couldn't blame him for not being a fan.

Since she arrived, there had been a shooting, attacks and now a fire. Even she was starting to view her presence as a curse.

"Is there a problem with my continuing to stay here?" Not that she could do much about that until Damon got back.

"Of course not. But you're not going to find what you need." He passed by her on the way to what was left of the front porch. His body lurched and his balance faltered when he lifted his leg then put it down without stepping up.

Pity bubbled up inside her but she squashed it down. He might be all stooped-shouldered, sad and lost now, but he'd made choices in the past that sent him down this path. "What if I told you I already did?"

He turned to stare at her. "You mean my son?"

Damon was a man worth finding but he wasn't a consolation prize.

She stood slightly behind Steven, forcing him to turn to face her. "I'm here about my sister."

"But you're with my son."

She glanced back to the yard and saw Trevor staring at her. She treated him to a short wave to let him know all was well. "I am."

"Is the plan to use him to get to me?"

Her gaze drifted back to Steven. If he wanted to offend her, it didn't work. What she felt for Damon was tumbled up and confused in her head, but real. She hadn't planned for him and couldn't figure out where he fit in her life. She just knew he did . . . and that he probably hadn't figured that out yet.

"If so, you should know it will only work one way." Steven shook his head. "I won't let you use him, but he won't care if you use me."

She wondered for what felt like the hundredth time how a man with his IQ could be so terrible at reading people. At loving them.

"Are you saying you'll protect him?" She hoped so because he deserved that.

"I already have."

She froze. "What?"

"That political clout he hates so much, the fact I knew powerful people back then who assisted the school . . ." Steven backed away from the house, giving it one last longing look before continuing. "Why do you think he's not in prison now?"

That quick, the calm in her head disappeared. A churning anxiety bounced around in her stomach as she tried to think a few moves ahead and figure out where he was going with this. "He was a kid."

"Twenty. An adult under the law."

The words cut into her. He wasn't guessing. He knew. "But the whole shoot-out was messed up, maneuvered by your brother."

"The man you know as Damon still shot an FBI agent."

He sounded so matter-of-fact, as if he were reading from a fact pattern involving a stranger. She had no idea how he compartmentalized and cut up the pieces of his life that way, or why he would want to. The Sullivan men really did hold on to the dead-inside argument no matter what.

"He was in the middle of a chaotic situation. No one could have been expected to know what was happening." She hadn't looked up the facts because she trusted the ones he told her. She'd watched the emotions pass over his face as he described the events of that day. She could feel the pain thumping inside him at the idea he was responsible for a man's death.

"The man he killed wore a jacket with FBI stamped on it." Steven folded his arms across his chest as he glanced down at his shoes. "Nearly everyone else heard him introduce himself on the megaphone."

Bile rushed up the back of her throat. She breathed in deep, trying to center her body. "Are you saying your son was guilty and got lucky?"

His head shot up and he faced her. "We both know he shouldn't have gone to prison. There were too many variables and all of them combined to set him up for this awful situation." He started shaking his head as the warm wind blew over the property, kicking ashes into the air. "But under the law, he was guilty. The excuses might have lessened his sentence but there is no denying he pulled the trigger."

The words clinked in her brain. The trigger . . . she didn't want to imagine a younger version of Damon, cocky on the outside but confused and turned around inside, shooting in panic.

No, that's not what happened. He didn't lose control or mishear. He was under siege. "He shot in self-defense."

"I pulled every string I could to make sure that was the answer that stuck." Steven tightened his arms around his chest. "*I* did that for him because he's my son."

And he possessed that type of power back then. He could make questions disappear. Make people stop asking them. "You realize you're basically saying you have the connections to make crimes go away, which is exactly what I think you did to my sister."

"They called her Sunshine." Steven's arms dropped to his sides. "Her friends did, I mean."

Her gaze shot to Trevor again. She didn't want him to walk in on this because she didn't want Steven to stop talking. Then she looked back to him. "You remember Shauna?"

"As I do every person who passed through here. I made it a point to know them all because the school was important to me and if they were here I assumed it mattered to them, too." He smiled as he kicked a loose piece of sod under his foot. "She had this dream about setting up a food co-op."

A food . . . Why hadn't *she* known that until she arrived here? "Stop."

This time, he dropped his head back and let the sun beat down on his face. He wore a small smile as he spoke, one of affection. Almost fatherly love and respect. "She talked about not having enough food growing up and coming up with ways for the kids to help out then take food home on the weekends because that's when things were tight. Away from the school lunches."

Cate knew. Every kid without enough to eat knew. The beginning of the month was okay. The middle was filled with the same two dinners—pasta and peanut butter and jelly. The end was a scramble to find anything.

"Why are you telling me this?" she asked.

He dropped his head forward and looked at her again. "I didn't have anything to do with your sister's death."

"I want to believe you." Cate ached to believe it.

"Do it, because while you're focusing on me, the person who killed her—and I now believe someone did—just tried to burn my house down."

He walked up to the house then. Hesitated by the porch but stepped up after a few seconds of delay. As she watched, he skipped the front door and headed for one on the side, away from the fire.

He shouldn't have been at the house. The investigation continued and the building's structure and safety were still questions. But she needed a minute, so he would have to save himself.

With one last glance at Trevor she walked back toward the front of the house. She'd circle one more time. Walk off some of the energy racing through her as Trevor finished up his call. Damon would be back soon and she'd talk all this through with him, but reality was, she was no longer convinced Steven had anything to do with her sister's death, except for his failure to protect her.

The idea of her finding guns or something else on the property that she shouldn't have still held a lot of merit. Cate couldn't think of much else that would have gotten her sister climbing up the side of the water tower. But nothing obvious stuck out to her. By all reports she'd been happy here until the one day she wasn't.

Cate walked in circles, letting the warm sun hit the back of her neck. The damp grass squished beneath her sneakers as she walked along the side of the house. This part of the property, opposite of where she stood a few minutes ago, had been spared most of the fire damage. Smoke and water were the main problems here. These issues can be fixed but the undertaking was no joke. Good thing Steven had a commune full of people with skills.

The thought made her smile as she bent down to touch a stray flower that likely had once been in one of the window flower boxes. She heard the footsteps behind her and thought about Trevor and how much he must have hated getting stuck on a call about technical fire details for the last fifteen minutes.

"Did you find out anything new?" When he didn't immediately answer she looked up and saw Trevor's elongated shadow rising from behind her. "Hey?"

She shifted as the shadow moved. Then she smelled it. *That* scent.

Before she could call out, a striking blow knocked her flat. She slammed down to her knees as she struggled to drag in air. Her skull tingled, which had never happened before.

She had one last thought before the bright day went black—not Trevor.

DAMON NOW KNEW what frantic felt like. His heart hammered in time with the pounding in his head. He'd been back at the old house for ten minutes and spent every second of that searching for Cate.

Trevor swore and apologized. He said she'd been right there, talking with Steven. That had to be the answer. His father. Maybe he said something rude and upset her, though that wasn't really his style. But Damon had to hold on to that story because any other option was too damn scary to think about. He couldn't let that into his head.

He rounded the house for the second time and stopped cold. Trevor had crouched down, staring at the grass and rubbing two of his fingers together.

"What is it?" Damon had been around enough to know but he hoped Trevor didn't say the word.

"Blood."

There it was. Hearing it was worse than he'd thought possible. The air rushed out of him and he doubled over. He could hear Trevor scrambling to his feet and the thud of footsteps on the broken porch.

Damon lifted his head. Let the anger wash over him, fuel him as he looked at his father. "Where is she?"

He walked to the edge of the porch. "What are you talking about?"

"I have turned this place upside down." Damon slowly stood up straight again. "Trevor saw you with Cate and now she's missing."

"She probably went for a walk."

"She promised she'd stay here." His fury built with each word. "She's not answering her phone." His back teeth slammed together and he forced the words out through the clenching. "So, I'm asking again."

"I don't—" Steven's words cut off when Damon took out his gun. "Put that down."

He professed to hate weapons yet he'd stockpiled them on the property. Well, he could look at this one until his memory returned. "I am done playing with you, Dad."

Trevor took a step forward. "Damon, not this way."

His father shook his head. "Do it. If that's what you need, just finally do it."

Damon held the gun steady. There were times over the years that embarrassed him, when the rage spilled through him and he didn't see a way out, that this would have made sense. When it wouldn't have mattered if he took the final step and careened over the edge. But now he needed to stay focused for Cate.

"Enough." Trevor put his hand on the top of Damon's gun and slowly lowered it until it aimed at the ground. Then he turned to Steven. "Where is she?"

He stepped off the porch and joined them in the grass. "Tell me what's going on."

"Cate is missing."

Trevor answered and Damon was grateful that he didn't have to say the words again. They sounded too awful to bear.

"We talked about Cate and her sister." His father lifted both of his hands. "That's all."

"I'm not buying it." She wouldn't run off after that. Something had her moving or someone came and grabbed her. But to take her when Trevor stood right there was ballsy. Stupid. Damon searched his mind for the person that fit that description and he came up empty.

"I have opened this property to you. You ran away and still I've done everything I can to help her, a woman I don't even know. A woman who openly threatened me if I didn't turn over information I didn't have." Steven blew out a ragged breath. "I even gave up my house—"

"That." That was it. He moved out and that tipped someone off, or at least scared them enough to make a terrible decision. "Who knew about you temporarily moving out?"

"I'm sure people saw the two of you going in and out."

In one step, Damon was on his father. He had a fistful of shirt and pulled tight. "Answer the question. Give me the details. The specifics. Who knows about the room and the paperwork and that you're sleeping somewhere else?"

Steven shook his head. "I don't know."

"Since he's holding a gun you should make an educated guess," Trevor said, not doing anything to hide the rough edge to his voice.

"It was just . . ." All of the color drained from Steven's face.

Damon let go of the shirt. "Yeah, exactly. You figured it out. Now talk."

"Liza." Steven swallowed a few times. "I needed to fill her in on some of the details so she could get me a cabin to temporarily stay in while you were here."

She hated him, made a face every time he talked. And now she had Cate. "Where is Liza now?"

Trevor pulled his cell out of his back pocket. "Call and get her over here."

"Liza wouldn't hurt Cate." Steven reached for his own phone instead, nearly dropping it twice in his shaking hands, and started pushing buttons. "There's no reason for her to do something like this."

Damon knew that was wrong. "For once in your life, be right."

CHAPTER 25

Cate tasted metal in her mouth. Maybe it was blood? She wasn't sure. She had no idea where she was. She looked around the dark cave-like structure, smelled the dankness and a hint of moldy water, she didn't know what had happened to her either. Not exactly.

The afternoon had been a push and pull of emotions. Listening to Steven Sullivan talk about his form of fatherly love—getting Damon out of prison—had been surreal. The rest was a bit hazy. Standing in the grass and Trevor and then . . . nothing.

Her shoulder ached from laying on it, pressing the fleshy part into a stone tucked underneath her. She struggled to sit up but when she reached out to support her weight, her hands snapped back again. Twist ties or rope. Something bound her, keeping her right there.

Her eyes hadn't adjusted but she did a mental inventory there on her side with the dirt scraping against her face. She moved her ankles in circles, trying to bring the circulation back. Except for the ache at the back of her head, all of her other injuries were old. She almost cried at the idea that she had become a person who had old and new bruises.

With her palm against the dirt floor, she pushed up again. This time her body stopped in a seated position. She strained and squinted as she tried to get her eyes to adjust to the lack of light.

The darkness suggested night but she'd been outside in the sun. It felt like minutes had ticked by as her body bounced around in the back of that truck but maybe it had been hours.

A few more minutes of lonely quiet passed before she heard a heavy noise that sounded like *ca-chunk*. Possibly a lock or something with hydraulics. Very loud no matter what it was. Then light beamed across her lap. She looked up and made out a heavy metal door and a room beyond. An immaculate room with shelves and lockers. A cement floor. Lights and tables. Clipboards tacked to the wall.

That part of the room looked professional. One that was locked and structured. The weapons room. The same one built into the side of the hill near the firing range. It had to be. Nothing else made sense, though this was still pretty mysterious to her.

She'd expected panic to overtake her the second the grogginess started to fade. The danger had ratcheted up and now being out of sight made her position even more precarious. But there was this other side of her. The part that tamped down the whirling in her stomach and tried to gulp in big breaths in an effort to calm down.

She needed to be smart and stay sharp. There were people out there who would help her. And she could kick and shoot. She'd use any advantage and any person who would help her to get out of this. This was not the time to be a hero or a martyr.

She inched her arms apart, trying to get enough room between her wrists to break the tie. She and her friends had spent a whole Friday night once, watching videos on how to escape bindings. They'd flicked their wrists and broken the hard plastic. She hoped she didn't need wine to make it work.

But her attention kept returning to the partially open door. She thought back to who had access. Likely Steven. Maybe Liza. She really couldn't remember anyone talking about it because everyone talked about it. Being prepared and talking firing lessons mattered here. It was one of the reasons she didn't buy the story that this place was all about studying again. She hadn't needed a Glock to get through statistics.

The crunching sound of work boots against a gravelly dirt floor hit her first. Forget the being-calm thing. Anxiety whipped through her until she thought she might throw up. She tried to rock back and forth and breathe out of her mouth. Anything to stay in control for as long as possible.

When no one burst through the door, she leaned forward, trying to spy her attacker. The person had slammed something into her head. She could hardly wait to repay that gift.

"Cate." Roger stepped into the room and closed the door behind him.

Roger, not Vincent. But the scent . . .

Before his face could fully register, the room was plunged back into darkness. Then with a click, lights came on. They hung from the walls at set intervals and were connected by wires.

The vault. The answer came to her. He'd put her in a vault in the weapons room. And now she remembered the main problem . . . it was a locked-down weapons room.

Her gaze went to Roger. He crouched down, balancing on the balls of his feet in front of her. He wore the same expression he'd aimed at her when they first met. There was something open and welcoming about his face. Now she knew that was a big fat lie.

"What's happening?" She wanted to kick him but went with that instead.

His hands dangled in front of him. He held what looked like some sort of electronic keycard.

As he crouched down there, not saying a word, he shook his head. "I ran out of options."

Poor freaking baby. "You're the one behind all of this?"

"No."

Liar. "You hit me over the head at the water tower then pretended to rescue me?" For some reason that infuriated her. "What is wrong with you?"

"Don't blame me for that one." His keycard bounced

as he shifted around in his squatting position. "I was cleaning up someone else's mess."

The answer made no sense. Her mind raced with the possibilities. She tipped from believing him to hating him every two seconds. The only thing she knew for sure was he couldn't afford to let her go now. It would be impossible to call this a mistake and move on. He'd extended his crimes to kidnapping . . . or whatever it might be called. She wasn't a legal expert, but she was no longer calm either. Panic coursed through her as her brain filled with a jumble of thoughts she couldn't grab on to.

"All you had to do was stay away." He let the edge of the keycard drag in the dirt. "You had every chance, were given every hint to go."

"Yeah, well, sorry."

He choked out what sounded like a fake laugh. "You are stubborn. Possibly worse than Damon."

She hated hearing Damon's name come out of this guy's mouth. He'd pretended to be the solid brother, the charming one. That was before he stuffed her into an oversized dirt closest.

"My sister died." She thought she'd point that out since the fear she would be next in his killing spree threatened to swamp her.

"I know, Cate. Trust me," he said in a singsongy voice. "You keep repeating it. You tried to get in here before, demanded information. Then you dragged Damon into this."

"Can you blame me?"

"Yes! I do. Why couldn't you leave it alone?" He stood up and started pacing. "That night was a simple accident."

The word vibrated through her. It was the one everyone used to push her away. Cate feared he used it because he knew the truth about what happened to Shauna and was desperate to cover it up.

"If that were true I wouldn't be sitting in . . ." She glanced around again, grateful for the light. "This is the weapons vault, right?"

"All that matters is you're under my control." His voice took on a heavier edge. His jaw clenched as he went back to walking in the small space.

"Like Shauna was?" It was worth a shot. Maybe he would talk. Maybe he wanted to brag. She couldn't really read him.

He skidded to a halt and looked at her. That reaction told her jumping in like that had him off stride.

"What? No."

She'd always suspected he knew more. Now she guessed he knew everything. "But you were there, right? You heard something or saw something."

Helped to cover something up after.

His steps sped up. It was as if he were locked in some sort of battle in his head. He mumbled as his outer shell crumbled. He went from cool and calm to jumpy. Sweat gathered on his forehead and chest. Guilt, terror, panic—something had him in its grip and refused to let go.

His anxiety touched off hers. It shot through her in

waves now, rolling over her, shoving her stomach to the floor. It was as if her body started to shut down. A case of dizziness had her head spinning. After two assaults in less than two weeks she felt breakable for the first time in her adult life. After years of planning every move to prevent feeling vulnerable, she now wallowed in it.

"At first I thought you two were really different. She was flirty and carefree. Not the type to care about studying all night because she had a test the next day." Roger listed it all out as he walked. "She took things in stride. God, she was fun. And stunning. That dark hair."

Cate waded through all the pieces he'd shared. One stuck out. "And your brother had a thing for her."

"Vincent thought she was pretty. A lot of guys did." Roger waved off that concern. "It wasn't a big deal."

"It was if it made him kill her."

"She . . ." Roger spun around to face her. "No. Wrong. You don't get it. Nothing now relates to her."

She tried to make that make sense in her head and failed. "Explain it to me."

"You need to let the past go."

As if that would ever happen. "Are you saying two people have been after me?"

He snorted. "That's a big ego you have."

She heard it. He evaded. Went right up to the edge then pulled back.

But she was close. She could feel it and kept poking. "Who is your partner in all of this?"

"I don't have one. You've got this all wrong."

The coolness of the cave seeped into her bones. She sat on a cold floor in damp dirt in a place without any air. Her brain rushed to compute the probability of being rescued versus dying here. She didn't like the odds. If she didn't have Damon and Trevor on her side, probably zero percent. With them, she stood a chance.

"Tell me."

When Roger stared at her, she thought she'd see a coldness there but didn't. He was the handsome guy-next-door. Evil didn't ooze out of him. She wouldn't have picked him out of a crowd as the person to worry about. She'd watched true crime shows and been lulled in by the idea of dead eyes. Naïvely, she assumed she would be able to tell when she came up against the person who took her sister's life because of those eyes.

Now she knew better.

"Roger." She leaned forward. "What happened that night?"

"It was an accident."

The word grated across her nerves as much this time as before.

"I believe you." She forced the words out. Asking didn't work and she assumed begging wouldn't either. Maybe giving him a straight chance to clean his conscience would work.

"I thought we were . . ." He shook his head. "Vincent was so upset."

The partial sentences left so much unanswered but a picture started to form in her head. Two brothers with a crush on her sister. Living away from home, having fun. Discovery and making bad decisions. Normal stuff for people just out of their teens, but something went very wrong that night. A sick image of her sister scared and beating back panic that Cate hoped wasn't accurate.

"She kept running that night, all out of control." He pushed the door shut, locking them inside.

"Roger?"

He focused on her then. "Are you going to do the same thing she did?"

She stepped carefully into this rough talk. "What?"

"Run."

DAMON GLARED AT Liza. He didn't care about her campus tours or her big dreams. Right now he didn't even care that she hated him, because she'd made that clear during every discussion they'd ever had. She had intel on Cate and if someone didn't get him to her soon, he was going to rip every building on the property down with his bare hands.

"You have two seconds to tell me where Cate is." He didn't even want to give her that long but Trevor and his father were there and they looked more willing to negotiate if it meant finding Cate. He was much more ruthless. It surged through him now.

Her gaze traveled between the men. "I don't know."

Before Damon could start yelling, his father stepped in front of his assistant. "Liza, this isn't the time. It's not about Damon coming back or the future of Sullivan. Cate could be in danger and I will be very upset if any harm comes to her."

"Why?"

"Because she's my son's girlfriend."

Damon didn't know if that was the right answer, but he didn't care. Apparently, Liza didn't care about much either since she emotionally flatlined at the idea of Cate's life being important enough to save.

"What are we talking about here?" But Damon knew. Liza wore her jealousy over his return like a blanket. She wanted to be the one his father turned to and he was fine with that. He didn't have any intention of staying. He was only back now because of Cate, and look how that turned out.

Right now he wanted to burn it all down. Liza could have it. Have the Sullivan name.

Standing there with her feet shuffling and her gaze bouncing to her feet, she looked delicate. Terrified. It took her a few beats of silence to work up whatever nerve she needed.

She looked up and pulled her shoulders back. "I only wanted to scare her."

The words slashed through Damon. *Scare her.* "When?"

"I . . . I realized the other stuff wasn't working. I begged Vincent to hunt you down and he talked to you at the diner, but that didn't work." She couldn't hold his gaze and switched to looking at his father. "I thought if she was separated from you and scared she'd back down but she just dug in."

Damon didn't know exactly what she was saying, but it didn't sound good. Looking over at Trevor, he saw the same wariness mirrored there that he felt deep inside. His control unraveled the longer this dragged on.

"Liza, listen to me." His father put his hands on Liza's shoulders and pitched his voice low and soothing. "Who has Cate now?"

"Say it." Trevor practically barked out the order.

"The thing with Shauna was an accident. He promised me."

Jesus. She sounded so sincere. Not like she was talking about the killing of one sister then the other.

Damon took a step back. It was the only way he could guarantee he wouldn't shake Liza. There had to be common sense in there somewhere. That she could write Cate off as not being worth worrying about and go about her usual day . . . Damon didn't get that at all.

"Are we talking about Vincent?" Trevor asked.

She shook her head. "Roger."

Damon's stomach dropped. They were talking about a guy he'd known forever. Someone he once considered a friend. And he did something to Shauna. Might have hurt Cate to keep her quiet.

Damon couldn't take it all in.

"You and Roger are together. Dating, right?" his father asked.

"We share the same dream." Liza smiled. "Your dream."

His father shook his head and his voice echoed the confusion in his eyes. "But you hurt Cate."

"I wanted to scare her. The water tower. I mean, I stopped. She was shaken up but fine." Liza made it sound as if that counted for something.

Damon could barely breathe. "That was you?"

"It was supposed to be a warning." She winced. "Then Roger showed up on his way back from the shooting range. He was furious. Said it was too obvious and would only make things worse." She looked at Damon and didn't show one ounce of fear. "Make it more likely you would stick around and ask more questions about Shauna's death."

Damon took a threatening step toward her this time. Trevor caught his arm, but it wouldn't have mattered if he hadn't. Damon didn't care about this woman. He wanted to get to Cate and refused to let anyone stall that process. "You have three seconds to tell me where Roger is."

"Wait." Trevor snapped his fingers. "Forget her. I know the answer. It's the only place no one else can go due to the security protocols, and Steven here doesn't check there."

Then the answer clicked in Damon's head, too. "The weapons room."

CHAPTER 26

Cate sat with her back balanced against the vault wall. She watched Roger pace, keeping him in her sights at all times. She had to because she kept twisting her hands, working the zip tie. Of course, if she got it off that still left her in a windowless locked room without the key.

"What's the plan here?" That's the part she didn't get. People would notice her going missing. She had friends and a life. Heck, even Steven Sullivan would notice something that obvious.

Attacking her meant starting the clock all over again. This would be one more time Sullivan landed at the center of a scandal. With Steven's clout diminished and Damon partnered up with Wren, Sullivan would end this time. She couldn't imagine anyone riding in to save it.

Damon. She thought his name and her mind went to him. The long body, those sexy hands. The scratch of his scruff against her inner thighs. Imagining him soothed her. With that memory she could go back to a point in time where she felt powerful and happy.

She needed that again. With him and far away from Salvation, Pennsylvania.

While she thought about the man who wouldn't leave her head, she tried to get through to the one who wouldn't leave the room. "Roger?"

He rubbed his forehead. "I'm thinking."

No plan. That thought hit her and she was happy she was already sitting. The idea that the kidnapping or any part of this series of attacks had been random or spur-of-the-moment made her want to cry. Her life derailed on a fluke. That's all she was to him. A nuisance he could push aside.

Forget crying. She wanted to punch him.

"Let me go." She debated begging but worried he might like that. She still didn't understand what had derailed him or how far gone he was. A firm request was the right answer, though she doubted that would work either.

He lifted his head and pinned her with a you've-got-to-be-kidding glare. "You blew that."

It had been worth a try, especially since she had more questions. "What did I do to you exactly? We didn't know each other until . . ."

Was it really two weeks? The time spun past her. She'd shared so much with Damon, fell so deep, that it felt like they'd been together for months.

"I told you."

She twisted the plastic back and forth, trying to cause a bend. A bend meant a weakness. She could work with that. "Were you the one in my condo?"

"Huh. Impressive." His expression matched the awe in his voice. "How did you figure that out?"

"I recognize the scent you're wearing."

"See, I knew it." He actually smiled. "Liza told me she didn't like it, that it lingered, so I gave it to Vincent then took it back. She was right."

"You were setting him up? Had him wear it to throw me off?"

Roger's mood sobered. "I wouldn't do that to my own brother."

"Because you're so honorable and all."

"That was a friend who works in the computer lab who owed me a favor." Roger leaned against the wall right across from her. "You'd picked up the pressure on Shauna's investigation. I needed to know if you had learned anything. He had the talent to know where to look."

The reason he needed to know more could not be more clear. Because he killed Shauna.

Since he'd started sharing she tried again. "Was the water tower you?"

"Liza." He shook his head. "That wasn't part of the plan."

It made her sick to think of her life reduced to that level. A part of a plan. Part of *their* plan, because she now knew there were two of them. "Was I in the wrong place at the wrong time?"

"She panicked. She worried Damon was using you as an excuse and that he really was back to claim his birthright." Roger leaned his head back against the rock. "She felt like she needed to scare you off and keep him away. Damon taking over would have ruined all of it."

"She was wrong about everything." That floored Cate. All of the fear and danger over nothing. "Damon isn't claiming any birthright."

Roger shrugged. "Maybe not now, but possibly in the future."

When he turned she got a good look at Roger. At the gun he carried. She wasn't sure where the keycard had disappeared to but one option had opened up— trying to get the weapon away from him. She decided to use that as her last resort.

"You were in the way. I mean, going through the files at the house? What the fuck was that? Steven and his son were estranged for years but suddenly they were working together? Even I started to buy Liza's birthright theory." Roger slipped his gun out. He held it, didn't wave it. Didn't aim it either. But it was in his hand and he knew how to use it. "I couldn't have you finding something or have Shauna's death trace back to me."

"You burned the house down."

"You're damn right I did."

He stared at her and this time she saw it—dead eyes.

TREVOR INSISTED THEY grab Vincent and drag him along. That turned out to be a good plan because the one other person who might get Roger to open the weapons room was Vincent. He didn't have an updated keycard, because Roger didn't share those, but he had an older one and Trevor was convinced he could make it work.

As far as a security system went, Damon wasn't impressed. But his father did have the entire Sullivan computer team working with Trevor on opening the door. Most of them from a remote location, which meant getting around Roger's vault. The brothers ran it, handled it and apparently treated it as their personal property.

And Damon had to get in there. He'd claw his way in if he had to.

"I'm telling you he wouldn't hurt Shauna or Cate. This is a mistake," Vincent said for the third time.

They stood twenty feet from the vault. They could probably stand in front of it and shout. It was supposed to produce a soundproof seal when closed. He planned on asking his father why something like that would ever be needed. Maybe it would open his eyes to the overuse of guns here.

Trevor had Vincent pushed against the wall. He held out his hand. "Give me the keycard."

"I don't—"

Enough of this shit. "I'm not playing, Vincent." The guys were a minute away from having a knock-down fight. Adrenaline soared through Damon. He'd be happy to burn off the excess right now.

"He has killed before," Trevor pointed out.

Vincent shook his head. "It wasn't like that. Fourteen years ago was a mistake. He's not really a killer."

At that moment Damon felt raw and lean. Like he could take anyone. He could survive being accused and confined. And he would if that's what it took to end this.

"You think I won't go to prison again?" Damon shoved Vincent against the wall and held him there with a hand on his chest. "See, she's one of the only people I would lose everything for."

Pain and desperation mixed in Vincent's eyes. He didn't try to struggle out of Damon's hold but his pleading voice suggested every second of this confrontation was killing him. "He wasn't with Shauna when she fell. He promised me."

That's what this was about. The brothers being attracted to the same woman. Damon had no idea if she returned either of their feelings but the hurt in Vincent's voice struck Damon as real. "He *was* with her."

"Vincent, you might want to be prepared for the fact your brother has lied to you," Trevor said.

He had cleared out the area with Steven's help. Makeshift guards were posted around the area. No one could get back there, near the weapons, except them. And for that part to even happen, Roger had to open the door or they had to force their way in. Damon hated both options.

After standing and listening, Vincent clearly had enough. He shrugged out of the hold and stepped away from the wall. "You don't know what you're talking about."

"When it comes to Shauna, they do." Liza put a hand on Vincent's arm. "Roger told me himself."

"Enough strolling down Memory Lane." They would never convince him of his brother's betrayal, if that's what the relationship even was. Damon didn't know and didn't care. He needed to get on the other side of this door, to see Cate and know she was okay.

Then he might beat the crap out of Roger.

Trevor walked over with an electronic gadget. It looked like a small box, less than half the size of a laptop, and a card. He insisted he could get the right code with this. Steven's computer guys backed him up. That was all fine but there were a lot of weapons in the vault. Going in might mean being wildly outgunned.

Just as Trevor stuck the card in the security panel outside the main door to the building, Vincent piped up again. "Please don't hurt him."

The desperate plea chipped away at Damon's determination not to think about anyone but Cate and getting her to safety for the next few minutes.

But then Trevor's device found one of the numbers and clicked it in. "I'm not promising that."

"SHE WAS MY sister, Roger." Cate read somewhere that it helped to make a connection with an attacker. Try to get the person to talk, see you as human. It sounded like nonsense to her but she didn't have many options.

"We went out." He sighed. "Vincent thought he liked her, but that wouldn't have worked."

"Why?"

"Come on. Him with Shauna?" Roger started walking again. He stepped over to the wall of lights and fiddled with the one closest to him. It wasn't as bright as the others and that seemed to upset him.

She was about to try another tack when the door flew open. Damon and Trevor charged inside, guns up and ready. Roger scrambled to his feet. He dove for her but didn't reach her and then tried to crawl the rest of the way.

But Damon got there first.

He moved in a blur and crashed right into her. She could hear him issuing orders and shouting. He landed half on top of her, half shielding her as he fired. Roger and Damon were so close that she waited to feel the dreaded thud of his body as bullets plowed into him. But it never came.

For a few seconds, bullets pinged around her. Damon's weight pushed against her, shoving her harder against the wall, covering her body with his. She knew that he was sacrificing himself, and that had her moving.

She shifted and flailed and tried to cover him like he was covering her. But when the shooting stopped Roger sat against the wall. He looked as if he were pinned there as Trevor walked over and kicked his gun away.

Heavy breathing lifted Roger's chest and a small gurgle rose from his throat. She saw blood but not as much as she expected. Vincent fell to the floor next to him and Liza screamed. People flooded the room now. Cate didn't recognize any of them.

"Damon?"

He glanced over his shoulder. "You okay?"

She wasn't sure she'd ever be okay again. "No blood."

"What?" He flipped over and stared at her then. His gaze wandered over her, caressed her face without touching her.

The most obvious question floated through her mind. "How did you not get shot?"

"Trevor and I hit him at the same time." Damon winced. "He didn't stand a chance."

She watched as Trevor talked with the newest group of lethal-looking men to enter the room. It dawned on her that they must be Wren's people. That was good, comforting in a way. But she wanted Damon. She expected him to hold her but he turned away as quickly as he looked at her.

Medics shuffled past the carnage and men with guns. She felt someone put a coat over her shoulders. She hadn't realized she was shaking to the point where her teeth clicked together until right then.

When Damon got up and went over to Roger, part of her wanted to yell at him, tell him to go somewhere safe. The other part wanted to jump up and wrap her legs around his waist and let him carry her out of here.

Roger's head dropped to the side as the ambulance workers checked the wounds. He glanced at his brother. "Why are you here?"

"Shauna."

The soft way Vincent said it broke her heart. It also sent a shot of guilt moving through her. She'd liked Roger at first but not Vincent. Now she knew how far off her radar was. She wondered if Shauna suffered from the same thing.

"You threatened Cate. Stalked her. Tried to set fire to her and kidnapped her." Damon nodded toward Liza, who was standing by Roger with a guard watching over her now. "And your girlfriend here hit her at the water tower."

That made sense. Cate could see it now. The two of them in a relationship. The lies from the past getting in the way. Their ambition screwing things up. Then there was their general distrust of everyone.

Vincent shook his head. "Roger, what the hell?"

"We have invested so much in this place and in Steven," Liza explained.

"In me?"

Cate didn't even realize Steven was there until he started talking.

"With your son gone, you needed an heir," Liza said. "You needed people to step up and take over. To blow your vision up until it was this huge reality."

Trevor shook his head as he swung into the room. "I'm thinking that dream is gone. For good this time."

Cate couldn't take much more of this. "But that's not why Roger did all of this."

She saw the truth now. He might hide behind Liza's

determination and running Sullivan, but his real goal was to save his butt.

"Easy," Damon said as he helped her to her feet.

That simple touch eased some of the tension racing through her. "All he wanted to do was cover up Shauna's death. Did you come on too hard and she ran? Maybe she didn't want to play your games that night and you chased her."

"She flirted." The lightness in Roger's voice made it sound like none of this mattered, as if he wasn't talking about an actual person. "We were having fun and then she went stone cold without warning. I thought it was a game and then she tried to run and wouldn't listen."

The color left Liza's face. "Roger? That's not what you told me."

"I grabbed her, thought it was some weird thing she was into. Like, she needed the chase." He shook his head. "And the ladder was right there."

Cate could see every piece. She wondered if the day would ever come when the awful scene wouldn't play in slow motion in her head. "You pushed her."

"She lost her footing."

Cate didn't believe him, but she wasn't even sure that the specifics mattered. Roger scared Shauna. He chased her and because of him she was dead. That's the information he hid and fought so hard to protect. He or his overeager hands or inability to hear the word *no* set the whole thing in motion. And that meant Roger was at fault. Cate had her answer.

She closed her eyes and let her sister's name echo in her head.

"It was a sick game to him." Damon wrapped his arm around her. "I'm sorry, Cate."

For a second, nothing else mattered. In a room filled with chaos and people, she hung on to him. Pretended no one else stood there and there wasn't blood on her shoes. She held on for all that happened today and in the past. Mostly, she buried her face in that sexy spot between his neck and shoulder because it was her favorite place in the world.

When his hold tightened around her shoulders she looked up. She didn't expect to see Steven standing nearby, but he was. His mouth had pulled into a flat line. Somehow, he'd aged ten years in the last few hours. Pale and drawn, sad and, for the first time since she met him, defeated.

This might have been the thing that ended it all. His assistant and longtime member locked in a criminal enterprise to hide a murder and slowly take his business. There was only so much a human could take and she truly wondered if he'd reached his limit.

"Thank you." Damon held out his hand. "For what you did for Cate."

Steven nodded his head as he shook his son's hand. "I didn't know about any of this. Not about Shauna's death or what Liza was planning."

"I know, Dad."

Cate bit back a sob. It was just the way he said it. Real and honest. In a moment of clarity, he accepted his father's word. She doubted that the peace would last, but they'd moved forward a small step, but still a step.

Without another word, Steven walked away. He ignored Liza calling out his name. After a quick check on Roger, he helped Vincent off the floor and walked out the door with him.

So much pain. A history full of it. She sighed, sinking in deeper against Damon.

"I'm so sorry," he whispered the words again, this time against her hair.

She looked up at him. Saw the blood but knew most of it wasn't his. She could see the small nick on his arm from a bullet. A wound like that would put her in the hospital but he didn't even get a bandage. But that seemed to be his only injury, which was nothing short of a miracle. "Why are you apologizing?"

"Because of Sullivan. Because of what happened here. Because I'm part of it even though I wish I weren't."

It looked like she had one more battle to fight today.

She turned until they faced each other and rested her hands on his hips. "Damon, I need you to hear me."

"About what?"

"Your father isn't evil. Willfully ignorant, purposely uninformed and emotionally vacant—yeah. All of those. I could list many more weaknesses but those are the obvious ones. He's the guy who lets things happen and there should be blame for that. There's a price he should pay."

He nodded. "Damn right."

He said the words but he still wasn't getting her point. "Maybe he already paid it. He lost a son to disease. Lost his wife. Now he's lost the only thing he had left."

"The school?" Damon shrugged. "I'm sure he'll figure out a way to salvage his demented dream one more time."

She was going to have to spell it out. For a smart one he was missing big clues. Since he'd just survived a shoot-out, she didn't make a big thing of it. But she didn't ignore the point either. "You, Damon."

His head shot back. "He doesn't care about that."

"You are smarter than this." She planted a quick kiss on his mouth and had to hold firm when he tried to deepen it. "The trust is gone. The relationship shattered. If he had hope, he can't have it now. Not after all of this. He likely feels that this time he lost you for good."

"You're giving him too much credit."

People still moved in and out around them. The medic was trying to get Damon's attention but he ignored it all. Everything but her. She loved the heat and intensity of that look, when he turned it full wattage on her.

"He's an empty shell. There is nothing inside him." She flattened her hand against his chest. "Sometimes loss burns life out of people. Sometimes hatred."

Damon's eyes narrowed but he didn't say anything.

"When that happens, when there's nothing left, the only thing to do is move on. Accept what can't be and push forward." And that was her life lesson for the day.

She gave him one more kiss, letting this one linger a bit more, then pulled away. With one last look, she headed out of the claustrophobic part of the vault and into the sunshine.

CHAPTER 27

Damon had no idea what just happened. They were touching and kissing. She talked about his family. He heard every word but his focus was on her voice. Alive and sexy and even in the middle of a shoot-out that could have killed her, more concerned about his relationship with his dad.

She was a hell of a woman.

Trevor came up to stand next to him. The two of them watched Cate walk into the much larger weapons storage room. "She seems okay. Is it an act?"

"I'm not sure." Despite the relief, he felt numb. Without her next to him, seeing her wander around thanking the people who were there to help, made him long for something more.

"She's impressive. Shitty things happened to her, but she's not alone." Trevor slipped his hands into his front jeans pocket. "How are you doing?"

"Not great." He should be celebrating. They conquered the danger and got through it . . . and the hollowness in his stomach refused to budge.

Then it hit him. She walked away from him.

"Wait a second." He didn't mean to say the words out loud, but he did.

"Where are you going?" Trevor asked.

"To start a fight."

"I don't know anything about dating women, but—"

Neither did Damon but he vowed to learn.

He caught up with her outside. "Hey, hold up," Damon called out to her. When she ignored him or didn't hear the first try, he yelled much louder the second.

She turned around. "What's wrong?"

He was full-on pissed now. Not just annoyed or frustrated. She'd given him this big speech, and a good one, then tried to ride off into the sunset. No fucking way. "What the hell was that?"

She looked at him like he'd grown a fifth head. "I don't understand."

"That speech. The empty-inside thing. The shell." He was shouting now. He knew because people were watching. Some of them not even being subtle about it. "Was that about me or my dad?"

Trevor snuck up close and put his hand out for Damon to quiet down. "Uh, Damon."

He ignored his friend's help and focused on Cate. "Are you dumping me?"

Her eyebrow lifted. "Are we even together?"

She had to be kidding. "I'm still here, aren't I?"

"That is not a real answer, Damon." Her shouting matched his now. They stood in front of the hill, not moving while people shifted around them. Law enforcement or Wren's people or someone moved out the weapons. People from Sullivan gathered to see what was going on. And Damon and Cate waited at the center of it all.

"You don't think I could have left at any time? Trevor was here." Damon gestured toward his friend then toward the house. He'd pretty much lost control of the conversation and his body by this point. "He might look useless but he's the one you want protecting your back. Wren wanted to pull me out. Garrett would have stepped in. I stayed for you."

She snorted at him. "Because I asked you to."

He was starting to hate that noise. "Because the idea of you being hurt, being in danger, made me sick." He touched her then because it felt wrong not to. He cupped her cheek. Ran his thumb over her bottom lip. "Somewhere along the line, you being okay mattered more than me having to deal with all of this shit from my past."

"You needed closure." Her voice was softer now. It dipped low but all trace of anger had disappeared.

"I really hate that word. It's meaningless." He rested his forehead against hers for a second and tried to block out the audience that had gathered. "You don't get closure after you kill someone. After you watch your mother bleed out. After you figure out your father, your family's history, is nothing but a path to destruction." His words started to falter. Not because he didn't believe them but because his energy was waning. "Oh, it has a pretty outer shell but it's garbage inside and people have paid over and over again for it."

She played with the top button of his shirt, slipping it in and out of the hole there. "There are good people here."

"And some bad ones. They almost got to you. I was standing right here and still you almost paid the ultimate price."

She sighed at him. "You are not responsible for my choices. I wanted to come here. You are not my protector or my savior."

"Is it so wrong I want to be?" Because that was the point. That's why he'd landed here. Wanting to be with her, help her and make sure no one hurt her.

"Since when?"

It was a fair question. And an easy one for him to answer. There were some times he practiced in the mirror, but this one came from the heart. "Why do you think I'm still here? It's not the sex or because I love the way you look, or how you stumble over the end of your sentences. Or even that expression you get when you want to punch me, though that is pretty sexy."

She shot him a look that suggested he was right on the edge with those examples. "Are you seeing that expression right now?"

"I admit I've messed this up, but I was honest with you. That stuff about not feeling anything—all true. I've been locked in this shell for over a decade, pounded by guilt every fucking day. The only light—only—has been a few friends and some assignments where I thought I actually did some good." Now that he started talking he wanted to tell her everything, to share everything.

She pulled back. Just a little. "I get it. You survive on work. You're an island."

"Was." No way was he allowing distance between them. He made that clear when he brought her in close. "Then you stormed into my life."

"I did not storm." But she smiled as she said it.

"You had your cause and your loyalty to your sister. You refused to back down."

"This is about me now?"

"Every time I told you that I'd lost the ability to connect, you fought me. Maybe not always out loud but I could hear your voice in my head. *Get over yourself.* See the eyeroll even if you didn't look at me and do it." He didn't even have to try hard to hear the sound. Her voice floated right into his head.

"Because it's ridiculous."

He felt something inside him explode. "I know that now!"

"What are you saying?"

He'd lived with his defenses for so long. It scared him to step out and be who he was . . . or it did. She made him want to try it. "You turned that light on. You broke through the barriers, you refused to just go away."

She looked him up and down, as if sizing him up to determine if he was a good risk. "I can do that now."

"Absolutely not. You don't get to give up on me now that I'm falling for you." She had him shouting and generally making a fool of himself. He didn't act like this. He didn't make scenes. He did now. "Damn it, Cate."

"Falling . . ."

The catch in her voice stopped him. "This is not the time for you to drop off the end of your sentence."

"I don't know what to say."

But he could hear it in her voice. She was starting to believe and he'd never been so relieved.

"I know I'm a bad risk. My past is fucked-up. That will always be there, the wrestling with guilt will not go away." His hands slipped up her back to bring her in closer. "But you made me believe in something."

A small smile played on her lips. "What?"

"You." The last of his ego shattered. He would get on his knees, agree to squeeze the toothpaste her way. Whatever she needed. He couldn't stand the idea of being apart. "Please don't leave me. Agree to make this fake relationship real."

She cupped his face. "Damon."

He couldn't tell from that tone if she intended to back away. She sounded soft but he didn't want a martyr. "All I'm asking for is a chance."

"Of course." She threw her arms around his neck.

Wait . . . That seemed too easy, as if she was waiting to unleash that reaction. "What?"

"You think I came to Salvation, Pennsylvania, looking for a boyfriend? I never expected you. I couldn't have predicted I would find you."

"I can't figure out if that's a good answer or not." But he loved it. Really loved it.

"You're not the only one falling, Damon." Some of the amusement left her face. She still smiled but her words hit like a pledge. "The pretty face, the grumpy attitude, the insistence on eating too many burgers. I'm in for all of it."

"The father, the family mess?" He couldn't imagine taking it on.

"Those, too, but with a bit less excitement."

He sat on the verge of happiness. He could see Trevor out of the corner of his eye, smiling and looking ridiculous. His father hovered. A few of the men he knew from other Wren cases hovered. He didn't get it at all. Part of him still knew that the risk of picking him was extreme. "God, why?"

"I've always been so focused, so clear, all my life. Get an education, stay out of debt, find the answers about Shauna, help my mom. I love my friends and having fun, but there's always been so much other baggage that I tried to hide in the corner and deal with on my own." She rested her forehead against his mouth for just a second. "I'm tired but when I met you I knew, maybe for the first time, that you were someone who could help me carry that load. That you wouldn't walk out or run away."

He shook his head, not understanding her but so

grateful that she saw something he doubted was really there. "I don't understand what you see when you look at me."

"A good man who tries really hard to hide it." She pulled him down for another kiss. "Hope. A future."

"Then why were you walking away from me?"

A smile burst across her face. "I was giving that man his coat back."

There's no way he heard that right. "What?"

"I had his coat." She pointed at the younger man who had a coat over his arm.

"You weren't leaving me?" Here he was, making a scene and saying things he never thought he'd say to anyone . . . and she wasn't going anywhere. He knew that should make him cranky but he just couldn't get there.

"My plan was to ask Trevor how to get through to you and if he didn't have any ideas, lock you in my apartment until you came to your senses."

Trevor leaned in. "For the record, I would have recommended something with fire."

Damon didn't even spare him eye contact. "Shut up."

"You're stuck with me."

"Bodyguard, burger eater, protector . . . you're in for all of it?"

Her smile could light up a room. "Boyfriend. The real kind."

He loved the sound of that. "You are the hottest thing ever."

"And that's the other reason I'm keeping you. Because you make me feel like I really am the hottest thing around."

"I can show you."

On that note, some of the crowd disbursed. Not Trevor, because he was Trevor.

"Okay, kids. Let's keep this respectable," he said. "And, for the record, that was the weirdest *we're really dating now* declaration I've ever seen."

Damon forgot about one very important problem with his big disclosure. He glared at Trevor. "If you tell the guys, I will kill you."

"Recorded it on my phone." Trevor held up his cell and shook it. "Already sent it to them."

She wrapped her arms around his waist. "I'm going to meet them all eventually."

"Trust me, they're happy you're willing to take him on." Trevor looked Damon up and down. "He's a fucking mess."

She wasn't having it. She stretched up and kissed Damon on the cheek. "But he's my mess."

Damon couldn't help but smile. "Let's get out of here."

THREE WEEKS LATER, Cate had to fight the urge to dance around the luxurious hotel overlooking the White House. She sat next to Damon on the bed, wearing matching white robes.

"I can't believe I'm finally going to meet all of your friends." She couldn't wait to put faces and names together. She'd met some but not all.

"I can't believe Emery finally agreed to marry Wren." Damon put an arm around her shoulders and pulled her into his side. "Could be she just wanted to see us all and figured an engagement party would get us all there."

She loved this position. All tight against his side.

"Well, we have been in hiding for two weeks. You even went a day without a burger." She was pretty sure that was a record.

He frowned. "I'm still pissed about that."

"The rest of it was worth it."

His lips found her hair. "Are you talking about the sex? Because my favorites are sex, food and being with you."

She snuggled into his side. As far as she was concerned, the party could come to them while they spent the night sitting like this. "I notice how you put sex first on your list."

"I'm a smart man." He kissed her forehead. "An appreciative one, too."

"We need to get packed."

"Soon."

"Don't you want to get home?" The one they would be sharing. It was new and exciting and she could hardly wait to try it.

"Depends, do I still have to be there when you have all of *your* friends over?"

Yes, that would be her turn. They suggested brunch, so he was stuck. "They're coming to meet you."

"So, that's a yes?"

"You'll like the house. You'll like them." She hoped that was true. She didn't see why it wouldn't be. Despite his sometime grumpiness she'd found that he loved lounging around the house with her.

"I feel like I already am home without traveling anywhere." He exhaled. "You do that for me. Make me feel centered and capable."

He meant it. She could hear it in the intensity in his voice. He'd said pieces before, so the thought had been there. But she loved hearing it. "You sweet talker."

"I love you. I'm no longer just falling. I'm fully in." He just dropped it. Firm and clear and filled with honesty.

She sat up and bit and looked at him. "Wow."

"Right? The guy who weeks ago swore he was dead inside."

She'd be fine never to hear that sentence again. "That statement was always ridiculous."

"Not until I met you."

"Then it's a good thing I love you, too."

He hooked his hand under her thigh and dragged her onto his lap. "That didn't take long."

"You're pretty loveable." She shifted until her legs fell on either side of his hips and she faced him. "Two weeks of constant talking and being together without interruption likely fast-forwarded the 'falling for you' process."

He winked at her. "You kind of sound like an actuary right now."

"An actuary who wouldn't mind getting naked to celebrate being in love."

His sexy smile promised that they would absolutely do that. "I'm starting to really like math."

"Then try this." She reached down and tugged on the end of the bathroom belt. "What is the probability of me getting your robe off before I can take mine off?"

"We should test that."

She laughed at the seriousness in his voice. "At least twice. I am a bit of an overachiever."

He rolled her onto her back and hovered over her. "Show me."

ACKNOWLEDGMENTS

I grew up in Lancaster County, Pennsylvania. It is gorgeous and green there, filled with rolling hills and farms. The kind of place where kids play outside until well after the sun goes down in the summer and the smell of freshly mowed grass is a guarantee. But there isn't a cult there. That part, along with every character in this book, is pure fiction. It just so happened the area around my childhood home provided the perfect setting for this book. To keep every relative and every person I went to high school with from getting ticked off, I changed the town names. For the record, I grew up in New Holland, Pennsylvania.

So, thank you to my parents for not being part of a scary commune. Also, thank you to May Chen, my amazing editor, for seeing the plot holes in the draft of this book and helping me to fill them. Any remaining mistakes are my fault because she likely wrote a revision comment to try to get me to fix them and I ignored her because I was tired.

As always, thank you to my readers. You guys make all of this possible. So does James, my patient husband, who rarely panics when he comes home to find me glassy-eyed and writing . . . and obviously in need of a shower.

**Don't miss the rest of HelenKay Dimon's
Games People Play series!**

THE FIXER

He's known only as Wren. A wealthy, dangerous man,
he specializes in making problems disappear. A professional fixer, Wren hides a dark past, but his privacy is
shattered when Emery Finn seeks him out. He's the only
person who can solve Emery's own personal mystery
but tracking down the sexy, brooding Wren is difficult
enough. Resisting her body's response to him will prove
completely impossible.

THE ENFORCER

Security expert Matthias Clarke hunts people who
don't want to be found. His latest prey: the sole survivor of the massacre that killed his brother. Kayla Roy
claimed she was a victim but then she disappeared.
Matthias thinks Kayla may be the killer—and he wants
justice.

Kayla never lets a man get close, but keeping Matthias away might be impossible. She knows nothing about
his connection to her past; only that their attraction feels
overpowering—and very dangerous.

THE PRETENDER

They say it takes a thief to catch a thief, and Harrison Tate is proof. Once a professional burglar, he now makes a lawful living tracking down stolen art. No one needs to know about his secret sideline, "liberating" artifacts acquired through underhanded methods. At least until one of those jobs sees him walking in on a murder at Gabrielle Wright's palatial family estate.

Available now from Avon Books!

At Avon Books, we know your passion for romance—once you finish one of our novels, you find yourself wanting more.

May we tempt you with . . .

- **Excerpts** from our upcoming releases.

- Entertaining **extras**, including authors' personal photo albums and book lists.

- Behind-the-scenes **scoop** on your favorite characters and series.

- **Sweepstakes** for the chance to win free books, romantic getaways, and other fun prizes.

- Writing **tips** from our authors and editors.

- **Blog** with our authors and find out why they love to write romance.

- **Exclusive content** that's not contained within the pages of our novels.

Join us at
www.avonbooks.com